The Loner:
THE BIG GUNDOWN

The Loner:
THE BIG GUNDOWN

J. A. Johnstone

PINNACLE BOOKS
Kensington Publishing Corp.
www.kensingtonbooks.com

PINNACLE BOOKS are published by

Kensington Publishing Corp.
119 West 40th Street
New York, NY 10018

All Kensington titles, imprints, and distributed lines are available at special quantity discounts for bulk purchases for sales promotions, premiums, fund-raising, educational, or institutional use. Special book excerpts or customized printings can also be created to fit specific needs. For details, write or phone the office of the Kensington special sales manager: Kensington Publishing Corp., 119 West 40th Street, New York, NY 10018, attn: Special Sales Department; phone: 1-800-221-2647.

ISBN-13: 978-0-7860-2277-9
ISBN-10: 0-7860-2277-9

First printing: February 2010

10 9 8 7 6 5 4 3

Printed in the United States of America

Chapter 1

The sound of horses made the boy look up from the puppies squirming in the basket. He saw three riders coming toward the isolated adobe ranch house. The morning sun was behind them, so all the boy could make out were the black, centaur-like shapes of men and horses.

He was on his knees beside the basket. He'd been playing with the month-old pups. A coyote had gotten their mother a couple of days earlier, and the boy's father had said that the critters were too small to survive without her. Best just to smash their heads in and be done with it, he'd said.

The boy was already crying over what had happened to the mama dog, and his sobs had gotten even harder when he heard his pa say that. Then his mother had put a hand on his shoulder and said, "Don't take on so, Cyrus. We'll see if we can't nurse them through. I can soak a rag in milk and let them suck on it."

The boy's father had just shaken his head as if that

was the most loco thing he'd ever heard, but he didn't argue. The boy was only five years old, but he had already figured out that when his ma's back stiffened up like that and she got that look in her eye, his pa never argued with her. The boy was just glad that he still had the pups, and so far, they seemed to be doing fine.

He stood up, hurried to the open door of the low, sprawling ranch house, and called, "Riders comin', Ma!"

She came out of the house, wiping her hands on a rag, and looked at the three men on horseback, who were now about fifty yards from the house. Then she said in a low voice, "Go fetch your pa, Cyrus."

That was his ma's don't-mess-with-me voice. Cyrus nodded and ran around the house. His pa was in the barn out back, tending to chores. The four Mexican hands who rode for the spread were already out on the range.

Cyrus was halfway to the barn when he heard a gunshot and saw a muzzle flash from the shadowy interior, which was visible through the open double doors. He skidded to a stop, his eyes widening in surprise and fear as a man he had never seen before stepped out of the barn. Smoke curled from the barrel of the gun in the man's hand as he looked at Cyrus and a grin spread across the hardened, beard-stubbled face.

Cyrus whirled around and ran back toward the front of the house. He heard a boom and recognized it as the sound of the family's shotgun.

"Ma!" he screamed as he rounded the corner and came to an abrupt halt again. He saw that the three riders had reached the house and dismounted. One of them had hold of Cyrus's mother while another wrenched the shotgun out of her hands. All three of the men were laughing, and none of them appeared to be hurt. Cyrus knew that if his Ma had shot at them with the greener, she must have missed.

He wished she hadn't missed.

The man holding the reins of all three horses noticed Cyrus and grinned at him, just like the man who had come out of the barn. This man motioned toward him and said, "Come on over here, boy. These your pups?"

Cyrus's ma struggled in the grip of the man holding her. "Run, Cyrus!" she shrieked. "Run!"

The man who had just spoken to him drew his gun and said in a warning tone, "Don't you do it, son. Not if you don't want something bad to happen to your ma."

Cyrus was scared, but he was outraged, too, and he couldn't hold that in. "You leave her alone!" he yelled. "And don't you bother them pups, neither!"

That show of defiance brought more laughter from all of them, including the man from the barn, who had just come around the corner of the house behind Cyrus. He gave Cyrus a hard shove that sent the boy stumbling forward.

"You take care of that fella we saw goin' in the barn, Brentwood?" asked the man standing beside the basket with a gun in his hand.

"Sure did. He won't be bothering us."

"Good. I reckon we can take our time, then, and enjoy these folks' hospitality for a while before we ride on to Bisbee to meet up with the colonel."

Cyrus knew that a colonel was some kind of soldier.

He had heard his pa talk about how his grandpa had fought in a big war with a colonel named Custer. But these men didn't look like any soldiers he had ever seen. They were all dirty, and wore rough clothes, and they were mean. You could just tell it. The meanness came off them like a stink.

"Just—just take what you want," Cyrus's ma said. "Only don't hurt us. That's all I ask of you. Don't hurt us."

The man holding the horses seemed to be the leader. He chuckled and said, "Why, we wouldn't think of it, ma'am. But we'll sure enough take what we want. You can damn well count on that."

The other three seemed to think that was funny for some reason. The one holding Cyrus's ma ran his hand over her chest, squeezing so hard it hurt. She gasped and turned pale under the tan that the Arizona sun had given her since she and her husband had started the ranch five years ago. She had given birth there, a long way from town or any other woman, with no one but her man to help her. Cyrus didn't know all that and wouldn't have understood it if he did, but he knew that his ma was really, really brave, and if these men had her scared, they had to be mighty bad.

"Culp, come over here," the leader said. The man holding the empty shotgun tossed the weapon aside, onto the ground. Cyrus's pa would have been upset if he had seen that. He always said you had to keep guns clean, that you had to take care of them if you wanted them to take care of you.

The leader was grinning down at the puppies in the

basket. "Any of you boys need some target practice?" he asked.

"Culp, get one of those pups and you heave it as high in the air as you can. I reckon that'll be some target."

Horror washed over Cyrus as he finally realized what was about to happen. He stared as Culp bent over and took one of the puppies from the basket. The little black and tan dog squirmed and whimpered in the man's rough grip.

Cyrus ran toward Culp. "Leave my puppies alone, you . . . you son of a bitch!"

He knew that was a mighty bad thing to call somebody. He had heard his pa say it a few times, when he'd hurt himself and Ma wasn't around. He'd grin at Cyrus and tell him never to repeat that, and while he was at it, don't tell Ma that he had just heard Pa use it, neither.

Right now, though, Cyrus didn't care if he got in trouble. He was mad clean through. That son of a bitch was messing with his puppies!

Brentwood lifted a foot and kicked Cyrus in the side as the boy went past him. The kick hurt like blazes and sent Cyrus rolling across the ground. He tasted dirt in his mouth and heard his ma screaming even harder. Cyrus came to a stop on his belly and looked up to see Ma trying to get loose from the man who held her. She would run to Cyrus' side, but the man wouldn't let her go.

The leader wiggled the fingers of his right hand over the butt of the gun that stuck up from the holster on his hip. "I'll bet I can blow that pup to pieces before it ever hits the ground," he boasted. "There's enough of 'em in that basket we can all take a turn."

"Then we'll take turns with the boy's ma!" Culp said.

"You're damn right." The leader crouched slightly, ready to draw. "When I say go—"

"Go ahead and say it."

That was a new voice, a flat, hard voice Cyrus had never heard before. He looked back over his shoulder and saw a stranger standing at the corner of the house. A tall man in a buckskin shirt and a broad-brimmed brown hat, who stood there with his thumbs hooked in his gunbelt like he didn't have a care in the world. The hat shaded his face so Cyrus couldn't see it all that well, but he saw blond hair curling around the man's ears and down the back of his neck.

The smile on the leader's face went away. An ugly snarl replaced it. "Who the hell—"

"Go ahead," the stranger said again. "I'm betting I can kill all four of you before that puppy hits the ground. What do you think?"

"Kill him!"

Chapter 2

It was amazing how much easier it was to live when you weren't afraid to die. The man called Kid Morgan had learned that lesson and learned it well. He had been through hell on earth already. The next world couldn't hold anything worse than the crucible of fire through which he had already passed.

Now, whenever he faced death a great calmness descended upon him. At the moment, the only thing that concerned him was getting lead in all four of the men before they killed him, so that they couldn't hurt the woman or the boy after he was gone.

With a whisper of steel on leather, the Colt on his hip came out of its holster, seeming to leap into his hand of its own accord with a flicker of movement faster than the eye could follow. He went for the loud-mouthed leader first, the man who thought it would be funny to blast a helpless puppy out of the air. If there had been time, The Kid might have permitted himself a second of satisfaction at the way the man's face caved in on itself as a .45 slug pulped his nose and bored into his brain.

By the time that happened, The Kid had already shifted his aim and fired again, sending a bullet into the chest of the man holding the horses. As that man collapsed, The Kid pivoted and went for the hombre with the puppy. The man didn't toss the little dog into the air as the leader had told him to. Instead, he dropped the pup to the ground and clawed at the gun on his hip. He hadn't cleared leather by the time The Kid's third shot punched into his guts and doubled him over.

Three of the bastards down and not one of them had gotten off a shot. Not bad. But the fourth man's gun roared and The Kid felt a hammerblow on his left thigh. The slug's impact knocked him halfway around, but he stayed on his feet and swung his Colt toward the fourth man.

The Kid's finger froze on the trigger. The man had one arm looped around the woman's neck, holding her in front of him. The Kid couldn't fire without hitting her, and the son of a bitch knew it.

The gunman didn't have any such worries, and a vicious leer appeared on his face as he drew a bead to put his next bullet dead center in The Kid's body.

A man whose face was covered with blood lurched through the open door of the ranch house behind the would-be killer. He held something in his hands, and the morning sun reflected off it as he plunged it in the gunman's back. The gunman screamed and staggered forward. The woman twisted out of his grip and threw herself on the ground, covering the little boy's body with her own. The Kid's revolver slammed out another shot. The fourth gunman jerked and pitched forward, landing on his face. The handle of a pitchfork stuck up from his back, the tines buried deep.

"Sean!" The woman leaped up and ran to the man with blood all over his face, throwing her arms around him. "Oh, my God! You're alive! I thought— but you're hurt!"

The man shook his head as he embraced her. "It's not as bad as it looks. Cyrus! Cyrus, boy, are you all right?"

The youngster scrambled to his feet and dashed over to his parents. They both went to a knee to fold their arms around the sobbing boy.

The Kid took a deep breath. He still had one round in the Colt's cylinder. Limping heavily as he felt blood trickling warmly down his wounded leg, he went to each of the gunmen in turn and checked to make sure that they were all dead.

Three of them were. The man who was gutshot was still alive, but he was unconscious and would never wake up again . . . if he was lucky. If not, he would come to and then die in agony in an hour or so.

With the threat over, at least for the moment, The Kid opened the gun and dumped the empties into the palm of his hand. He took fresh cartridges from the loops on his belt and thumbed them into the cylinder, leaving one chamber empty for the hammer to rest on, as usual. Then he pouched the iron and turned toward the family.

The pup that had been taken out of the basket sniffed and fumbled around his feet. The Kid leaned over, fighting the dizziness he felt from the loss of blood, and scooped up the little animal.

"Here you go, son," he said as he held the puppy out to the little boy. "Your pup's fine."

The man stood up, leaving his wife and son kneeling on the sandy ground with the now-frolicking puppy. "I—I don't know how to thank you, mister."

"I told you to stay in the barn." The Kid shrugged. "Under the circumstances, though, I suppose it's a good thing you didn't. Appreciate you giving me a hand."

"You—you save the lives of my family, and my life, too, and you're thanking me?" The man looked down in concern at The Kid's wounded leg. "And you're hurt!"

The Kid was about to say it was nothing, when he realized how stupid that was. He had a bullet hole in his leg—a couple of them, actually, since the slug seemed to have gone all the way through—and it hurt like hell. He had lost a lot of blood and the world was starting to spin funny.

He started to say something, but before he could get any of the words out, the ground seemed to tilt sharply under his feet. He felt himself falling and crashed to the ground. The last thing he was aware of before he passed out was a tiny wet tongue licking his cheek.

Consciousness began to seep back into The Kid's brain. He wasn't sure where he was, but he knew the place was warm and soft, and he wanted to just keep his eyes closed, settle down into those comforting surroundings, and never leave. He imagined this was what death must be like.

The pain brought him back. Pain was life. Life was pain.

He opened his eyes.

The boy was staring at him from a distance of a couple feet.

"Ma! He's awake!"

At least Cyrus had turned away before he yelled. The Kid was grateful for that much. Even so, the boy's voice struck his ears and made him wince.

Cyrus turned back to The Kid and said, "Howdy, mister. How do you feel?"

The Kid's head hurt, and his leg felt even worse. It had a dull throb that went through him with every beat of his heart. But he managed to put a faint smile on his face as he husked, "I'm all right."

"No, you're not." That comment came from the woman, who now leaned over him with a concerned expression on her face. The Kid was vaguely aware that she was pretty, with deep brown eyes and a mass of brown hair around her face and shoulders. She rested a hand on his forehead and went on, "You've got a fever. That wound in your leg must be infected."

"You've got to . . . clean it out good." The Kid's voice was weak. He didn't have as much strength as he had thought at first. "Carbolic acid . . . or if you don't have any . . . plenty of whiskey."

"That, we've got." It was the man's voice. He moved up on the other side of the bed where The Kid lay. Crimson still stained his face here and there, but most of the blood was gone. The woman must have cleaned it and then wrapped a bandage around her husband's head where the bullet had grazed him. The man had been bleeding like a stuck pig when The Kid found him in the barn, but that was common with head wounds. It had taken only a second for The Kid to determine that the injury probably wasn't serious. The man had been stunned, only half-conscious, and The Kid had told him to stay there while he went to deal with the men who'd invaded the ranch.

Those bastards were all dead now. The Kid remembered that much. He remembered being shot in the leg, too. He couldn't afford to lose it. A crippled gunfighter was a dead gunfighter, and there were already too many men in the world who wanted to test their speed against the man called Kid Morgan.

"Get a cloth," he rasped. "Soak it in whiskey . . . run it all the way through the hole . . ."

"That'll hurt like blazes, mister."

The Kid moved his head from side to side. "Don't care. Just . . . do it. Then pour . . . more whiskey . . . on the wounds."

The man and woman looked at each other, and the man shrugged. "I reckon he probably knows what he's talking about." A glance at The Kid. "Man like him's probably been shot before now."

A man like him . . . The fellow probably didn't mean anything by it. He was right, though. The Kid had been shot before. He knew about cleaning wounds and how to patch them up. It was a necessary skill when a man lived the life of a lone, drifting gunfighter.

"Cyrus, you go outside and play now," the woman said.

"Aw, Ma, can't I stay and watch?"

"No, you can't. Now do like I told you and scoot!"

When the boy was gone, the woman pulled down the sheet that covered The Kid. He felt a momentary surge of embarrassment when he realized that he was pretty much naked, but the woman was brisk and businesslike about what she was doing, which helped. She went to fetch a clean cloth, and the man came back with a bottle of whiskey and what looked like the ramrod from an old muzzle-loading rifle.

"This ought to do," the man said.

The woman leaned over the bed. "Let me take this bandage off."

When she lifted the bandage, The Kid thought he smelled the rot setting in already. That was probably just his imagination, as there hadn't really been time for the wound to fester that much. At least, he didn't think so.

"What . . . day is it?"

"The same day it was you got shot, mister," the man replied. "You were out for a couple hours, that's all."

That was long enough. The Kid didn't like the idea that he'd been helpless during that time, although clearly he had nothing to fear from these people. He had saved their lives, after all.

The woman drenched the cloth with whiskey, wrapped it around the end of the ramrod, and said, "Are you sure about this?"

The Kid nodded. "Go ahead."

"Wait a minute," the man said. He took the bottle from his wife, slipped his other hand under The Kid's head, and lifted it. "Take a swig of this first."

"Good . . . idea."

The man tipped the bottle to The Kid's lips. The Kid took a long swallow of the fiery liquor. It burned all the way down his gullet, but that fire was nothing compared to the blaze that seared his leg as the woman pushed the whiskey-soaked rag through the wound. The Kid's head tilted back against the pillow. He closed his eyes and felt the cords in his neck standing out as he clenched his teeth against the pain.

"Oh, God, Sean, he's bleeding again!"

"Of course he is. Don't worry about it, Frannie. The blood will help clean the wound."

The Kid opened his eyes to look up at them. "Sorry about . . . your sheets."

"Don't worry about that," Sean said with a shake of his head. "That's a small price to pay for the lives of my family."

The Kid winced as the woman withdrew the ramrod, and he nodded toward his leg.

"Pour the whiskey on it. Soak it good."

Sean did so. The fresh surge of pain brought a grunt from The Kid's lips. As the woman wrapped fresh bandages around his thigh a wave of drowsiness began to steal over him.

"I'm Sean Williams," the man said. "This is my wife Frannie. And you've met our boy Cyrus. You don't have to tell us your name, though. I know it's sometimes not considered polite to ask about such things."

"I . . . don't mind . . . Name's Morgan . . . They call me . . . Kid Morgan."

Sean's eyes widened. "The gunman?"

"Yeah . . . Lucky for you . . . right?"

"Damn right. We owe you our lives."

Frannie had another wet cloth, wet with water this time, not whiskey. She wiped its cool softness across The Kid's brow. The gentle touch felt wonderful.

"You sleep now, Mr. Morgan. Just rest, and we'll take care of you."

"Those men . . ."

"Don't worry about them." Sean's voice was grim. "I've already dragged them off behind the barn. I'll bury them, although it's more than they deserve. I ought to just leave them for the buzzards."

Whether the dead men were buried or not wasn't what concerned The Kid. What he was worried about was that they might have friends who would come looking for them.

But the darkness came up and carried him away again before he could say anything more.

Chapter 3

For an unknowable time after that, The Kid drifted in and out of consciousness. He woke up once and it seemed that he had been lying there in the bed for years. He woke up the next time and it was if only moments had passed since the thunder of guns and the acrid tang of gunsmoke filled the air. Sometimes he recognized the blurry faces of the man and woman who fed him and changed his bandages and took care of him, and other times they seemed like perfect strangers to him.

And there was the little boy—Cyrus? Was that his name?—who stood and watched with a tentative smile on his face, sometimes with a fat little puppy clutched in his arms. The Kid remembered . . . something . . . about a puppy, but he wasn't sure just what it was.

He knew he was sick because he could see the fear in the eyes of the woman as she leaned over him and wiped his forehead with a cool, damp rag. She was afraid he was going to die.

The Kid wasn't afraid. The only thing death meant

to him was that he would see the woman he loved again. He would see Rebel . . . unless, of course, all the blood on his hands meant that he would be headed down instead of up. It might be the Devil waiting for him on the other side, instead of St. Peter.

To be honest, The Kid wouldn't be surprised either way.

Finally, the time came when The Kid opened his eyes and not only was his vision clear, but his mind was, too. He remembered everything in detail: the way he had approached the ranch, just drifting, looking for a place where he could water his horse and maybe get a hot meal; the man he had seen sneaking into the back of the barn; the ominous sound of the shot he'd heard a moment later. Curiosity had driven The Kid to slip through the rear door of the barn himself. He had found a man who looked like a rancher, probably the owner of this place, sprawled on the ground with a pool of blood around his head. The wound wasn't as bad as it looked, and as the man began to come around, The Kid had told him to stay put, then gone to see what the screams and the other shots were about.

Rage had filled him as he saw how the woman was being manhandled. When the intruders threatened the pups and kicked the little boy, The Kid knew that if he didn't step in, those bastards wouldn't leave anybody alive when they rode off and left the ranch behind them.

The Kid didn't go out of his way to look for trouble. He didn't have to. It always seemed to find him. But he didn't turn his back and walk away from it, either.

He heard yipping and looked toward the open

doorway. The boy was just outside, playing with the pups. He had a short piece of rope in his hand, and all four puppies had hold of it, trying to pull it away from him. The Kid smiled. It looked like fun.

Growing up in a fancy house on Boston's Beacon Hill, he'd never had a dog. His stepfather, the man he had believed for many years was his real father, was a good man, but he hadn't been much for animals, especially not in the house. That was just one of the things The Kid had missed growing up and had not even realized until years later.

Frannie Williams laughed and came into The Kid's view as she crossed the room to stand in the doorway and look out at her son playing with the puppies. "I swear, Cyrus, you spend so much time with those pups I think you're going to start growling and yipping just like them."

The boy looked up at her and grinned. "I wouldn't want to be a dog, Ma. I like eatin' the food you fix for us!" He glanced past her skirts then and spotted The Kid watching them. "Ma! Mr. Morgan's awake again!"

Frannie turned quickly from the door and came across the room toward the bed. She wore an anxious expression as she bent over The Kid.

"Mr. Morgan, how do you feel?" She rested a hand on his forehead. "You're cool! The fever's broken at last."

The Kid's brain was working again, but his mouth didn't want to, at least at first. He struggled to say, "How . . . how long . . ."

"How long have you been here?" Frannie guessed. "Four days. You were so sick we thought we were going to lose you."

The Kid let his head sag back against the pillow. He wasn't surprised by what she had just told him. He had sensed that he'd lost a considerable chunk of time while he was out of his head with the fever.

"But you're going to be all right now," she went on. "The fever's broken, and I'll bet you'll be up and around before you know it."

The Kid hoped that was true. For a man who lived the life he did, to be flat on his back was just asking for trouble.

"Those men . . ."

Frannie's expression clouded at The Kid's words. Cyrus had come inside and followed her over to the bed. She looked at him now and said, "Run on back outside and play, Cyrus."

"But, Ma, I want to talk to Mr. Morgan," he protested.

"There'll be plenty of time for you to talk to Mr. Morgan later. Now, scoot like I told you."

Cyrus went outside, but on the way, he muttered, "I'm all the time havin' to *scoot*."

Frannie turned back to The Kid. Keeping her voice low, she said, "If you're talking about those horrible gunmen, Sean buried them, like he said he would."

"Where?"

"Up in our north pasture."

"But still on your range."

She frowned. "Of course. He wouldn't have taken them onto somebody else's land to bury them."

"Why didn't he . . . take them to the nearest town?"

"That would be Bisbee, which is two days from here by wagon." Frannie shook her head. "It may not be the height of summer yet, Mr. Morgan, but it's still too warm to spend two days on the road with some dead men."

The Kid couldn't argue with that. He was worried, though, that if friends of the dead men came looking for them, they might find the graves and figure out what had happened. That could mean bad trouble for the Williams family.

"Did he dig four graves . . . or just one?" The Kid didn't know Sean Williams, didn't know how smart the rancher was.

"He didn't actually dig any graves. He hollowed out under the bank of an arroyo a couple of miles from here and then caved it in on top of the bodies. No one knows they're there except for the vaqueros who work for us."

"You can trust them?"

Frannie nodded. "Of course. All four of them have been with us for five years, ever since we came here. I'd trust them with my life. More importantly, I'd trust them with the lives of my husband and son."

"That's just what you're doing," The Kid muttered.

Frannie crossed her arms. "I know that. Sean said we might be in danger if anybody found out what happened here. That's why he was so careful to put the bodies where nobody would ever find them. He led their horses about five miles from here and turned them loose, too." She sighed. "It's ridiculous. We're only a few years away from a brand-new century, and yet out here, it seems like nothing has changed. We have to worry about Apaches and banditos raiding from across the border, we have gunmen like those four passing through, and the only law that really means anything . . ."

"Is the law of the gun," The Kid finished for her as her voice trailed off.

"I mean no offense, Mr. Morgan, truly I don't," she said quickly. "You saved our lives, and I can't ever repay you for that. But if you hadn't been faster on the draw than those men . . . if you hadn't been better at killing than they were . . . well, I guess none of us would still be here. It's a shame that life comes down to that."

"Yes, ma'am. I agree with you. But it's always been like that, and I suppose it always will be, at least to a certain extent."

She smiled at him again. "You don't exactly talk like a gunfighter, Mr. Morgan. You seem more like an educated man."

"A man can be handy with a gun and still be educated."

"There I go again, saying things that sound worse than I really intended them."

The Kid shook his head wearily. "Don't worry about it, ma'am. I'm in your debt as much as you are in mine. You and your husband saved my life."

"You wouldn't have been hurt if it wasn't for us."

"No, ma'am, that's not right. I wouldn't have been hurt if it wasn't for those four men who rode in just before I did. They're the ones who caused all the trouble, and it doesn't make any sense to blame yourself for what they did."

"I know." Frannie paused. "My goodness, I'm about to talk your ear off, and here you are just now starting to recover from the awful fever. I'll bet you're thirsty."

The Kid's mouth was like cotton, and talking hadn't help. "Yes, ma'am. Parched."

"I'll get you some water. And how about some food?"

The Kid hadn't realized it until she mentioned it, but he was starving. "I could do with something to eat," he admitted.

"Stay right there."

He smiled. "I don't think I'll be going anywhere just yet."

But soon, he hoped. He needed to be back on his feet just as soon as he could.

Before trouble came calling again, as it always did.

Chapter 4

By evening, The Kid was sitting up in the bed with pillows propped behind him. When Sean Williams came in, the rancher grinned to see him doing so well and came over to shake hands.

"I haven't had a chance to properly thank you yet, Mr. Morgan," he said. "You've been, uh, out of your head for a while, at least most of the time."

The Kid nodded. "I know. There's no thanks necessary. You and Mrs. Williams saved my life."

"After you saved ours."

The Kid gestured toward the bandage that Sean still wore around his head. "How's that bullet graze?"

"Just about healed up. I probably don't even need the bandage anymore." Sean inclined his head toward the stove, where Frannie was stirring a pot of stew with her back to them. "But she thinks it's a good idea."

"I heard that, you know," she said without turning around.

Sean grinned. "Anyway, I'm fine, and I'm glad to see that you're on the mend, too, Mr. Morgan."

"Call me Kid."

"That's all? Kid?"

"It's enough."

"Sure. I didn't mean anything by it."

The Kid waved a hand to show that he wasn't bothered by what Sean said. "You haven't had any blurred vision, double vision, anything like that?"

Sean frowned and shook his head. "No."

"Any loss of memory?"

"Nope. Those sound like questions a doctor would ask. You're not—"

"A doctor?" The Kid shook his head. "Not hardly. I've just been around men who had head wounds before, and sometimes they didn't realize just how badly they were hurt until a few days later."

"Well, I'm fine. I had a headache for the first day, but once that went away, I've never been better." Sean lowered his voice again and held up his hand with his thumb and forefinger almost touching. "There's something about coming *this* close to dying that makes a man really appreciate living, you know?"

The Kid nodded. He knew, all right. Despite the fatalism that gripped him most of the time, he had experienced those moments of sheer exhilaration that sometimes followed a brush with death. He had drawn in a deep breath and realized that the air had never smelled sweeter, even though a tinge of gunsmoke might linger in it.

"I was wondering about my horse."

"I found him picketed up on the hill behind the barn. He's in there now with my horses. Don't worry, we've been taking good care of him. Heck, Cyrus brushes him twice a day."

The Kid smiled. "I'm much obliged." He and the buckskin had been through a lot of hardships together in a relatively short time. His expression grew more serious again as he went on, "Mrs. Williams told me about what you did with those four men . . ."

The young rancher's face stiffened into a grim mask. "Seemed like that would be the smart thing. I didn't want anybody to know that those varmints had even been here."

"That's right. If anybody comes looking for them, you never saw them."

Sean nodded. "I've talked about that with Frannie and the boy, and with the fellas who work for me. We're all agreed. We'll keep our mouths shut."

"No other strangers have been around?"

Sean shook his head. "Nope. It's been peaceful around here—just the way I like it."

The Kid hoped it stayed that way.

"The stew's ready," Frannie announced. She stepped to the doorway and called, "Cyrus! Supper!"

There was no response.

Frannie frowned. "That's funny. I thought he was just right outside with the puppies. The pups are here, but I don't see Cyrus."

The Kid felt his gut clench suddenly.

Sean looked worried, too. He left the bedside and went over to the door as Frannie walked farther outside.

"Frannie!" His voice was sharp. "Get back in here."

She turned to look at him. The expression on her face was a mixture of confusion and fear. "But I can't find Cyrus—"

"I'll find him." Sean picked up the Winchester he had leaned against the wall beside the door when he came in. He strode out, took Frannie's arm, and gently steered her back into the house.

The Kid's jaw was tight. He wished he could go out there with Sean. His eyes went to the gunbelt that was coiled nearby and placed on a chair beside the bed, along with the holstered Colt. The gun was in reach if he needed it. He looked around the room for something he could use as a crutch if he had to.

Holding the rifle slanted across his chest, Sean walked away from the house, calling, "Cyrus! Cyrus!"

"I'm here, Pa!"

Relief washed through The Kid as he heard the little boy's voice call from somewhere fairly close by.

But then Cyrus went on, "We got company!"

The Kid tensed again. Out here, company wasn't necessarily a good thing. In fact, chances were it could mean trouble.

He watched through the open doorway and saw Cyrus emerge from some brush about a hundred yards away from the ranch house. As the boy had said, he wasn't alone. A man on horseback followed him, and then several more riders came out of the brush. As Cyrus ran toward the house, the men followed him, riding single file in a slow, deliberate pace.

"Mrs. Williams," The Kid said, "is there another rifle here in the house?"

"There is," she said. "I'll fetch it . . . for myself."

"I was thinking you'd better let me have it—"

"I can handle a gun, Mr. Morgan. I know one of those men managed to knock the shotgun aside just as I pulled the trigger the other day, but they took me by surprise."

Three guns were better than two, he decided. He

jerked his head in a nod and said, "All right." He reached over, slipped the Colt out of its holster, and held it at his side, just out of sight under the sheet.

He didn't like this at all. If trouble broke out, he would have a limited field of fire, just what he could see through the doorway. And the boy was out there, along with Sean.

It was possible that there was nothing to worry about, he reminded himself. The strangers might be peaceful. They could be just passing through, as he himself had been a few days earlier.

The Kid didn't believe it for a second . . . but it was possible.

Cyrus pounded to a stop next to his father and looked up at Sean. "See, Pa? I told you we had company!"

The man who was in the lead reined in. He reached up and tugged on the brim of his hat as he nodded. "Good evening to you, sir," he said. His voice was deep and powerful. "I hope we didn't interrupt your supper."

"We were just about to sit down and eat," Sean said. "You're welcome to join us."

It was the sort of invitation you issued out there on the frontier as a matter of habit, no matter who had come to call. If a band of Hottentots showed up on your doorstep at dinnertime, The Kid thought, you'd just naturally ask them to light and sit a spell and have something to eat.

The man shook his head. He wore a fringed shirt of soft buckskin, blue cavalry trousers with a yellow stripe up the outside of the legs, high-topped black boots, and a cream-colored hat with a couple of tassels attached to the band. The hat also sported the crossed sabers insignia that meant the wearer had been part of a cavalry outfit at one time. He might still be in the army, although the men with him all wore civilian clothes.

From what The Kid could see of them, he didn't like them. They looked like the same sort of hard cases as the ones who had invaded the Williams ranch a few days earlier.

"We're much obliged for the offer," the leader said. "We wouldn't want to put you out any, though, and we have our own supplies."

Sean shrugged. "Suit yourself. You're welcome to water your horses, though."

The stranger smiled. Dark hair curled out from under the cavalry hat, and he sported a pointed goatee of the same color. "Now, we'll take you up on that kind offer," he said as he gestured for his men to move their horses up to the water trough and let them drink.

The man went on, "I'd like to ask you a question, too, if you don't mind."

"I reckon that would be all right."

"We're on our way up the San Pedro to the Santa Catalinas, and some friends of ours were supposed to meet us in Bisbee and come with us. They didn't show up, and I was wondering if you might have seen them pass through here. Four men . . . Hudgins, Culp, Brentwood, and Dobbs."

Sean shook his head, and The Kid had to admit that the rancher's voice and attitude were convincingly casual as he replied, "Those names don't mean a thing to me, mister, but I can tell you there haven't been any strangers pass through here for a month or more. Sorry."

"They didn't stop just to water their horses or anything like that?"

"Nope."

The stranger nodded. "Well, it was worth asking, I suppose. If they do happen to come by here, can you tell them that the colonel was asking about them?"

"That would be you?"

The man smiled and touched a finger to his hat brim again. "Colonel Gideon Black, at your service, sir."

From his place just beside and behind Sean's leg, Cyrus asked, "Are you a real soldier, mister?"

Colonel Black smiled down at the boy. "I was, son. I'm no longer in the army, though."

"But you were a real colonel?"

"Yes, indeed."

Sean said, "That's enough, Cyrus. Run on in the house."

The rest of the men had watered their horses and the light was fading from the sky. Frannie hadn't lit the lamps inside the house yet, and The Kid thought that was a good thing because the men outside probably couldn't see him watching them from the shadows. Nor would they be able to see Frannie standing beside a window where the shutter was open a couple of inches, clutching a rifle in her hands, ready to use it if she needed to.

Colonel Black let his horse drink as well, then lifted a hand in farewell. He called, "Move out!" to his men as if they were an actual military detail, and the group trotted off to the east, toward the San Pedro

River. Sean stayed outside for quite a while, watching them go. Finally, he came back inside.

Then, and only then, did The Kid holster his gun.

"Well, they're gone," Sean announced.

"You're sure of that?" The Kid asked. "They're not doubling back?"

"I don't think so. I could see their dust for quite a ways. If they plan on doubling back, they went to a lot of trouble to make me think they weren't."

Cyrus said, "They didn't look like soldiers, Pa."

Sean hung the Winchester on a couple of pegs near the door. "That's because they weren't."

"But that man was a colonel."

"Yeah, and he said he wasn't in the army anymore. That means he's not a real colonel anymore, no matter what he calls himself."

"Oh. I understand . . . I guess."

The Kid understood. Colonel Black was something of a wild card, but he had seen plenty of men who looked like the ones who'd been with the former officer. He knew without anyone having to tell him that they were outlaws, and that didn't surprise him a bit, considering the circumstances under which he had killed their four missing friends.

The question now was whether they had believed Sean and would ride on . . .

Or whether they would be paying a return visit to the Williams ranch.

Chapter 5

To The Kid's relief, the men didn't come back. Laid up as he was, he wasn't sure if he would have been able to handle them, even with help from Sean and the four vaqueros. The rancher and his men were tough, sure. They had to be in order to survive out there.

But those men with Colonel Black were killers. Stone-cold killers.

Sean called his vaqueros into the house when they rode in a short time later and told them what had happened. He gave orders for them to set up guard shifts so that someone would be awake and keeping an eye on the place all night. That was a smart move, The Kid thought, and he hadn't even had to suggest it to the rancher. Sean seemed to be a pretty canny young man.

The stew tasted as good as it smelled, and as The Kid ate, he felt strength flowing back into him. It would take a while, but he was confident that he was on the mend.

He slept soundly that night, a good honest sleep instead of the unconsciousness that had gripped him before. The rest revitalized him, so that when he awoke the next morning, he was actually anxious to get out of bed and try his legs again.

Frannie wouldn't hear of that, however, and The Kid sensed that she was so strong willed that arguing wouldn't do any good. So he didn't bother. He just lay there and rested and let her fill him full of good food for a couple more days. While that was going on, he checked frequently with Sean to find out if he or any of the ranch hands had seen any sign of Colonel Black and his men. Sean reported that they hadn't.

On the third day after he regained consciousness, The Kid was too restless to stay in bed any longer. Frannie brought him a heavy hickory cane with a carved wolf's head for a grip.

"This cane belonged to my grandfather," she told him. "Be careful when you use it."

"I'll take good care of it while I'm borrowing it," The Kid promised.

"I'm not worried about the cane. I don't want you falling down and hurting yourself even worse."

"That's not going to happen." The Kid grinned at Cyrus, who stood nearby watching with a rapt expression on his face. "I'll have Cyrus close by to give me a hand if I need one, won't I, son?"

"You bet, Mr. Morgan!" the boy replied.

The Kid talked Frannie into turning around while he pulled his clothes on. Cyrus helped him with his boots. Then The Kid got a good grip on the cane and pushed himself to his feet. He felt a twinge of pain in his wounded leg, but it didn't buckle. He took a tentative step, then another and another, keeping as much of his weight off the injured leg as he could.

Suddenly he swayed a little, but Cyrus was right there so that The Kid was able to rest his free hand on the boy's shoulder and balance himself. "Ma . . ." Cyrus said.

Frannie turned around and fixed The Kid with a stern stare. "I think that's enough for now, Mr. Morgan."

"I'm going to the door and back," The Kid said. He knew he was being stubborn, but he didn't care. He wanted to push himself, to find out just how much he could do.

"All right, but take it slow and easy," Frannie said with obvious reluctance.

With the cane in one hand and the other hand on Cyrus's shoulder, The Kid walked slowly to the door. By the time he got there, his heart was pounding and he felt dizzy. He stood there looking out and catching his breath for a moment and then turned to make his way back to the bed. Frannie was there to take his arm and help him lie down again.

"You tried to do too much, didn't you?"

The Kid answered without hesitation. "No. A man's got to push himself. If he's satisfied with what's easy, that'll never be enough."

She smiled down at him. "You're talking to a woman who married a man determined to start a ranch in the middle of nowhere. I know all about a man pushing himself."

The Kid tried to keep his eyes open, but the lids sagged closed anyway. Next time he would walk farther and do more. And the time after that, and the time after that . . .

He dozed off with that thought in his head.

* * *

By the time three more days had gone by, the pain in The Kid's leg was almost gone. Using the wolf's-head cane, he could get around everywhere in the ranch house and in the yard outside. With Cyrus keeping an eye on him and helping him if necessary, he walked over to the barn to check on his horse and was glad to see that the buckskin was being well cared for. He hadn't expected anything less from Sean and the ranch hands, but it was good to see that with his own eyes.

Cyrus never went far from his side, and the boy was full of questions. One thing he wanted to know was where The Kid was from.

"Oh, here and there," The Kid told him.

He didn't mention that once he had been an Eastern-born-and-raised businessman named Conrad Browning. Nor did he say anything about his real father being Frank Morgan, the notorious gunfighter known as The Drifter, or explain that he had once been married to a beautiful young woman named Rebel, who had been taken from him tragically because of greed and a lust for vengeance. All those things had gone into shaping the man who was now known only as Kid Morgan, who had developed a reputation of his own as a gunfighter. Only a handful of people knew the truth, knew that he had turned his back on a whole other life, and that was the way The Kid wanted it. He was content to drift, a loner who wasn't headed anywhere in particular.

But even a loner could not live totally isolated. He had to run into people from time to time, just as he had come across this ranch, and where there were people, there was trouble. The Kid knew that, and he felt a nagging curiosity about the man called Colonel Gideon Black. It was none of his business, of course, but he wondered why an ex-army man would team up with a bunch of gun-wolves like the men who had accompanied him the other day . . . not to mention the ones now buried in that arroyo, who had planned to meet the colonel in Bisbee.

A youngster like Cyrus wouldn't understand any of that, so The Kid didn't try to explain it to him. He just gave noncommittal answers to Cyrus's questions about who he was and where he had come from.

There was the time Cyrus asked, "Can you teach me how to use a gun like you, Mr. Morgan?"

They were standing by the corral fence, watching one of the vaqueros work with a balky horse, trying to get it used to wearing a saddle. The Kid looked down at the boy and said, "It ought to be your pa's job to teach you to shoot, Cyrus."

"Yeah, but Pa can't shoot like you do, Mr. Morgan. I never saw anything like it when you killed those four men! That's what I want to do."

The Kid shook his head. "You don't want to kill anybody, Cyrus. Not unless you have to, to protect your life or the life of someone you love."

"Well, then, I want to be able to do that."

It was certainly a worthwhile ability to have, The Kid reflected. Even though civilization had made a lot of inroads and people liked to talk about how the turn of the century would mark the beginning of a new, kinder and gentler era, The Kid knew that was a bunch of bullshit. Life was still harsh and dangerous, especially out here on the frontier, and that wasn't likely to change any time soon. In many ways, so-called civilization just meant surrendering to the wolves and hoping that they wouldn't devour you. That never worked.

As his father had once told him, "The meek aren't going to inherit anything west of the Mississippi."

."Maybe you should start by learning how to shoot a rifle," The Kid told Cyrus. "Have you ever used one before?"

"Nope. Ma says I'm too little."

"What's your pa say?"

"Whatever Ma says." Cyrus grinned. "Whenever she's around, anyway."

The Kid chuckled. "I'll have a talk with him. Can't hurt."

"Thanks, Mr. Morgan! I really would like to learn how to draw and shoot a handgun like you, though."

"I hope you never have to," The Kid said softly as he watched the half-wild horse trotting around the corral, trying to avoid the vaquero.

That evening, when Sean Williams went outside to have a last look around the place after supper, The Kid followed him. The Kid didn't take the wolf's-head cane with him since he didn't need it anymore. He felt a little twinge of pain in his leg from time to time, but the wound had healed and his leg was strong again.

"Cyrus told me he wants to learn how to shoot," The Kid said as he and Sean walked toward the corral. An arch of reddish-gold in the western sky marked the place where the sun had set.

Sean glanced over at him. "I intend on getting around to teaching him one of these days."

"I figured as much. The thing is, he wants to learn how to shoot like I do."

A frown creased Sean's forehead. "No offense, Mr. Morgan . . . you know how much we appreciate what you did for us . . . but I'm not sure I'd ever want Cyrus learning how to be a, well, a . . ."

"Gunfighter," The Kid finished for him as Sean's voice trailed off.

"To be honest, yes. I thought your name sounded familiar, so I asked the hands if any of them had ever heard of you. Pablo said he thought you were the man who killed Jack Trace over in New Mexico Territory a while back."

The Kid nodded slowly. "That was me, all right. Didn't have much choice in the matter."

"I never said you did. But I know how trouble seems to follow a man like you."

"Not always. Sometimes I walk into it," The Kid said pointedly.

Sean grimaced. "I know, what I'm saying sounds bad. Sounds like we're not obliged to you for saving our lives—"

The Kid raised a hand to stop him. "One thing doesn't have anything to do with the other. I saved your lives, but you and your wife saved mine. We're even on that score."

"You wouldn't have gotten hurt if not for us."

The Kid shook his head. "I already had this conversation with Mrs. Williams. Look, Sean, don't worry about it. I don't want to teach Cyrus how to be a gunfighter, either. In fact, I'm thinking it might be a good idea for me to pull out early in the morning, before he gets up."

"He'd be really disappointed if he didn't get a chance to say good-bye to you."

"And that might not be such a bad thing," The Kid said.

Chapter 6

This part of Arizona Territory, not far from the Mexican border, could be blistering hot during the day, but at night the dry air cooled quickly and by morning, there was often a little chill lurking around the edges of dawn.

That was the way it was the next morning when The Kid slipped out of the house and went to the barn while the sky was still just gray in the east. His breath even fogged a little in front of his face.

Sean and Frannie would be glad to get their bed back, he thought. They had put a corn-shuck mattress on the floor next to Cyrus's bed in the part of the room where the boy slept, that was closed off by a blanket hung from a rope. After the first couple of nights, The Kid had offered to bunk in with the youngster, but Frannie wouldn't hear of it. He would recuperate better in a real bed, she had declared, and as usual, there was no arguing with Frannie.

The buckskin tossed his head in greeting when The Kid walked into the barn and came up to the stall. "You're ready to get back on the trail again, aren't you, old boy?" The Kid asked. "So am I."

Sean hadn't tried to argue him out of leaving this morning. Although The Kid hadn't spelled it out, they both knew that it wasn't a good idea for Cyrus to be idolizing The Kid just because he was particularly good at killing. If leaving like this made Cyrus angry at him, that was fine. Cyrus didn't need to grow up wanting to be like Kid Morgan. He'd do better to follow in the footsteps of his father.

The Kid had the buckskin saddled and ready to ride when a soft footstep made him turn swiftly toward the double doors of the barn. His hand moved with blinding speed to the butt of the gun on his hip. The reaction was all instinct, no conscious thought at all.

"Whoa!" Sean took a step back. "Easy, Kid. It's just me."

The rancher had a cup of coffee in one hand and a canvas bag in the other. The Kid felt a little foolish when he saw that. He took his hand away from his gun and forced himself to relax.

"Sorry, Sean. I didn't think anybody else was up and around yet."

"You can't do anything in that house without Frannie knowing about it." Sean smiled as he came closer and offered the coffee to The Kid, who took the cup and sipped the strong black brew gratefully. "She thought you might want some food to take with you." He hefted the bag. "It's just some biscuits left over from last night."

"Your wife's biscuits are mighty good."

"And a couple of fried apple pies."

The Kid smiled. "Even better." He paused. "You told her I was leaving this morning?"

"No, but she figured it out pretty quick when you got up and slipped out. I never told her what Cyrus said yesterday. Didn't want to worry her. But if she knew, I figure she'd be grateful to you for what you're doing, Kid."

The Kid shrugged. "I had to be moving on sometime. Today's as good a time as any."

"Well, we both appreciate it. I thought I'd give you a hand saddling up, but I see you've already done it. How's your leg?"

"It's fine."

"You know, most men would've been laid up for at least twice that long with a bullet hole in their leg."

"I don't like to stay in one place for too long."

"Because of the chance that trouble might catch up to you?"

"Something like that," The Kid said.

"Don't you get, well, lonely, always drifting by yourself like that?"

It wouldn't do any good to tell Sean that he was never really alone, The Kid thought. A beautiful blond ghost rode with him everywhere he went, always at his side even when he wished she wasn't.

So he just shook his head and said, "Not to speak of."

"Well, I would. Once you've got a family, I don't reckon you'd ever feel right being alone again."

The Kid turned toward the buckskin. The shadows were still thick in the barn, but they might not be thick enough to conceal the look of pain and loss that he felt come over his face. He didn't want Sean to see that. Nobody could see it.

It was his, and his alone.

He drank the last of the coffee, handed the empty cup to Sean. Then he took the bag of food and said, "I'm much obliged to you and Mrs. Williams. For this, and for everything else."

"You reckon you'll ever come back this way again, Kid?"

The Kid shrugged. "*Quien sabe?* I never know where the trails will take me."

"Well, if you do, be sure and stop in for a visit, you hear?" Sean stuck out his hand. "Best of luck to you."

"Thanks." The Kid shook hands with the young rancher, then took hold of the buckskin's reins, put a foot in the stirrup, and swung up into the saddle. He looped the cord attached to the bag of food around the saddlehorn.

Sean stepped back to let The Kid ride out of the barn. The Kid looked around in the doorway and lifted a hand in farewell. He didn't look back again, as he rode away.

And he pretended he didn't hear the sudden banging of a door and the plaintive sound of a little boy's voice somewhere behind him.

There was an old saying about the dawn coming up like thunder. That's the way it was out there. One minute the sun was still below the horizon. The next it was a brilliant orange-red ball floating in the sky and flooding the landscape with light.

The Kid kept the buckskin moving at an easy pace

toward the San Pedro River. He was only a couple of miles from the Williams spread, but already he had put the place behind him. It was a part of his past, a part that he would remember fondly in some respects but not in others.

Out of habit, he kept a close eye on the landscape around him, alert for any sign of trouble. It was pretty dry country, but there were small grassy valleys here and there, where the ranchers in the area grazed their stock. Ranges of low hills framed the valleys. Miles to the north lay the grayish-blue peaks of the Dragoon Mountains. The Kid had never been through those parts before, but he had talked to people who had, including Sean Williams. Up ahead were the towns of Sierra Vista, right on the river, and Bisbee a few miles beyond it. He wasn't sure he wanted to visit either place, although it might not hurt to replenish his supplies.

Because he was watching everything around him, he spotted the buzzards circling in the air to his left. The Kid reined in and studied them for a moment as they wheeled through the blue sky and then dropped toward the earth, one after the other. Whatever was down there, the buzzards had decided that it was already dead, not just dying.

As The Kid studied the terrain from under the broad brim of his brown hat, his eyes suddenly narrowed. He saw a line meandering in a jagged path across a broad flat and recognized it as a dry wash, a common feature in that part of the country. There was nothing unusual about it.

Frannie Williams had said that her husband Sean had taken the bodies of the four gunmen to an arroyo about two miles from the ranch house and buried them by caving in the bank. The Kid whipped around in the saddle and gazed back toward the Williams spread. He had come about two miles.

And there were more buzzards arriving in the vicinity, even as he sat there.

"Son of a bitch," The Kid muttered under his breath. He tugged on the reins and turned the buckskin toward the arroyo. His boot heels prodded the horse's flanks and sent it forward at a fast trot.

When he reached the arroyo, The Kid dismounted and hauled his Winchester from the sheath strapped to the saddle. On the other side of the saddle, an old Sharps rode in a similar sheath, but he used it for long-distance work. He was more likely to need the repeater.

The Kid stepped to the edge of the wash and looked down, grimacing as the stench reached him. Somebody had been digging down there, and now more than a dozen buzzards were clustered around what had been unearthed, their bald, ugly heads dipping and darting as their sharp beaks ripped strips of rotting flesh off the four corpses. The Kid couldn't have recognized the men. Their tattered clothing was the only thing that still marked them as human since the skeletons hadn't been fully exposed yet. The way the carrion-eating birds were working on them, it wouldn't be true much longer.

A bitter, sour taste of revulsion welled up The Kid's throat and filled his mouth. He pointed the Winchester at the sky and cranked off three fast rounds, yelling as the shots blasted out. The racket sent the flock of buzzards soaring into the sky with angry cries and the flapping of leathery wings. The Kid lowered the rifle and wiped the back of one hand across his mouth. It didn't make the bad taste go away.

This was a waste of time and bullets, he told himself as the echoes of the shots rolled away over the Arizona landscape. He wasn't going to bury those bastards. Might as well let the buzzards have them. Buzzards had to eat, too, The Kid supposed.

The question was, who had come along and uncovered the bodies?

One obvious answer suggested itself, and The Kid didn't like it at all.

He liked it even less a moment later as his head jerked up and he realized that the shots he was hearing weren't the echoes of the ones he had fired to chase off the buzzards. They were a fresh burst of gunfire, followed by some sort of heavy boom, and they seemed to originate in the direction he had come from.

The direction of the Williams ranch.

Chapter 7

The wind tugged at The Kid's hat as he leaned forward in the saddle, over the neck of the hard-galloping buckskin. Without really thinking about what he was doing, he reached up to tug the hat down tighter on his head. It was just a reflex action. His brain was full of worry for the family he had left.

He had covered about a mile, so he was only halfway there. Despite the way the buckskin's long-legged pace ate up the ground, it seemed to take forever to get anywhere. The Kid's lips pulled back from his teeth in a grimace. He shouldn't have ridden off like that, he told himself. He should have stayed to make sure Sean and Frannie and Cyrus were safe. He should have known that the colonel would be suspicious and would come back to the Williams spread sooner or later.

The Kid shoved those thoughts out of his head. He knew from tragic experience that all the "should haves" in the world meant nothing. All that mattered was what actually happened.

A column of black smoke climbed into the Arizona

sky that had turned a brilliant blue with the advent of morning.

The Kid bit back a curse and lashed the buckskin with the reins, trying to get more speed out of the horse. The buckskin responded gallantly, stretching out even more. The landscape flashed by in a blur. Man and horse were one, racing across the flats, bounding up and down the gentle hills, wheeling tightly around obstacles.

Finally The Kid realized that the horse's heart might burst if he kept up this pace. The buckskin would run himself to death, if that was what The Kid asked him to do. The Kid hauled back on the reins, slowing his mount a little even though the smoke curling into the sky called out to him with a terrible urgency.

It wouldn't do any good if the buckskin collapsed underneath him, he told himself. He held the horse at a hard run instead of the full-out sprint.

He couldn't hear the shots anymore, but it was unlikely he'd be able to hear them over the buckskin's pounding hoofbeats, even if they continued.

A long rise loomed in front of him. The Kid knew that the ranch headquarters was on the other side of that rise. There was no longer any doubt about where the thick black smoke was coming from.

He pulled the Winchester from its sheath as he started up the rise. If whoever had attacked the ranch was still there, he intended to make them pay for what they had done.

As he topped the rise, he saw that the raiders were gone. Nothing was moving around the ranch. Smoke poured up from the house, the barn, and the bunkhouse. Those structures were made of adobe, but their interiors could burn. The corral was empty and its gate open. The raiders had taken the horses with them.

The Kid's heart slugged heavily in his chest as he spotted several dark shapes sprawled on the ground near the bunkhouse. The vaqueros must have run outside when the shooting started, only to be cut down. Another body lay face down near the house. The Kid rode hard toward it. Maybe somebody was still alive. He knew it was a forlorn hope, but he couldn't abandon it.

As he came closer, he saw a big hole in the wall of the house, as if something had smashed through it. He didn't know what could have inflicted the damage but it didn't really matter. He hauled back on the reins and slowed the buckskin, swinging down from the saddle even before the horse came to a halt. The Kid landed running, with the Winchester held ready for instant use if he needed it.

He recognized the man lying facedown as Sean Williams. The Kid dropped to a knee beside the young rancher and set the rifle on the ground. He took hold of Sean's shoulders and carefully rolled him onto his back. The Kid's hard-planed face took on an even grimmer cast as he saw how sodden with blood Sean's shirt was. The rancher was shot to pieces.

But somehow, he was still alive. His eyelids flickered open. The Kid slipped an arm under his shoulders and lifted him a little. He peered up at The Kid without seeming to recognize him. "F-Frannie?" he husked.

"It's Morgan, Sean," The Kid said. "What happened?"

Blood dribbled in a crimson stream from the corner of Sean's mouth. He still didn't seem to know who The Kid was, but he answered the question.

"Men . . . rode up . . . started shooting . . . we'd just sat down . . . to breakfast . . . I ran to the door . . . oh, God!" His face twisted, either from pain or the memory of what had happened or both. "There was . . . a terrible noise . . . something came through the wall . . . Frannie and Cyrus were still at the table . . . Oh, God! No! No!"

The Kid glanced at the hole in the wall. If whatever had caused that destruction had gone on through and hit Frannie and Cyrus, there was no way they had survived. And if they were still in the burning house, there might not even be anything left of their bodies.

Sean's fingers clutched at The Kid's arm. "You've got to . . . save them . . . get them out . . ."

"Sure," The Kid said. "I'll do what I can, Sean. I swear."

But he didn't get up, knowing that there was no point. He had already seen the light fading in Sean's eyes, and a moment later, the young man's grip relaxed and his fingers slid off The Kid's arm. His breath came out of him in a long, final sigh. The Kid closed Sean's eyes and eased him back to the ground.

The Kid stood up and looked toward the house. He had promised Sean that he would do what he could for Frannie and Cyrus, and he fully intended to keep that promise. He would also do the one thing that was within his power.

He would avenge their deaths.

The Kid checked on the three vaqueros who lay near the bunkhouse and found that they were dead, also shot full of holes just like Sean. He didn't see the fourth member of the crew, but he assumed the man's body was inside the bunkhouse, being consumed by the flames. He couldn't put out the fires. They would just have to burn themselves out.

In the meantime, he covered the bodies with blankets from his bedroll to keep scavengers off them, then mounted up and rode in a large circle around the ranch headquarters. He saw numerous hoofprints, and while he wasn't an expert tracker like his father, he could tell that the men who'd attacked the ranch had approached the place from the southeast.

The Kid noticed something else that was odd—two parallel lines etched into the sandy ground that looked like the tracks of wagon wheels. They were too close together to be wagon tracks, though. He wasn't sure what had made the marks, but he was reasonably certain it was something the raiders had brought with them, then taken away again, because the marks turned and went back in the other direction.

The place where they turned around was on top of a small ridge that commanded a good view of the ranch house. The Kid sat there on the buckskin for a long moment, frowning as he thought about what he was looking at. An idea played around in the back of his mind, but he didn't know if there was any truth to it.

The fires inside the buildings were starting to die down. The roofs had collapsed, but the adobe walls still stood. The Kid rode back down there, dismounted, and started looking around for a shovel. He found one in a small shed that stood near the barn but wasn't attached to it. The fire hadn't spread that far.

He walked up a small, aspen-dotted hill behind the ranch house that looked like it might be a good place to dig some graves. He figured Sean and Frannie and Cyrus would like to be laid to rest overlooking the home where they had lived for too short a time. He hadn't started digging, though, when he heard a sudden rustling noise in some nearby brush. Instinct made The Kid drop the shovel and whirl toward the sound, palming out his Colt as he did so.

A weak voice said, "P-Please, señor . . . h-help me . . ."

Wary of a trap, The Kid approached the brush carefully, gun in hand. He crouched, moved some branches aside, and saw a man he recognized as one of the Williams vaqueros lying there covered with blood.

No one else was around. The Kid holstered his gun and moved quickly to the injured man's side. One glance was enough to tell him that the vaquero was in the same shape as Sean Williams had been—shot to pieces and not long for this world.

"Did you see the man who did this to you, amigo?"

The vaquero's tongue came out and licked blood-smeared lips. His hands moved aimlessly around his bullet-shredded midsection. "The hombres . . . Señor Sean . . . warned us about . . . a dozen of them . . . maybe more . . . they had . . . *artilleria* . . ."

The Kid wasn't sure he had heard right, but what he thought the vaquero had said fit in with the theory he had come up with. On one knee next to the man, he leaned closer and said, "You mean a cannon?"

"Sí, señor . . . a c-cannon . . ." A shiver went through the man, and he cried out, "Aii, Dios mio!"

Those were his final words. His head slumped to the side. His eyes were open and staring without seeing anything.

The Kid closed this man's eyes as he had Sean's, then came to his feet and looked down at the ranch house. A cannonball had caused the hole in the wall. The words of the dying vaquero had confirmed his suspicions. The cart on which the big gun was mounted had left those tracks.

What sort of men would attack a peaceful ranch with a cannon and brutally wipe out a family that had done nothing wrong?

Even as that question went through The Kid's mind, he knew the answer.

The sort of men who rode with Colonel Gideon Black.

He had known as soon as he saw them that they were evil, cold-blooded killers. The colonel himself had seemed different, polite and well-spoken. But he had been in charge, and he had to know the kind of men who were riding with him. To The Kid's way of thinking, that made Colonel Black just as bad or worse. The Kid had no doubt that it was Black who had ordered the attack on the ranch after finding the bodies of the men buried under the bank of the arroyo. Black hadn't asked any questions. He had just assumed that those on the Williams ranch were responsible for the deaths of his men, and he had acted quickly and ruthlessly to settle the score for them.

Colonel Black was going to discover that he wasn't the only one who could avenge some deaths. The Kid intended to make the colonel and his men pay for what had happened there that morning. He didn't care how many of them there were, and he didn't give a damn that they had a cannon. The big gun didn't matter.

Before this was over, The Kid vowed as he stood on the hill and looked at the thinning smoke from the ruined ranch, there was going to be one hell of a big gundown.

Chapter 8

Bisbee, Arizona Territory, was nestled in the Mule Mountains, not far from the Mexican border. It was stretching a point to call the low peaks around them mountains, but in that generally flat country, The Kid supposed they qualified. Dusk was settling down, and lights from the buildings were spread across the lower slopes.

The discovery of copper in the area almost twenty years earlier had led to the founding of the settlement, and it had grown as miners realized that smaller quantities of gold and silver could be found along with the copper. The Kid recalled that as Conrad Browning, he had owned a stake in a copper mine near there. Still did, he supposed, but he had never visited the operation and it had represented nothing to him then except some figures on a balance sheet. Now it was even less than that to him. He had no reason to go there, at least none that he knew of.

The first time Colonel Black came to the Williams ranch, he had said that he and his men were headed up the San Pedro. That might have been a lie, or it might be that the killers had indeed gone up the river and then returned to the ranch to wipe out the Williams family. Either way, The Kid didn't know where they were now, and since he wanted to pick up their trail, the best place to start seemed to be Bisbee. He knew from what Sean and Frannie had told him that the four men he'd killed on the ranch had been planning to rendezvous with Colonel Black in Bisbee.

Somebody there would be able to tell him where to find the colonel.

Once The Kid knew that, his plan was simple: kill the son of a bitch and everybody with him.

It was all he could do for Sean and Frannie and Cyrus.

In the early afternoon he had found the bodies of mother and son in the charred ruins of the ranch house, once the heat had subsided enough for him to go inside. The ashes were still hot under his boots, so he moved quickly as he wrapped the bodies in blankets and carried them out to place them gently next to Sean's body. He had already dug seven graves up on the hillside. He was drenched with sweat, his muscles ached and there was still work to be done.

The metal framework of the wagon that had been inside the barn was still relatively intact. Only some of it was twisted from the heat of the flames. The Kid shook out his rope, tied the vehicle to the buckskin, and used the horse to pull it out of the ruins. He found enough scraps of charred lumber and cobbled together a new bed for the wagon. Once he had done

that, he placed the bodies on the wagon and used it to
carry them up the hill to the gravesites.

Earlier, he had spotted the basket where Cyrus had
kept the pups. A glance into the basket told him that
someone had emptied a six-gun into it. The Kid took
the basket up the hill, too, and put it into the grave
with Cyrus. Then he started filling in the seven holes.

It was mid-afternoon by the time he finished, and
he still had a long ride to Bisbee. But he paused long
enough to stand for a moment over the graves. He
wasn't a praying man—he didn't think *El Señor
Dios* would look too kindly on words from a man
who had so much blood on his hands—so he said to
the people he had just buried, "I can't make it right.
But I can make the bastards pay."

He was settling his hat on his head when he saw
movement down at the ranch. A couple of small dark
shapes darted around the ruins. The Kid frowned,
wondering if they were rats.

When he heard the faint yipping he knew that he
was looking at a couple of Cyrus's pups. Somehow
they had escaped the massacre of their brothers and
sisters. Probably off wandering around somewhere
when the attack came.

The Kid thought about it for a long moment, then
heaved a sigh. He mounted up, rode down the hill,
and called and whistled until the puppies came to
him. He made room in his saddlebags, scooped them
up, and put them in there. As the buckskin walked
along Bisbee's main street a few hours later, they
were still there, their heads sticking out the top of the
saddlebag as they looked around. They didn't weigh

more than a few pounds each, little squirming bundles of black and gray and brown, and The Kid didn't know what the hell he was going to do with them. All he knew was that he couldn't leave them on the death-haunted ranch to survive on their own. Cyrus wouldn't have wanted that.

The Kid angled the buckskin toward the hitch rail in front of a general store that was still open. He saw two men walking along the planks of the boardwalk toward the store but didn't pay much attention to them as he dismounted. He took the pups out of the saddlebag and cradled them both in the crook of his left arm as he started up the steps to the high loading dock in front of the store.

"Would you look at that, Rawley? Fella's got hisself some little dogs."

The Kid glanced toward the men, saw them elbowing each other and laughing as they looked at him and the pups.

"Naw, them ain't proper dogs, Paxton," the one called Rawley said. "Look how little they are. I think maybe they're prairie dogs."

Paxton giggled. "You ever had fried prairie dog? It ain't bad."

"Yeah, and I'm hungry." Rawley grinned at The Kid. "Say, mister, you want to sell us those little varmints? We'll fry 'em up and see how tasty they are."

The Kid recognized the two men for what they were with a single look. Rawley wore a Mexican sombrero with little balls dangling from the brim, while Paxton sported a dusty black suit and Stetson. Both men carried Colts in cut-down, tied-down holsters. Would-be hard cases and desperadoes, men who fancied themselves fast with their guns. They'd been drinking, but their steps were steady enough and they didn't sway as they stood on the store's loading dock grinning at The Kid. The combination of all those things made them dangerous, although The Kid wasn't particularly worried. He just didn't want to be bothered with them.

"Sorry, boys," he said. "These pups aren't for sale. I'm looking for a good home for them, though."

"We'll give 'em a good home," Paxton said. He grinned and rubbed his belly.

"Hand 'em over, mister," Rawley added, "and there won't be no trouble."

This was ridiculous, The Kid thought. The two men didn't really want the puppies. They were just looking for an excuse to bully somebody, and the pups had provided it.

"There won't be any trouble," The Kid said flatly. "I'm going in the store, and the pups are coming with me."

Rawley's lips pulled back from his teeth as his mouth curled in a sneer. The Kid's response was just what he'd been waiting for.

"What if we say they ain't?"

"Then you'll be wrong."

"You know who we are?" Paxton demanded in a blustering tone. "You got any idea who you're messin' with here, boy?"

"I think I do." The Kid paused. "A couple of damned fools looking for somebody to run roughshod over. Well, I have to tell you, I'm in no mood for it."

Both gunnies stiffened in outrage at The Kid's words. "Why, you little piss-ant!" Paxton spat. "You can't talk to us like that!"

"Sure as hell can't!" Rawley added.

The Kid took a step toward the store's entrance. "Go somewhere and finish getting drunk. And leave me alone while you're at it."

He wasn't trying to pick a fight with them. He honestly wanted them to go on and leave him alone. If they had done so, that would have been the end of it.

But Paxton yelled, "You son of a bitch!" and reached for his gun, and Rawley made his draw in silence.

The confrontation wasn't worth killing over, but both men were fairly fast and The Kid knew he wouldn't have the time for anything fancy. He pivoted toward them as the Colt leaped into his hand as if by magic. The two hard cases had called the tune. Time for them to dance to it.

Both men cleared leather, but The Kid's gun was level while their weapons were still coming up. The Colt roared and bucked in his hand as he put his first shot in Rawley's chest. The impact rocked the man back a step, but he stayed on his feet. The Kid switched his aim and fired again, this time at Paxton. Paxton was moving, darting to the side as The Kid drew, so that the bullet intended for Paxton's heart shattered his left arm about halfway between the elbow and shoulder instead. Paxton screamed in agony as the shot spun him halfway around.

Rawley was still trying to get a shot off, so The Kid planted another round in him. Rawley's head jerked, and the sombrero with its dangling, decorative balls went flying off his head. He finally managed to pull the trigger, but his gun was still pointed down and the slug smacked harmlessly into the loading dock at his feet. Rawley fell to his knees and pitched forward onto his face.

Panting in pain through clenched teeth, Paxton stood at the edge of the dock and tried again to raise his gun. The Kid fired for a fourth time, and this bullet sent Paxton plunging off the dock into the street. His face plowed into the dirt as he landed. He didn't move again.

The pups had been squirming before the shots began to roar, but the thunderous reports had stunned them into stillness. The Kid glanced down at them to make sure they were all right and saw them staring up at him wide-eyed, with almost human expressions.

"Sorry," he said.

He turned his attention back to the two men he'd just shot. He was pretty sure they were both dead, but he still had one round left in the revolver's cylinder in case he needed it.

Neither man was moving. The Kid stepped over to the edge of the loading dock to take a closer look at Paxton, then used the toe of one of his boots to roll Rawley onto his back. The man stared up sightlessly into the night.

Bisbee had a reputation as a tough town. Most settlements that had sprung up because of their proximity to mines were like that. But even so, an outburst of gunfire was enough to draw considerable attention. A number of men converged on the general store to see what all the commotion was about.

He glanced over his shoulder when he heard a clicking sound behind him. He saw a man standing in the store's doorway, pointing a double-barreled shotgun at him. The sound he'd heard had been both hammers of the greener being cocked.

"I want to see both hands empty, mister," the man holding the shotgun grated, "or I'll blow you plumb in two!"

Chapter 9

"Take it easy, Sheriff." The Kid had spotted the badge pinned to the shotgunner's vest right away. "The shooting's over."

"Damn right it's over. If there's any more guns goin' off, it's gonna be this greener o' mine! I said show me your hands!"

The Kid slid his Colt back in its holster. He didn't like pouching the iron without reloading it first, but under the circumstances he supposed it was the best thing to do.

"I'm not going to drop these pups," he told the lawman. "I can't very well shoot anybody with them, though, so I reckon you'll have to be satisfied with one empty hand."

The sheriff stepped out farther onto the loading dock. "Don't you go gettin' smart with me, boy. You're gonna march right down to my jail. I'm lockin' you up."

A tall, thick-bodied, balding man in an apron followed him onto the dock. "Why would you do that,

Stewart?" he asked. "We both saw what happened. The stranger killed Paxton and Rawley in self-defense."

"I don't abide killin's!" the sheriff snapped. "I'm puttin' this fella behind bars until there's an inquest."

"Yeah, well, you know what the coroner's jury is going to say. I'll testify that Paxton and Rawley drew first, and that the stranger was just defending himself. You'll be wasting your time and the county's money locking him up."

Sheriff Stewart turned his head to glare at the store owner. The Kid figured that's who the man in the apron was. Stewart said, "I don't like anybody tellin' me how to do my job. You may be the mayor of Bisbee, Carmichael, but I work for the county, not the town!"

"I know that," Carmichael said, "and I'm not trying to tell you how to do your job. I'm just saying that it's pointless to put this man in jail tonight and turn him loose tomorrow." He glanced at the bodies of the two dead gunmen. "Besides, nobody's going to lose any sleep over those two. They were born troublemakers."

"Well, you're right about that," Stewart admitted grudgingly. He looked at The Kid again. "You plannin' on ridin' out of town tonight?"

"No. I'll be here for a day or two, at least."

"You'll be here until after the inquest tomorrow, that's for damn sure. I want your word on it."

"You've got it," The Kid said.

The sheriff finally lowered his scattergun, and once the twin barrels were pointed toward the ground, he eased the hammers back down. He was on the short side, a middle-aged man with a brushy mustache and what seemed to be a perpetual glare. He gave The Kid a curt nod and said, "I'll fetch the undertaker. Don't give him any more work while you're in Bisbee, if you know what's good for you."

If The Kid knew what was good for him, he wouldn't be in Bisbee on the trail of a gang of vicious, murdering sons of bitches armed with a damned cannon, of all things, but he didn't explain any of that to Sheriff Stewart. Instead he just returned the lawman's nod.

The store owner, Carmichael, motioned to The Kid as Stewart headed up the street with the greener tucked under his arm. "Come on in. I'd like to talk to you."

The Kid had been headed into the general store anyway, so he followed the proprietor inside. A few customers were clustered just inside the entrance, peering out curiously.

"It's all over, folks," Carmichael told them. "You can go on about your business now, especially if your business is buying merchandise from me." He grinned.

The little knot of people dispersed. Carmichael gestured for The Kid to follow him toward the back of the store, where there was a long counter. Carmichael went behind it and pointed to a stool in front of it.

"Have a seat, Mister . . . ?"

"Morgan," The Kid supplied, without adding the rest of it. He held on to the pups.

"You can set 'em down if you want. I don't think they'll get into too much trouble."

"That's all right. They're pretty hungry. They might start looking for something to eat."

"Well, we can take care of that. Got some beef

scraps they can have. Are they big enough to eat something like that?"

"I don't know. They're not really my pups. I sort of . . . inherited them. I'm looking for a good home for them, as well as some information."

"About dogs?"

"About a man," The Kid said. "Colonel Gideon Black."

A scowl appeared on Carmichael's normally friendly face. "I know the name. Don't really know the man, though. Don't want to, either."

"Why not?"

Carmichael hesitated. "I don't want to say anything against the man, in case he's your friend."

"He's not," The Kid assured the storekeeper. "I never met the man." Technically, that was true, although he had laid eyes on the colonel once. "I promised some people I'd look him up, and I was told that he's been here in Bisbee lately."

"That's true. He's been in and out of town several times in recent weeks. I don't really know the man myself, so I shouldn't make any judgments as to his character. I'm just going by the company he keeps."

"Bad company, huh?" The Kid asked, even though he already knew the answer.

Carmichael nodded toward the street. "Those two gunnies you just tangled with out there . . ."

"Colonel Black's men?" The Kid asked, somewhat surprised.

"Not really. They wanted to be, but I reckon Black turned them down. They didn't ride out with him the last time he left. Plenty of other hard cases did, though. That's why I don't care much for the colonel.

He's surrounded himself with gunmen. Outlaws and hired killers, if you ask me."

The Kid nodded. So far, Carmichael hadn't really told him anything that he didn't already know, except that Paxton and Rawley had been would-be members of the colonel's gang, and that Black had found them wanting for some reason.

They hadn't been fast enough and tough enough, more than likely, and Black had sensed that somehow. The Kid hadn't had much trouble disposing of them. Black's men had to have more bark on them than those two.

"You think he's liable to take offense at what happened to Rawley and Paxton?" The Kid asked.

"I don't know. Like I said, they didn't actually ride with him. They're the reason I wanted to talk to you, though."

"What about?" The Kid asked warily.

Carmichael placed his hands flat on the counter. "There's getting to be more and more of that sort of men around here. Bisbee's always been a pretty rugged place, but it's getting worse. The county sheriff has always handled law and order here in town, too, but the town council and I have been thinking that it's time to hire a city marshal. To be blunt, I'd like to offer you the job, Mr. Morgan."

The proposition took The Kid by surprise. "You just met me. You don't really know anything about me."

"I know you're mighty slick on the draw, and you didn't even think about backing down when those two started to ride you. That's the sort of man we need to keep the peace here in Bisbee."

The Kid's first impulse was to laugh. Pinning on a

lawman's badge was just about the last thing he ever wanted to do. Wearing a badge meant wearing a cloak of responsibility and respectability, too. He didn't want to be tied down, and he didn't want anybody looking to him to solve their problems. Whenever he stepped in and took a hand in something, he did so because it was his own choice, not because it was his duty.

He settled for shaking his head and saying, "Sorry, Mayor. I'm not looking for a job right now. Not that kind, anyway."

Carmichael's eyes narrowed. "That's right, you said you were planning to look up Colonel Black. I reckon maybe I misjudged you, Mr. Morgan."

"Maybe you did." The Kid paused. "But I'm still looking for a good home for these pups."

"Well . . . I might be able to help you out there. It so happens I've got an eight-year-old grandson here in town, and I think he'd love to have a couple of fine little pups like these."

"He'll take good care of them?"

"I'll see to it." Carmichael held out his hands, and The Kid gave him the puppies. The storekeeper shook his head. "No offense, Mr. Morgan, but I never figured a man who can handle himself in a gunfight the way you did out there would be so worried about a couple of pups."

"Like I said, I inherited them from somebody special. I want them to have a good life."

"They will. You've got my word on it."

The Kid nodded and started to turn away. "I'll probably be back before I leave town to stock up on some supplies."

"You'll be welcome. And Mr. Morgan . . . ?"

The Kid looked at him.

"I don't know why I'm doing this," Carmichael said, "but if you're bound and determined to meet up with Colonel Black, he spends a lot of time at a place called Augustine's when he's in town. It's a couple of blocks up on the right."

The Kid nodded. "Thanks."

"Don't thank me. Maybe I'm hoping that when the colonel finds out you killed Rawley and Paxton, he'll try to even the score for them."

A cold smile tugged at The Kid's mouth. "You're thinking that he'll kill me?"

"Or you'll kill him." Carmichael shrugged. "Either way, I think Bisbee might be better off."

"You could be right," The Kid said.

Chapter 10

The Kid scratched the pups behind the ears by way of farewell, then left Carmichael's store and headed up the street, leading the buckskin. It didn't take him long to spot Augustine's. The place was big and brightly lit, obviously one of the leading saloons in Bisbee. In a mining town like this, where there were probably more saloons than all the other businesses put together, that was saying something.

After looping the buckskin's reins around a crowded hitch rail in front of Augustine's, The Kid stepped onto the boardwalk and pushed through the batwings. Not surprisingly, it was loud and smoky inside the saloon. Chandeliers made from wagon wheels hung from the ceiling, each with half a dozen oil lamps mounted on it casting a harsh glare over the big room. The long hardwood bar ran down the right side. Poker, faro, and roulette were set up on the left. The area in between was filled with tables and chairs where miners with grimy faces and hands and equally grim clothes sat and drank so they wouldn't think about the tedious, dangerous life they led underground. At the far end of the room, a staircase with an ornately carved banister led up to the second floor with its balcony that overhung the bar. As The Kid paused just inside the saloon's entrance, he watched two whores in gaudy, spangled dresses leading customers upstairs, while a miner came down the stairs with a big grin on his face and fewer coins in his pocket.

The Kid had seen dozens of saloons like this, although to be fair about it, Augustine's was one of the biggest and best-furnished he had run across since he started drifting. Of course, it couldn't hold a candle to some of the establishments he had patronized in Boston, New York, Chicago, Denver, and San Francisco, back when he hadn't cared who knew that he was a rich man.

He was still a rich man, but he didn't flaunt his wealth now. Just like his father, the money was important to him only because it allowed him to keep drifting without having to worry about how he was going to pay for his next meal or the supplies to carry him over the next hill.

He spotted an empty place at the bar and started toward it. It had been a long, terrible day, and he intended to chase away not only his thirst but also some of his weariness with a mug of what a sign over the bar proclaimed to be ice-cold beer.

Before he could reach the bar, though, a man ran into his shoulder with a heavy jolt. The Kid had to take a quick step to the side to keep his balance and not fall down.

"Watch where you're goin'," the man growled. He was a miner, a tall man whose shirt bulged from the massive, slab-like muscles on his arms and shoulders, muscles that had developed from years of working with a pick and shovel.

"Maybe you're the one who should watch your step, mister."

The words came out of The Kid's mouth before he could stop them, but even if he had thought about it, he would have spoken up anyway. He had learned from Frank Morgan and from life itself not to go looking for trouble, but not to back down from it, either. The Kid came by that honestly.

The miner stopped and swung around to glower darkly at him. "What the hell did you just say to me?" he demanded. He had a faint accent that marked him as being English. A Cornishman, maybe, The Kid judged. He had been to England several times, but he was far from an expert on the accents of people who hailed from that island nation.

"I said you should watch your step." The Kid nodded toward the bar. "And while we were talking, someone else got that empty spot we were both after."

He had guessed that was the miner's goal, and the way the man's head jerked toward the bar confirmed it. "Blast it!" the man said. "If you hadn't run into me, you American lout, I'd be there drinkin' now."

The Kid didn't care for that "American lout" comment. After all, the miner was over here working in an American mine, being paid American wages. If he didn't care for the country and its citizens, he could always go back where he came from.

But The Kid wasn't going to start a fight. He started to step around the miner. "There's room for all of us."

The man's hand came down hard on his shoulder. "No, there ain't," he said as he hauled The Kid around and swung a mallet-like fist at his head.

The miner's problem was that all those muscles might give him incredible strength, but they also slowed him down. The crowd around the two men suddenly began to clear as the saloon's customers scrambled to get out of the way. The Kid weaved to the side and let the big fist sail harmlessly past his ear.

He stepped in and hooked a right into the miner's belly. That was usually where the soft spot was on big galoots like him.

In this case, though, it was like punching a brick wall. The Kid almost yelped from the pain that shot through his knuckles as he drove them into iron-hard stomach muscles.

The miner just grinned at him, grabbed him by both shoulders, and flung him hard against the bar.

The edge of the hardwood caught The Kid in the back, forcing him to bend over backwards. The impact against the bar knocked the breath out of him, and he was stunned and gasping for a second. That gave the miner time to lace his fingers together and lunge at The Kid, bringing both hands up and swinging them like a club at the young gunfighter's head.

The Kid recovered just in time to roll away from what would have been a devastating blow. The miner's fists crashed down on the hardwood. The Kid pushed away from the bar and threw a punch of his own. It caught the miner on the ear and stung. The man howled furiously.

It never occurred to The Kid to draw his Colt. The miner was unarmed. He was also just as tall as

The Kid, and was heavier and had a longer reach, giving him the advantage. The man waded in, swinging wild punches.

The Kid was able to block some of the blows, but some of them got through and rocked him. Luckily, the punches that landed were all to his body. If any of the miner's head shots had connected, in all likelihood the fight would have been over. As it was, The Kid was pinned back against the bar. He was vaguely aware that everyone in the saloon was shouting. They were probably yelling encouragement to his opponent, since the other miners would know him and The Kid was a stranger.

As he tried to slide along the bar and shift position, his left leg suddenly threatened to buckle. He had worked hard and then ridden a long way, and it had been less than a week since he'd been shot.

The Kid had seen the heavy, lace-up work boots the miner wore. He knew that if he went down, it was entirely possible the man would stomp him to death.

The little lurch he'd made when his leg twinged had caused one of the miner's punches to miss. The man was close, his breath hot in The Kid's face. The Kid lifted his right fist in a vicious uppercut that landed cleanly under the miner's chin. It might not have done too much damage if the tip of the man's tongue hadn't been protruding between his front teeth at that instant.

But as it was, those teeth came together sharply, and blood spurted as they bit completely through the tongue, severing about a quarter of an inch from the tip. The miner staggered back, roaring in pain as blood bubbled over his lips from the mutilated tongue.

The Kid went after him, not giving the miner a chance to recover. He swung a left and a right and another left to the man's jaw, rocking his head back and forth with each punch. A stiff right jab landed on the miner's mouth. The Kid kicked him in the knee, and as the miner started to bend over, The Kid bulled into him, driving him backward. The miner lost his balance and fell, landing on his back on a table that collapsed under him, its legs splintering. He crashed to the floor in a welter of debris and lay there stunned with his bloody tongue sticking out of his mouth.

Chest heaving, The Kid looked around. All he saw were unfriendly faces. He had been right in his guess about the shouts. The sentiment in the saloon was definitely against him. Angry, dirty-faced men began to sidle toward him. His hand moved toward his gun. There was no way he could fight more than a dozen miners, especially as beat up as he already was.

"That'll be enough, gentlemen!"

The deep, powerful voice cut through the angry muttering that filled the room. A stocky, heavy-jawed man in a dark suit came along the bar. The miners stepped back to let him by, even though he was unarmed and smaller than most of them. Judging by the man's expensive clothes and the air of command about him, The Kid pegged him as the owner of the saloon. As such, the miners wouldn't want to cross him, even though he was interfering with their fun.

"Next round is on the house," the man announced, confirming The Kid's hunch that he was the owner.

That offer was enough to defuse the situation. The miners dragged their fallen comrade into a corner and propped him up at a table. One of them reached down and picked up something from the floor, regarding it intently for a moment before he flicked it into a spittoon. The Kid knew that the item was the bitten-off tip of the miner's tongue. Oh, well, the hombre didn't have any use for it anymore.

"I'm Charles Augustine," the man announced as he stood in front of The Kid. "Why don't you come with me? I'd like to buy you a drink."

The Kid looked around until he spotted his hat lying on the floor. He picked it up, brushed off the sawdust, punched it back into shape, and settled it on his head.

"That's liable to get you in bad with this bunch."

Charles Augustine smiled. "You think I'm worried about that? I have the coldest beer, the finest whiskey, and the prettiest whores in Bisbee. As long as those three things are true, those miners don't care what I do."

The Kid knew that was probably true. He followed Augustine through the surly crowd. No one tried to stop them or even slow them down. Augustine led him through a door at the end of the bar, along a short hallway, and through another door into an opulently furnished office dominated by a big desk and a square, massive safe. Augustine went to a small bar in the corner and picked up a crystal decanter half filled with amber liquid.

"Brandy all right?"

"Fine," The Kid said. He had come into the saloon to get a beer and maybe find out something about Colonel Gideon Black, and instead his temper and some bad luck had gotten him into a brawl. He would settle for brandy instead of the beer, but he still hoped for some information about the man he was looking for.

Augustine poured brandy into a couple of snifters and brought them over to The Kid, who took one of them. Augustine clinked the glasses together and said, "To the best fight I've seen in here in, oh, at least a week."

The Kid sipped the brandy. It was like liquid fire and kindled a welcome blaze in his belly. "You have a lot of fights in here?"

"I don't discourage them. I always collect damages, from the mining companies if not from the miners themselves. They like to blow off steam when they come to town. A little fracas every now and then is good for business."

The Kid nodded and took another sip of the brandy. He noticed Augustine studying him with a canny expression but didn't really think anything about it until the saloon owner said, "You're not who you're pretending to be."

Chapter 11

That statement took The Kid by surprise. "What are you talking about?" he said. "I haven't even told you my name yet."

Augustine waved a well-manicured hand. "Your name doesn't matter. You come in here wearing buckskins and boots and a big hat, and you've got a Colt strapped on like you're some sort of gunslinger. But you sip that brandy like a cultured man who's tasted fine liquor before."

"You've got me all wrong, Mr. Augustine. I'm just a drifter."

Augustine smiled like he didn't believe that for a second, but he said, "Have it your way. So tell me what you're calling yourself."

"Morgan."

Augustine lifted his snifter of brandy in a salute. "I'm pleased to meet you, Mr. Morgan. It's not every man who can take Clyde Watkins in a bare-knuckles fight. In fact, I'm not sure anyone in these parts has ever done that before."

"That'd be that miner downstairs?"

"That's right."

The Kid shrugged. "There was a little bit of luck involved. If he hadn't bitten off the end of his tongue, I'm not sure I would have been able to put him down."

"I'm not sure I believe in luck. Strange thing for a gambler to say, isn't it?"

The Kid lifted his glass in acknowledgment of that point and took another sip.

"Over time, the man who's the best at what he does always prevails," Augustine continued. "That's why I like to surround myself with talented people, whether those talents involve dealing cards . . . or dealing other things."

"Are you working your way around to offering me a job, Mr. Augustine?"

"Would that bother you?"

"No, but I'd turn it down, just like I turned down Mayor Carmichael when he wanted to pin a city marshal's badge on me."

Augustine looked at The Kid for a moment, obviously surprised by what he'd just heard. Then the saloonkeeper threw back his head and laughed.

"You're the man who killed Rawley and Paxton over in front of Carmichael's store!"

"News travels fast," The Kid said.

"I heard about it almost as soon as it happened. I make it my business to hear about everything that goes on in Bisbee. I didn't know until now that you were involved in that shooting, though. That makes me even happier that I asked you to come back here and have a drink with me."

"I told you, I'm not looking for a job—"

"And I'm not offering you one," Augustine said. "But I know someone who might, and you'd be wise to reserve judgment on whether or not you'll accept, Mr. Morgan. Have you ever heard of a man named Edward Sheffield?"

Now it was The Kid's turn to be taken by surprise. He had expected Augustine to steer him to Colonel Gideon Black, since according to Mayor Carmichael, Black spent considerable time at this saloon whenever he was in Bisbee.

Augustine hadn't mentioned Black at all, though. Instead he had thrown out a name that was indeed familiar to Kid Morgan.

Or at least, Edward Sheffield's name was familiar to Conrad Browning.

Before the tragedy that had forever changed Conrad's life, the vast Browning business empire had included interests in both railroads and mining. It still did, of course, although The Kid no longer had anything to do with the day-to-day running of them.

Edward Sheffield was a financier who also dabbled in railroads and mining, among other enterprises. He and Conrad had held seats on the boards of some of the same companies, but never at the same time. So while The Kid knew the name, he had never actually met Sheffield.

Cautiously, he said, "Some sort of big business tycoon, isn't he?"

"You could say that. Between the railroads and the mines, he's played a large part in developing this part of the territory. He has a very successful copper mine up in the Dragoons that also produces significant amounts of gold and silver. There's a town up

there—Titusville, named after Mr. Sheffield's father—
that he owns pretty much lock, stock, and barrel. And
he's built a spur line from the Southern Pacific here
at Bisbee all the way to Titusville to carry in supplies
and carry out the ore from the mine."

The Kid hadn't heard about any of that. He supposed
they were fairly recent developments in Sheffield's
career.

"Sounds like he's pretty successful. I don't see
what that has to do with me, though."

Augustine threw back the last of his brandy. "I
happen to know that Mr. Sheffield is having some
trouble. Outlaw trouble. And he's looking for somebody to do something about it."

"You mean he's looking for hired guns," The Kid
said.

"Not just hired guns. He needs someone to take
charge of the effort to wipe out those desperadoes."

"And you think I could be that man."

Augustine shrugged. "You're fast enough on the
draw to kill a couple of men who were pretty gun-
handy, and tough enough to chop down a miner who's
been known to take on three or four men at once and
thrash them all. I think you're exactly what Edward
Sheffield is looking for. I think you should talk to him,
anyway."

The Kid was about to repeat that he wasn't looking for a job, when a hunch occurred to him.

"These outlaws . . . what do you know about them?"

"Nobody *knows* much of anything, but I have my
suspicions. I think they're led by an ex-army colonel
who's turned renegade, a man named Gideon Black."

The Kid didn't allow any reaction to show on his face. "I've heard of him," he said.

"He's been around these parts for a while. Sheriff Stewart doesn't have any proof that Black's involved in anything illegal, but from the looks of it, Black's been recruiting hard cases and putting together a pretty good-sized gang. Mr. Sheffield thinks that they're the ones who have held up a couple of his trains."

The Kid finished off the brandy in his snifter. "I didn't know that. I'd heard that Black was looking for some good men, though. As a matter of fact, that's why I'm here."

Augustine's rather bushy eyebrows rose. "Then I may have spoken out of turn, if you're planning on joining up with the colonel."

"I haven't made any plans," The Kid said. "Just heard the rumors and drifted into town to get the lay of the land. I'm open to the best opportunity . . . whatever it is."

"Then you'll want to talk to Edward Sheffield. He'll pay top dollar for a man who can put a stop to his trouble."

The Kid set the empty snifter on the bar. "You know, Mayor Carmichael told me that Black's been spending a lot of time in your place, Augustine. I got the impression that you and the colonel were friends. Now it seems more like you'd rather give Sheffield a hand."

Augustine smiled. "Just like you, Mr. Morgan, I'm open to the best opportunity. If Colonel Black and his men want to spend their money in my saloon, I'm perfectly willing to take it. At the same time, I wouldn't mind getting on the good side of a man like Edward

Sheffield. As I told you, he's probably the most important man in this part of the territory."

"In other words, you're playing both sides against
the middle." The Kid's words were blunt, and he
didn't soften his voice or smile as he delivered them.
He wanted to get a rise out of Augustine, if there was
one to be gotten. That was one thing he had learned
from his career in business: if you got under a man's
skin, he was liable to let more of the truth slip than
he intended to.

But Charles Augustine just chuckled in response
to The Kid's accusation. "Say it however you like.
I've never apologized for wanting to make money,
and I'm not going to start now."

"Fair enough," The Kid responded with a nod.
"Where do I find this man Sheffield?"

Augustine took a heavy gold turnip watch from his
vest pocket and flipped it open to check the time.
"You just got into Bisbee a little while ago, didn't
you, Mr. Morgan?"

"That's right. About an hour ago, I reckon." It
seemed longer ago than that, The Kid thought. But it
also seemed beyond belief that only this morning, the
Williams family and their vaqueros had still been
alive and happy. This day full of violence and death
had lasted a hundred years.

"Why don't you get yourself something to eat and
maybe find a hotel room, then come back here in
about an hour? The Bisbee House would suit all
those needs, since it's the best hotel in town and also
has a fine dining room. And a stable for your horse,
for that matter."

"How do you know I can afford a place like that?" The Kid asked with a faint smile.

"I don't, of course. But I assumed that a man who's familiar with fine brandy would also be accustomed to staying in the best places."

As a matter of fact, The Kid had plenty of money at the moment. During a recent stopover in Santa Fe, he'd had his attorney in San Francisco, Claudius Turnbuckle, wire him enough cash to cover his expenses for a while, and he hadn't spent much of it during the ride to Arizona Territory. And there was plenty more where that came from. The Kid's share of the Browning holdings generated enough revenue that he would never run out of money, even if he never earned another dime from his own efforts.

"All right, I'll check it out. My horse could use a good rubdown and something to eat." The Kid paused. "I suppose you want to send word to Sheffield and find out if it's all right for me to meet with him. Folks must tread lightly around him since he's the big man in these parts."

"That's right. But for what it's worth, Mr. Morgan, I'll put in a good word for you. I thought the way you handled Watkins was quite impressive, to say nothing of that shootout with Rawley and Paxton. As gunmen, they weren't quite at the same level as the men who ride with Colonel Black, but they were no slouches, either."

"All right, then. I'll be back in an hour or so." The Kid turned toward the door of the office.

"I'd better come with you. There may still be some resentment on the part of the miners over what happened to Watkins."

The Kid didn't argue with him. They walked out together. The Kid was aware of the angry glares sent in his direction by many of the saloon's customers. He saw Watkins still sitting at one of the tables. A man in a bowler hat was working on his tongue, either sewing it up or bandaging it or something. The black medical bag sitting open on the table told The Kid that the man in the bowler was a doctor.

Augustine paused on the boardwalk just outside the saloon's batwing doors. "The Bisbee House is in the next block. You can't miss it."

"Thanks," The Kid said. "For the brandy . . . and for that good word you're going to put in with Sheffield."

"I don't know that I'm doing you that much of a favor," Augustine said. "If you take the job, you'll be going up against heavy odds. I don't know how many men the colonel has now, but it could be more than two dozen."

Plus a cannon, thought The Kid. Those were heavy odds, all right.

Luckily, he didn't give a damn about things like that.

Chapter 12

The Bisbee House was a fine hotel, as Charles Augustine had said. A three-story building of adobe and brick, the upper two stories had wrought iron balconies along the front that overhung a broad porch where guests could sit in wicker chairs and sip drinks in the shade during the heat of the day. Gas lamps hissed softly as they filled the lobby with warm yellow light that gleamed on the brilliantly polished hardwood floors. Potted palms stood in the corners. Men in expensive suits sat on overstuffed divans and armchairs, reading newspapers. The place had the hushed atmosphere that came with money and power.

For that reason, the clerk at the desk looked a little askance at The Kid's buckskin shirt, denim trousers, high-topped boots, and broad-brimmed hat. The fact that he had a pair of saddlebags slung over his shoulder and was carrying a Winchester didn't help matters, either.

The clerk put his hands on the desk and leaned forward, saying, "Sir, I'm not sure—"

"I am," The Kid broke in. "I'll have a room, and I need someone to take my horse around to the stable and see that he's tended to. He's the big buckskin tied up right out front." He glanced through an arched doorway and saw people eating off fine china at tables covered with snowy linen tablecloths. "Good, the dining room is still open."

"Sir, I'm afraid I must insist—"

"On giving me the best accommodations in the house? I appreciate that." The Kid reached in his pocket and brought out several twenty-dollar gold pieces, which he stacked neatly on the desk in front of the surprised clerk. "There's a hundred dollars. Let me know when it runs out."

The clerk put his eyes back in his head, swallowed hard, and said, "Yes, sir."

The Kid smiled at him. "Go ahead. Pick one of them up and bite it. I know you're dying to."

The clerk shook his head. "No, sir. I'm sure your money is good." He banged the palm of his hand on a bell that sent a loud *ding* across the lobby. "You say your horse is a buckskin?"

"That's right."

"I'll have it taken care of, sir." The clerk turned the register around. "If you'd care to sign in . . ."

The Kid hesitated before reaching for the pen that rested in a holder with a black marble base. He didn't want to use the name Conrad Browning. He had put all that behind him. Most of the time it seemed to him like Conrad Browning was a completely different person. Besides, just as he had recognized Edward Sheffield's name, it was highly like that Sheffield had heard of Conrad. He didn't want word getting to Sheffield that Browning was in town.

Somehow it didn't seem right, though, to sign in as Kid Morgan. He had dubbed that dime-novelesque name on himself when he wanted the world to believe that Conrad Browning was dead, and the handle had stuck. The Kid had grown comfortable with it, and it was something of a tribute to his father, as well. But there was no getting around the fact that it was a little, well, melodramatic.

He settled for scrawling *K. Morgan* in the register, and in the space for his home address, he wrote *San Francisco*. That's where the offices of Turnbuckle & Stafford were, and that was as close to a home as The Kid had these days.

"Thank you, Mr. Morgan," the clerk said, reading the register upside down with a practiced eye. "If you need any help with your bags—"

"I don't," The Kid said. "This is all I have. Just see to the horse."

"Of course, sir."

It was amazing how much difference a stack of double eagles made in the way a man was treated, The Kid mused.

The clerk handed him the key to Room 28. "It's right on the front, with a fine view of the street."

From what The Kid had seen, the main street of Bisbee wasn't all that scenic. But he took the key, nodded, and said, "Much obliged."

A porter responded to the bell, and the clerk told him to get The Kid's horse and take it around back to the stable.

"See that he's well taken care of," The Kid added.

"Yes, sir," the porter replied with a nod. He grinned when The Kid pressed a fifty-cent piece into his hand.

The Kid was aware that some of the guests in the lobby were watching him curiously. To the eyes of those well-to-do businessmen, he wasn't the sort of man who normally patronized the Bisbee House. He felt them watching him as he went up the stairs carrying his rifle and saddlebags.

He climbed two flights and found Room 28 on the front of the hotel where the clerk had said it would be. The corridor had a thick carpet runner down the center of it, prints of landscape paintings on the walls, and ornate gas lamp fixtures.

The room itself was more of the same, except there was a large woven rug instead of the carpet runner. The paper on the walls had gold flecks in it. A pitcher and basin sat on a wash stand. The bed was heavy, the mattress thick. A wave of weariness came over him as he looked at it, and he wanted to just crawl into the bed and stay there for the next fourteen or fifteen hours.

Instead, he placed the Winchester and the saddlebags on the bed, tossed his hat beside him, and peeled off the buckskin shirt. He wanted to wash off the grime of the day.

When he had washed up as best he could, he pulled a white shirt, black whipcord trousers and a black vest and jacket out of the saddlebags. After shaking the wrinkles out of them, he donned them and then wrapped a black string tie around his neck.

He looked considerably different than when he had ridden into town. This garb was simple, far from the dandified get-ups he had worn as Conrad Browning, but it was more respectable than the trail clothes he usually wore. He wouldn't look as out of place in the hotel dining room or when he met with Edward Sheffield.

Not that The Kid gave a damn what people thought of him. The events of the past year had taught him how meaningless such things were. But he had already killed two men and had a knock-down, dragout fight with another since his arrival in Bisbee, and he figured he had attracted enough attention to himself for the time being.

He wasn't going unarmed, though. That would be too much, he thought as he strapped the gunbelt around his hips.

When he went back downstairs, the clerk glanced at him and then looked away, evidently not recognizing him. Then the man looked again, clearly surprised as he realized who the tall man in the dark suit was.

"Mr. Morgan," he said. "The dining room's right through there."

Morgan nodded. "Thanks."

He went into the dining room and sat at one of the tables with its snowy linen cloth. A pretty, brown-haired waitress came over and smiled at him, not bothering to keep the admiration and interest out of her eyes as she asked him what she could get him.

Morgan's tone was businesslike as he ordered steak with all the trimmings and coffee. He was hungry. He hadn't had much to eat that day, and the brandy on an empty stomach he'd had at Augustine's was making his brain a little fuzzy. The food and coffee would take care of that.

The meal was a good one, and by the time Morgan

finished with it, he felt human again. The hard, grim day had taken a toll on him, but he felt like he could keep going for a while now.

The waitress hovered around his table. "Are you sure there's nothing else you'd like, sir?" she asked.

"Not a thing," Morgan said. He knew that if he'd been of a mind to, he could have flirted with the waitress and there was no telling how far it would have gotten him. But that was about the last thing he wanted right now, and besides, he had an appointment with Charles Augustine. The saloon owner was going to take him to meet Edward Sheffield, and Morgan hoped that Sheffield would help him find Colonel Gideon Black and even the score for the Williams family.

He signed for the meal, then stood up and put on his hat. As he walked onto Bisbee's main street, he saw that the town was even livelier now that it was a little later in the evening. The saloons appeared to be doing a booming business, and the stores that were still open, including Carmichael's Mercantile, had customers going in and out of them, too. Morgan thought briefly about the puppies he had brought from the ranch and hoped that Carmichael's grandson took good care of them.

Then he put that out of his head and strolled toward Augustine's.

As he entered the saloon Morgan noted the big miner with whom he had clashed earlier was gone, or at least not at the same table where he had been. Surely some of the other customers who had glared murderously at him as he left were still there, but they didn't pay any attention to him. It was another reason he had changed clothes. He wasn't trying to duck trouble, but it didn't make sense to go out of his way to find it, either.

He made his way along the crowded bar to the door at the end of it. As he reached for the knob, one of the bartenders came down to that end of the bar and said, "Hold it, mister. You can't just—"

Morgan looked at him coldly. "Mr. Augustine is expecting me."

The man swallowed. "Well, uh, then you just go right ahead, sir. Sorry I bothered you."

"No bother," Morgan said. He opened the door and stepped into the corridor.

When he reached the door at the other end, he knocked on it. "Who's there?" Augustine called from within.

"Morgan."

"Ah. Come in."

When Morgan opened the door, he saw Augustine taking his right hand out from under his coat. He had a hunch that the saloonkeeper's fingers had been wrapped around the butt of a pistol in a shoulder rig. No man was as successful in a mining boomtown as Augustine appeared to be without making a considerable number of enemies along the way.

Augustine smiled as he got to his feet. He didn't comment on Morgan's changed appearance. He just said, "Are you ready to meet Edward Sheffield?"

"That's why I'm here." Morgan looked around the room. "I don't see him."

"Oh, he's not here. We'll have to go see him. That's the way it works."

Morgan wasn't surprised. Rich men were accustomed

to people coming to them, rather than the other way around.

Augustine took a soft felt hat from a hat tree. "We'll go out the back. You didn't have any trouble when you came in, did you?"

"Not a bit."

"How do you like the Bisbee House?"

"It's fine. Looks comfortable, and the food in the dining room was good."

Augustine chuckled. "I'm glad you liked it." He led the way into the corridor, where he opened another door that let them into an alley. Morgan stayed close to him, not expecting any sort of a double cross but knowing at the same time that it would be more difficult to ambush him if there wasn't much distance between him and Augustine.

He realized after a few minutes that they were walking toward the train station. Recalling what Augustine had said about Edward Sheffield building a spur line into the Dragoon Mountains to serve the company town near his mine, Morgan wondered if he would have to go all the way to Titusville to meet with Sheffield. Surely Augustine would have told him if that were the case, so that he could have brought his gear along with him.

That wasn't how it turned out, however. When they reached the depot, Augustine gestured toward a couple of railroad cars parked on a siding. "There it is," he said. "Edward Sheffield's home away from home."

Chapter 13

Morgan wasn't particularly surprised. He knew that a lot of tycoons had their own private railroad cars. When he was still Conrad Browning, he might have enjoyed such a thing himself.

The two of them went up a set of iron steps to the platform at the rear of the closest car, which was a thing of beauty, all polished brass and dark wood. Augustine knocked on the vestibule door, which was opened a moment later by a stout woman in a maid's uniform. "*Herr* Augustine," she said in a German accent, "please come in. *Herr* Sheffield is waiting for you."

"He hasn't been waiting long, I hope," Augustine said with a smile.

"*Ach*, no. He and *Frau* Sheffield just finished their dinner a few minutes ago."

Morgan thought back, trying to remember what, if anything, he had ever heard about Sheffield's wife. He didn't recall much, only that she was in bad health. He wondered if she had come to Arizona Territory with her husband because of the warm, dry climate.

Sheffield's home was in Chicago, Morgan remembered. The winters there would be hard on someone who was sick.

The maid took their hats and led them through the vestibule into an elegantly appointed sitting room. Morgan had seen plenty of hotel rooms that weren't as elegantly and comfortably furnished as this railroad car. A slender man rose from a divan to greet them. He held a drink in one hand, a long, thick cigar in the other. His gray hair was parted in the center and thinning on top. He had a mustache and rather bushy muttonchop whiskers.

"Augustine," he said with a curt nod, then gestured with the cigar toward Morgan. "This is the man you mentioned in the note you had delivered to me?"

"That's right, Mr. Sheffield," Augustine replied. "This is Mr. Morgan."

"No first name?" He looked at Morgan with a challenge in his eyes.

"Morgan will do."

Sheffield nodded again. "All right, then." He stuck the cigar in his mouth, clamped down on it with his teeth, and extended his hand. "Pleased to meet you, Mr. Morgan."

"Same here," Morgan said. He didn't mention that the two of them had traveled in the same circles for years and had almost crossed paths on numerous occasions. Sheffield might not have believed it, anyway. He thought he was meeting some sort of frontier gunman . . . which, as a matter of fact, he was.

Sheffield didn't offer him a drink, which wasn't surprising. This wasn't a meeting of equals. Sheffield was deciding whether or not to hire him. The man also didn't waste any time getting down to business.

"Did Charles here tell you about the trouble I've been having?"

"He said that some outlaws have been giving you problems."

Sheffield took the cigar out of his mouth, tossed back the whiskey that was still in his glass, and said, "That's right. I run a private train between here and Titusville, in the Dragoon Mountains. It's been stopped a couple of times by bandits. Passengers robbed, gold and silver shipments looted."

"I thought you made most of your money out of copper," Morgan said.

An impatient look came over Sheffield's face. He didn't like being interrupted.

"That's right. The Gloriana is primarily a copper mine, but we take out significant amounts of gold and silver, too. You don't have to have a very big shipment of those ores for its value to amount to something."

"No, I imagine not. Go ahead."

It was a subtle thing, that telling Sheffield to proceed as if Morgan were giving him permission. Morgan did it on purpose, once again trying to get under someone's skin so they would be more liable to blurt out the truth. Sheffield noticed, too, and an irritated flush crept over his face.

He went on, "I've put extra guards on the trains, but I think it's only a matter of time before those outlaws strike again. I want them stopped before that happens. Not only that, I also want them brought to justice for the crimes they've already committed."

Morgan didn't figure justice had a whole lot to do with it. Sheffield wanted vengeance because someone had dared to cross him. There was something else going on there, too.

"I imagine you'd like to have that stolen gold and silver back, if anything's left of it, that is."

"Of course," Sheffield snapped. "It's mine."

And that was the crux of it, Morgan thought. Sheffield couldn't stand anybody taking anything away from him. Morgan knew that . . . because there had been a time in his life when he had felt the same way, until someone took away everything that really mattered.

"What do I have to do with this?"

Sheffield gestured with the cigar toward the Colt on Morgan's hip. "Augustine tells me that you killed two men earlier this evening in a gunfight."

Morgan shrugged. "They drew on me. I didn't have much choice in the matter."

"Still, two against one . . . most men facing those odds would be dead now."

Morgan didn't say anything, just met Sheffield's eyes with a level stare.

"Not only that," Sheffield went on, "but you had some trouble with one of the men who work for me at the mine."

"Clyde Watkins," Morgan said. "He didn't give me much choice, either."

Sheffield smiled thinly. "Watkins has a reputation for violence. Since he's been at the Gloriana, no one has ever defeated him in a brawl. Is there anything you *can't* do, Morgan?"

"Plenty," Morgan said flatly.

Change the past. Bring back everything he had lost.

"No need to beat around the bush," Sheffield said. "I've hired guards, but what I really need is a hunter. Someone to hunt down those outlaws and deal with them."

"Deal with them harshly?" Morgan permitted himself a faint smile.

"Deal with them however is necessary to insure that they never bother me or anyone else again. Whatever it takes."

"And you want me to be that hunter."

"I think it's a job you can handle"—Sheffield paused to cock an eyebrow—"Kid."

Morgan wasn't really surprised that Sheffield had already looked into his background and discovered who he was. Not who he *really* was—or rather, had been—of course, but he knew that Kid Morgan had developed quite a reputation as a fighting man in a short period of time.

Augustine was a little taken aback, though. "You're Kid Morgan?" he said.

"That's what some people call me."

Augustine shook his head. "That didn't occur to me. When I heard your name, my first thought was about Frank Morgan, the famous gunman, but I knew you were too young to be him."

"Our young friend is a different Morgan, Charles," Sheffield said. "But no less notorious."

"I wouldn't say that," Morgan drawled. "Frank Morgan has had a lot more time to build his rep."

"But he's not here, and you are. I'm not sure he's

even still alive. I need help now, Morgan. I need someone to track down that damned colonel—"

"Colonel Gideon Black?"

"That's right. I know you've heard of him. Charles told me that you came to Bisbee with the idea that you might join his gang."

"I heard Black was looking for men who were good with a gun," Morgan said. "That's all. I didn't know he was putting together a gang to hold up your trains."

"And that makes a difference, doesn't it? You have a reputation as a gunman and a killer, but not as a desperado."

Morgan shrugged. "I'd just as soon be on the right side of the law if I can, so I won't have to spend the rest of my life looking over my shoulder for every sheriff and marshal and bounty hunter who'd like to take me in."

"Then it doesn't matter what brought you here. Take the job I'm offering you, Morgan. Hunt down Gideon Black and his gang and destroy them. I can provide you with men, weapons, horses, whatever you need."

Morgan didn't answer right away. He wasn't just pretending to be reluctant. He honestly didn't know whether he wanted to get involved with Edward Sheffield's problems. If he took the job Sheffield was offering him, then the tycoon would expect to be in charge of the campaign against Colonel Black. Morgan didn't much like the idea of taking orders from the man. In truth, he didn't much like Sheffield, period. And he wasn't that sympathetic about Sheffield's problems.

He just wanted to settle the score with Black for

what had happened that morning at the isolated ranch west of there.

Sheffield was starting to look impatient again. "Well, Morgan, what's it going to be?" he demanded.

Before Morgan could say anything, the door at the far end of the car opened, and a new voice said, "If Mr. Morgan needs some convincing to accept your offer, Edward, maybe I could help."

Chapter 14

Morgan turned his head to look toward the newcomer. The sight that met his eyes wasn't what he expected at all.

If it wasn't for the fact that the young woman had called the tycoon "Edward", Morgan might have thought that she was Sheffield's daughter. She didn't appear to be more than twenty-five years old. A bottle-green dress was buttoned up to her neck, but the decorous cut of the gown couldn't conceal the way it hugged a tall, sleek, well-curved body. Thick red hair was pulled back into an elaborate arrangement of curls behind her head. Green eyes met Morgan's gaze with an undisguised boldness.

Of course, calling Sheffield by his first name didn't have to mean anything, Morgan reminded himself. He called his father Frank, after all.

But as the young woman came forward, Sheffield grunted and said, "Mr. Morgan, my wife."

Morgan nodded to her. "Mrs. Sheffield."

He knew good and well this beautiful young woman

wasn't the semi-invalid Sheffield had been married to a few years earlier.

She stepped up to him and extended her hand. "I'm Gloriana."

He glanced at Sheffield as he took her hand and said, "Your husband's mine is named after you."

She smiled as she clasped his hand with a firm pressure. Her hand was cool and smooth. "Of course Edward named the mine after me," she said, "or renamed it, I should say. It used to be called something else. But when we married last year, that was one of his presents to me. By the way, you can call me Glory."

She held on to his hand too long and Morgan carefully disengaged his fingers from her grip. He saw a flicker of disappointment in her eyes, but the radiant smile on her face never wavered.

"We're discussing business here, my dear," Sheffield said with a slightly disapproving tone in his voice.

"I'm aware of that," Glory responded coolly. "You know how interested I am in your business, darling. I may be quite decorative, but I *do* have a brain, too."

"Of course you do, but I prefer to keep my business and personal lives separate. So if you'll excuse us—"

"Just go right ahead with what you were talking about," Glory said with a casual yet elegant wave of her hand. "I'll just sit over here."

She moved to a divan and sat down, where she continued to smile with maddening boldness at Morgan. Her husband's jaw tightened, but he turned back to Morgan and made a visible effort to ignore the fact that his wife was still in the room.

"What about it, Morgan?" he said. "Will you take the job?"

"You'd be putting a lot of faith in somebody you just met," Morgan pointed out.

Sheffield gave a short, humorless bark of laughter. "I didn't get where I am by being timid, or by not trusting my instincts. I'm an excellent judge of character. I can tell that you're the man I need to run this renegade colonel to ground. What do you say?"

It was a tempting offer. Sheffield could place a lot of resources at his disposal.

The problem was that Sheffield wanted what amounted to a military campaign carried out against Colonel Black and his men, and Morgan wasn't a general. He had never even been in the army, and while he had felt comfortable enough issuing orders in a business setting, this was different. This was life and death. He didn't want that responsibility.

Still, Sheffield might prove useful in locating the colonel. Morgan didn't want to turn him down flat.

So instead of answering Sheffield's question, Morgan asked one of his own. "When are you going up to Titusville?"

Sheffield frowned in confusion. "Actually, I'm scheduled to visit the mine tomorrow. My cars will be hooked onto a train that's leaving at eight o'clock tomorrow morning."

"Let me come with you," Morgan said.

"Then you're accepting my offer?"

Morgan shook his head. "Not just yet. I want to get the lay of the land first."

A look of irritation came over Sheffield's face. "See here," he snapped. "I'm not accustomed to people stonewalling me like this. Give me a simple yes or no answer, blast it."

From the divan, Glory Sheffield said, "I don't think Mr. Morgan is stonewalling, Edward. He's just being cautious. Why don't we take him up to Titusville with us tomorrow, as he suggested? That way he can get the lay of the land, as he put it."

As Morgan saw the lascivious light shining in Glory's eyes and heard the sultry tone of her voice, he wished he hadn't phrased it like that.

Sheffield either wasn't aware of those things or chose to ignore them. He said grudgingly, "I suppose we could finish our discussion in Titusville after you've had a chance to look around. But don't postpone your decision too long, Morgan. I'm not the most patient man in the world."

Glory got to her feet, uncoiling from the divan like a cat. "Now that you gentlemen have concluded your business for the time being, I think we should all have a drink."

Sheffield looked like he didn't care for that idea—he didn't drink with the hired help, after all—but evidently he didn't want to be ungracious. He shrugged and said, "All right. Morgan? Augustine?"

The saloon owner nodded. "That sounds mighty fine to me, Mr. Sheffield."

"Thanks," Morgan added.

Sheffield gestured curtly to the German maid, who had come into the room unobtrusively behind Glory. She poured the drinks and handed them around. Glory lifted her glass, smiled at Morgan, and said, "To new friends."

Morgan returned the smile but didn't say anything.

He wasn't the least bit interested in Glory Sheffield, although he was mildly curious about how she had come to be married to the mining and railroad tycoon, as well as what had happened to Sheffield's first wife. Edith, that was her name, Morgan recalled suddenly. She must have passed away, and Sheffield had wasted no time in remarrying.

Sheffield threw back his drink. The nod he then gave to Morgan was one of dismissal.

"We're much obliged to you for your time, Mr. Sheffield," Augustine said. "I hope things work out for you and Mr. Morgan and that you get those blasted outlaws taken care of."

Sheffield grunted.

Glory moved closer to Morgan and rested a hand lightly on his arm. "Don't be late in the morning, Mr. Morgan. I'd hate it if we had to leave without you."

"I'll be here," Morgan promised.

She smiled. "Good. I'm looking forward to getting to know you better. It takes several hours for the train to reach Titusville, so we'll have plenty of time to . . . get acquainted."

Morgan didn't know what to say to that, so he didn't say anything. He finished his drink and then left with Augustine. Glory came out onto the platform at the rear of the car to rest her hands on the railing and watch them walk away.

Morgan let out a low whistle of amazement. "Is she always like that?"

"You mean like a whore trying to drum up business?" Augustine laughed. "If you ever quote me on that, I'll deny it up one way and down the other. I'm just like everybody else. Nobody wants to offend Edward Sheffield, so nobody ever mentions that he married himself a real she-devil."

"He has to notice the way she acts."

Augustine shrugged. "I reckon he does, but he chooses to ignore it, and that's his right. For what it's worth, I've never heard any gossip about Mrs. Sheffield actually doing anything with other men except flirting. But she goes about that mighty serious-like."

"She's a very beautiful woman," Morgan mused.

"No doubt about that. She could make herself some good money if she wanted to come to work in a place like mine."

"She's not Sheffield's first wife, is she?" Morgan already knew the answer to that question, but he thought Augustine might be able to provide some more information and he was just curious enough to ask it.

"No, his first wife died about a year and a half ago, I reckon. He married the current Mrs. Sheffield six months after that."

"Where did he find her? Some cathouse some-where?"

Augustine shook his head. "That's not the way I heard it at all. She's the daughter of some politician. Mr. Sheffield travels in pretty high circles, you know."

Morgan knew, all right. He had traveled in the same circles himself, although those memories seemed to belong to another man entirely.

Augustine went on, "It could be that the marriage was some sort of business arrangement. Those fellas like to take care of each other, just like the old kings and queens did in Europe. If that's the case, then I'd say Mr. Sheffield got the better end of the deal. Mrs. Sheffield's one of the prettiest women I've ever seen."

Gloriana Sheffield was beautiful, all right, thought Morgan, but she couldn't compare to Rebel. No woman could.

They walked along in silence for a moment, then Augustine said, "You're going to take the job Mr. Sheffield offered you, aren't you, Morgan?"

"Does it matter to you whether I do or not?"

"Of course it does. I'm the one who suggested that Mr. Sheffield talk to you. He wants to hire you, and he's a man who gets what he wants. If he doesn't, he's liable to be upset with me, too."

"I'm not going to accept his offer just to keep you on his good side," Morgan said bluntly.

Augustine bristled. "You'd better think about that, Morgan. I have friends in this town, too."

Morgan didn't like the veiled threat in the saloon owner's voice, but he decided to let it pass. "I'll make up my mind when we get to Titusville and I've had a chance to look around. I'm not sure if I want to go up against this Colonel Black. If he's got a small army of gunmen working for him, he must be a dangerous man."

"That's why you need to take Mr. Sheffield's offer. He'll give *you* a small army, too."

And that was the problem. Morgan didn't want an army.

He just wanted Colonel Gideon Black in his gunsights.

Chapter 15

Augustine left Morgan at the saloon with a warning not to be late to the train station the next morning. "I'll be there," Morgan said, not caring for Augustine's tone of voice but deciding that the issue wasn't important enough for him to push it.

Morgan walked on to the Bisbee House and went into the hotel. A different clerk had come on duty, but the man paid no attention to Morgan. The dark suit made him look respectable enough that he wasn't out of place. He went upstairs, undressed, and turned in for the night.

This day, he thought, had been a thousand years long.

Despite his weariness, he didn't fall asleep instantly, as he'd thought he would. Instead, images played through his mind, some of them tragic and grisly—the fate suffered by Sean, Frannie, and Cyrus Williams, along with their ranch hands—and some of them un-accountably intriguing, such as Gloriana Sheffield. Morgan wasn't interested in her as a woman, but he was human enough to know that she was incredibly attractive. He responded to her beauty as any man would, just not to the same degree that most men would experience if they spent much time around Glory. He was still in mourning for everything that he had lost.

Even if he hadn't been, Glory would have been off-limits to him. Conrad Browning had been a pretty sorry son of a bitch at times, but even then, he hadn't been the sort to go after another man's wife.

No, he didn't have any romantic interest in her, Morgan thought, but he had to admit that she was a strong personality, the sort that you didn't forget. Even though he was sure they didn't mean it the same way, *he* was looking forward to getting acquainted with *her*, too.

With that thought in his head, Kid Morgan finally dozed off.

After breakfast the next morning in the hotel dining room, Morgan settled up his bill and then led the buckskin down to the train station. It was early, not quite seven o'clock. The train for Titusville with Edward Sheffield's private cars coupled to it wouldn't be rolling out for more than a hour, but Morgan wanted to be sure he could make arrangements to take his horse with him.

The conductor assured him that wouldn't be a problem. "Mr. Sheffield told us that you'd be traveling up to the mountains with him today, Mr. Morgan," the man said. "He didn't say anything about you taking a horse with you, but he asked us to accommodate anything you asked for, as long as it doesn't throw us off schedule. We've got a boxcar fitted out with stalls for livestock. You can put that buckskin of yours in any of them."

"I'm obliged to you," Morgan said with a nod. "Have you hooked on to Mr. Sheffield's cars yet?"

"No, we'll do that just before we pull out. Mr. Sheffield's up and about, though. I saw him just a little while ago, talking to the stationmaster."

Morgan nodded again and then led his horse over to the train. Some of the porters moved a ramp into place so that he could load the buckskin into the boxcar fitted out with stalls.

Once that was done, he walked toward the siding where Sheffield's private cars were parked. Activity around the depot had picked up as the hour approached the time when the train would leave. Bags were being placed into the baggage car and passengers were beginning to congregate on the platform. Some of them were miners who were returning to Titusville and the Gloriana Mine after having a few days off in Bisbee.

Morgan climbed the iron steps to the platform at the rear of the car where he had met with Sheffield the night before. He knocked on the door, expecting the maid to open it.

Instead, it was Glory Sheffield who stood there when the door swung back. She wore a dark green silk robe that was belted tightly around her trim waist. The robe was open just enough at the top to give a hint of the shadowed cleft between her breasts. Her thick red hair was loose around her shoulders.

She smiled a greeting as she stepped onto the platform. "Mr. Morgan," she said. "Right on time. Actually,

I think you're a little early." She put a hand on the breast of her robe. "You'll have to pardon me for not being dressed yet."

Morgan tugged on the brim of his hat. "Just wanted to let your husband know that I'm here, ma'am, and ready to go."

"You don't care that *I* know you're here?"

"No offense, Mrs. Sheffield, but I'm not doing business with you."

"You could be, you know."

"No, ma'am," he said. "I don't think so."

A trace of anger sparked in her eyes. "I meant, if Edward would give me some more responsibility, I could handle some of his affairs for him."

"I suppose he does what he thinks is best."

Green eyes regarded him coolly for a moment. Then Glory said, "Come inside. I'll tell my husband that you're here."

Morgan nodded. Before either of them could move, though, footsteps crunched on the gravel roadbed of the siding and a man stepped around the end of the car. He swung up a shotgun and yelled something incoherent.

In moments of danger, time seemed to slow down for The Kid. He recognized Clyde Watkins, the miner he had fought in Augustine's the night before. Watkins was probably shouting curses and threats, but his words weren't understandable because of his injured tongue.

The threat he represented was perfectly clear, though. At that range, the blast from both barrels of the shotgun would splatter not only Morgan but also Glory Sheffield all over the railroad car platform.

Morgan's instincts took over, allowing him to react in less than the blink of an eye.

He reached out with his left hand and shoved Glory backward through the car's open door into the vestibule. The Colt leaped into his other hand and roared just as the greener's barrels came to bear. The slug plowed into the vengeance-seeking miner's chest and knocked him backward. The shotgun's barrels kept rising, and by the time Watkins' finger contracted involuntarily on the triggers a heartbeat later, the weapon was pointed toward the sky. Both barrels went off with a deafening double boom, but the buckshot slashed harmlessly through the air.

Watkins sat down hard. His mouth worked, but again all that came out was gibberish, made even more incomprehensible by the blood that welled over his lips in a thick crimson flow. After a second, he fell to the side and lay still.

Morgan heard Glory gasping for breath. He turned to look at her and saw that his shove had sent her toppling to the floor of the vestibule. Her robe gaped open, showing more of her breasts. She didn't seem to be hurt.

"You weren't hit, were you?" he asked sharply.

She looked up at him, blinking, seemingly half-stunned by the sudden and unexpected outbreak of violence. After a few seconds, she swallowed hard, licked her lips, and was able to say, "No . . . no, I'm all right."

The door at the far end of the car slammed open. Heavy footsteps pounded. Morgan looked past Glory and saw Edward Sheffield rushing toward them. Sheffield wasn't wearing his coat and tie, his suspenders were down, and his shirt collar was open. Bits of shaving soap clung to his cheeks, and he still held his razor in his hand.

When he saw Morgan standing there, gun in hand, over Glory, Sheffield's face mottled with rage and he brandished the straight razor as he started toward them.

"By God, Morgan, if you've hurt my wife—"

"Stop it, Edward!" Glory said. "Mr. Morgan just saved my life." She raised a hand toward him. "If you'll just help me up, Mr. Morgan."

She recovered quickly from the shock of almost being shotgunned, Morgan thought. She was also making sure that he got a good view down that partially open robe.

"I'm sure your husband would be glad to help you, ma'am," he said as he opened the Colt's cylinder. "I need to replace that cartridge."

She glared at him as he thumbed a fresh round into the gun and snapped the cylinder closed again. Down on the ground, Watkins still hadn't moved. Morgan went down the steps to take a closer look. He kicked the empty shotgun aside and kept the Colt trained on Watkins as he circled the miner.

Watkins was dead. The blood that came from his mouth formed a small pool beside his head. Morgan didn't feel any real regret over the killing—any man who tried to blast him with a shotgun could expect the same thing—but he did have a bitter taste in his mouth for a moment at the sheer senselessness of it. The fight the night before had been over nothing but Watkins' injured pride, and now he was dead for the same reason.

Sheffield had helped his wife to her feet and both of them came onto the platform. Morgan noticed that Glory was holding her robe tightly closed at the throat.

"That's the man you were brawling with in Augustine's place last night," Sheffield said.

Morgan nodded. "Yeah."

"And now you've killed him." Sheffield's voice held a vaguely accusatory tone.

"When a man's pointing a shotgun at you, there's not enough time *not* to kill him," Morgan said.

Sheffield sighed. "I suppose not. Watkins' temper was always getting him into trouble. If he'd fired that shotgun, chances are that Mrs. Sheffield would have been wounded."

"He probably would have killed me, along with Mr. Morgan," Glory said. "Mr. Morgan really did save my life, Edward."

"Well, that's one reason for me to forgive him for killing one of my employees. And one more reason for you to accept my proposition and go to work for me, Morgan. You can replace Watkins on my payroll . . . but for a much higher salary, of course."

"We'll talk about that later"—Morgan slid his gun back into its holster—"once we get to Titusville."

"All right." Sheffield jerked his head toward the door of the railroad car. "Come on in. We'll be leaving soon."

Morgan went back up the steps and followed Sheffield and Glory into the car. "Welcome aboard," Sheffield added over his shoulder as he headed for the door at the far end of the car. Their living quarters were in the other car, and he needed to finish shaving and dressing.

Glory turned her head to smile at Morgan. "Yes," she said, "welcome aboard."

Somehow it sounded completely different when she said it.

Chapter 16

The train pulled out of Bisbee right on schedule. It had backed onto the siding so that Sheffield's private cars could be coupled behind the caboose. Then it rolled through a big curve, leaving the Southern Pacific tracks behind and heading north on the rails of the spur line owned by Sheffield.

Once they were out of the Mule Mountains around the settlement, the tracks followed the broad, flat valley of the San Pedro River. Because of the river, the mostly arid landscape to be found elsewhere in that part of the territory was relieved by broad patches of grass and scrubby trees and brush. The splashes of green were welcome sights in the primarily brown and tan and gray vistas rolling past outside the windows of the sitting room in Edward Sheffield's private car.

While Sheffield and Glory were in the other car, the German maid appeared and offered Morgan some coffee, asking him as well if he would like anything to eat. He smiled at her and said, "Just the coffee, thanks."

As she turned to leave, he added, "Have you worked for Mr. Sheffield for very long?"

"*Ach,* years I have taken care of *Herr* Sheffield and *Frau* Sheffield." The maid frowned. "The other *Frau* Sheffield."

Morgan sensed an opening and took it. "That's right, I remember hearing something about Mr. Sheffield being married before."

The maid nodded. "*Frau* Sheffield was a lovely woman. But not well. Sick, you understand?" She touched her ample bosom. "Her heart."

"That's a shame. At least Mr. Sheffield was able to find someone else"

"*Ja.* Someone else." The sound of the maid's voice as she repeated Morgan's words made it clear that she didn't care much for her employer's new wife. "Are you going to work for *Herr* Sheffield?"

The question took Morgan a little by surprise. "I don't know yet. Maybe."

"You be careful around that one. I did not say anything, you understand, but . . . be careful."

With that, she turned and left the car, and when she came back a few minutes later with a cup of hot coffee, she didn't say anything else.

Morgan sat in one of the armchairs and sipped the coffee as he looked through the windows. The Dragoon Mountains were already visible to the northeast, blue and gray on the horizon. They were bigger than the Mule Mountains, rugged peaks that contained valuable quantities of copper and silver and gold. The railroad tracks began another long, sweeping curve that would take the train into the mountains.

Glory Sheffield came into the car. She wore a

modestly cut, expensive dress again, but somehow on her, it didn't look all that modest. She had left her hair loose.

"Good morning again, Mr. Morgan," she said. "I hope the rest of our trip is more pleasant—and less dangerous—than it started out."

"I couldn't agree more," Morgan said.

She sat down in one of the overstuffed armchairs opposite him and demurely folded her hands in her lap. "I hope you'll agree to take Edward's offer, too," she said. "It would be nice having someone around who's closer to my own age."

"If I take the job, I won't be around all that much," Morgan pointed out. "I'll be on the trail of those outlaws."

"Well, I suppose that's true, but I'm sure we'd see each other some of the time."

"Do you know anything about this Colonel Black your husband suspects is the leader of the bandits?" Morgan asked idly.

He was surprised by the way Glory stiffened at the question, just enough for him to notice. "No, of course not," she said. "Why would I know anything about a bandit?"

"No reason," Morgan replied with a shake of his head. "I just thought you might have heard Mr. Sheffield talking about him."

"No, I don't know any more than you do. I'm sorry."

"No need to be sorry. I was just curious."

Glory stood up. "Would you like something to eat? I can have Dorothea prepare some breakfast."

"Already ate, thanks." Morgan held up the cup. "Coffee's fine."

"All right. I'll see you later, Mr. Morgan."

She left without giving him her usual flirtatious smile, and Morgan couldn't help but wonder if his question about Colonel Black had caused her sudden shift in attitude. The only reason he could see that it would was if she had lied to him.

And if she'd lied to him, then she really did know more about the renegade colonel than she was letting on. That was . . . interesting, he thought. Morgan didn't know what it meant yet, or whether it would prove helpful to him, but it was definitely interesting.

Sheffield came into the car a short time later, smelling of bay rum from the shave he'd had earlier. He sat down and said, "Before we left Bisbee, I made arrangements to have Watkins buried at my expense. I also sent word to Sheriff Stewart that you'd be available for questioning about the incident later, if necessary."

"The sheriff's not going to be happy with me." Morgan chuckled. "I was supposed to attend an inquest today for those two hard cases I shot last night."

Sheffield waved a hand. "Don't worry about that. My attorneys can smooth over any ruffled legal feathers. I don't consider myself above the law, Morgan, but I don't see anything wrong with using it to my advantage, either."

"You mean you take whatever advantages you can," Morgan said.

Annoyance showed in Sheffield's eyes. "Of course I do. I'm a businessman. No one is successful in business without learning how to seize opportunities. *Carpe diem.* That means—"

"Seize the day."

Sheffield's eyebrows rose. "You speak Latin?"

Morgan shrugged. "A little."

As a matter of fact, he'd had several years of instruction in Latin at the prestigious Boston academy where he'd been educated, as well as in college. But Sheffield didn't have to know that.

"At any rate," the tycoon went on, "you don't have to be concerned about Sheriff Stewart . . . if you go to work for me, that is. If you don't . . ." He shrugged. "Then any legal matters would be your own responsibility, of course."

Morgan wasn't worried. He could muster as much legal firepower as Sheffield could, if not more. But that was something else Sheffield didn't have any reason to know.

Changing the subject, Morgan asked, "How long has it been since the outlaws hit one of your trains?"

"Almost three weeks. As I told you, I put extra guards on the trains, and word of that could have gotten to the gang."

"You don't think that's going to scare them off for good?"

Sheffield shook his head. "No, I don't. In fact, it worries me that this much time has passed since the last robbery. The odds are that they won't wait much longer to strike again."

"How did they stop the trains?"

"They piled rocks and logs on the tracks at the spot where the line comes out of the mountains. The right-of-way is narrow there, with bluffs crowding in on both sides, and the tracks curve so that southbound trains don't have a good view of the gap until they're almost on top of it."

"Sounds like a spot almost tailor-made for an ambush and holdup," Morgan commented.

"Unfortunately, that's true. When my surveyors laid out the line, they concerned themselves only with engineering concerns, not on whether they were creating a bottleneck where a train could be stopped easily. No one realized the potential problem until later."

"After the first robbery, I expect."

Sheffield shrugged. "That's right."

"And by then, it was too late to do anything about it."

"Correct again. It would be prohibitively expensive to move the line now."

Morgan rubbed at his jaw and tugged on his earlobe for a second as he frowned in thought. "They only hit trains coming out of the mountains, bound for Bisbee from Titusville?"

"Of course. Those are the trains that have ore shipments on them. Northbound trains such as this one carry passengers and supplies, but not enough to make it worth the while of those outlaws to stop them."

"So you're not worried about them stopping us on the way up there?"

"Not at all." Sheffield smiled thinly. "But we'll be taking on an ore shipment while we're there, so there's a chance we might run into trouble on the return trip."

He sounded like he almost hoped that would be the case, Morgan thought. Sheffield probably thought there was a better chance he'd take the job if that happened.

It would take about two and a half hours to reach Titusville, Sheffield had explained, and during that time, Morgan talked to the tycoon about the previous robberies, finding out everything he could about them. The bandits had worn masks, so none of the witnesses had seen their faces. Because of that, there was no proof that Colonel Gideon Black was involved in the crimes, but Sheffield was convinced that was true anyway.

"I never had any trouble with holdups until Black arrived in Arizona and began gathering hard cases around him," Sheffield said. "I realize that's not enough proof for a court of law, but it's enough for me."

"Enough for you to hire your own gunmen."

Sheffield smiled thinly. "Fighting fire with fire is a time-honored tactic."

Morgan couldn't argue with that. "There's been shooting during the holdups?"

Sheffield nodded and said, "Yes, sad to say, several passengers and members of the train crews have been killed when they tried to fight back. Those outlaws are merciless, Morgan. That's one more reason they have to be dealt with severely."

After seeing what had happened at the Williams ranch, Morgan didn't have to be told how merciless the outlaws were. He had seen too much evidence of that with his own eyes, images that might haunt his brain forever.

Sheffield didn't mention anything about the gang having a cannon. Morgan supposed that might be a new development. If you were trying to stop a train, especially a heavily-guarded one, a big gun like that might come in really handy. A former military man like Colonel Black would know that, too.

By the time the train was approaching the mountains, Sheffield had excused himself and left the parlor car. The maid brought Morgan a fresh cup of coffee, and she was followed a few minutes later by Glory Sheffield. Morgan wondered if she had been deliberately avoiding coming back there while her husband was with him.

It appeared that was the case. Morgan had moved onto one of the divans, and as soon as Glory came into the car, she sat down beside him, close enough that he could feel the warmth from her hip through their clothes. A disturbing thought forced itself into his mind. How far would Sheffield go to get what he wanted? Would he actually send his wife to seduce Morgan, just to get him to agree to go after Colonel Black?

Or was it all Glory's idea? She leaned even closer to him and smiled.

"How are you enjoying the trip so far?"

"This car is very comfortable, and the coffee is good," Morgan said.

"What about the company?"

"Very pleasant."

"I'm glad to hear you say that." She rested a hand on his shoulder. "It could be even more pleasant, Mr. Morgan . . . or can I call you Kid? That's what Edward says you're known as—Kid Morgan. No offense, but it sounds like something out of a dime novel." She was close enough that he could feel the warmth of her breath on his cheek. "What's your real first name?"

Morgan was saved from having to answer by a sudden boom that was loud enough for him to hear over the rumble of the train's wheels on the tracks. At the same time, a sharp jolt went through the car, sharp enough so that Glory was thrown right off the divan with a little scream as she landed on the floor.

Morgan sprang to his feet and leaped to the window as the train slowed down and came to a lurching, screeching halt.

It looked like Sheffield had been wrong about them having nothing to worry about on the trip up to Titusville. Unless Morgan's hunch was wrong, the outlaws' big gun had just spoken.

And the big gundown had begun.

Chapter 17

Edward Sheffield rushed into the car and shouted, "My God, what's happened?" Then he spotted his wife on the floor. "Good Lord, Gloriana! Are you all right?"

Out of instinct, Morgan had drawn his gun as he peered through the window. He saw that the train had reached the gap where the spur line entered the mountains. Those bluffs Sheffield had mentioned loomed closely on both sides of the tracks.

Atop the bluff to the right sat the cannon that had boomed a moment earlier. Men clustered around it, reloading it. Morgan saw a man run a wet swab on a long pole down the barrel with practiced efficiency, putting out any lingering sparks from the first shot before a second charge of powder was packed into the weapon.

Other men armed with rifles clustered along the bluff, taking potshots at the train. Their intention was probably to make everyone in the cars keep their heads down until more outlaws could board the train and take it over.

Morgan grimaced. He couldn't do any good with

a handgun. He needed his Winchester, which was in the car with the buckskin, his saddle, and the rest of his gear.

"Stay here," he told Sheffield and Glory. "Get behind one of the divans and keep your heads down."

"What are you going to do?" Sheffield asked.

"I don't know yet. Something."

"Does this mean you're working for me?"

Morgan suppressed the surge of impatience he felt. "It means I don't like anybody shooting at me," he snapped as he strode past them toward the door at the front of the car.

He stepped onto the platform as a bullet banged off of the brass fittings on the car. He quickly dropped down to the roadbed through the space between the two private cars. Morgan stretched out and wriggled on to his back underneath the train. Then he reached up, grasped the rods that ran under the cars, and began pulling himself along. He was well-hidden from the outlaws up on the bluffs as he tried to reach the car where his horse was.

Since Sheffield's private cars were the last two of the train he had to make his way under the living quarters car and then the caboose. The converted baggage car where he had left the buckskin and his gear was right in front of the caboose. It wasn't that difficult pulling himself along the roadbed, but he lost his hat and the gravel ripped and tore at the back of his coat, gouging his flesh in places, as well.

It took him a few minutes to reach the front of the caboose. During that time, he heard shots continue to ring out from the bluffs. A few shots came from the train as well, as passengers and crew tried to mount a

defense, but from the sound of it, the resistance was
rather feeble.

He couldn't get into the car from the end, so he
would have to expose himself to the outlaws' fire.
He pulled himself along to what he judged was the
middle of the converted baggage car, as close as he
could get to the sliding door on its side. Then he rolled
out from underneath it and sprang to his feet, moving
as fast as he could in the hope that he could get inside
before any of the riflemen on the bluff noticed him.

That was a futile hope. Bullets burned through the
air as he reached up and grasped the edge of the door,
which had been left open a few inches to let in some
light and air for his horse. Slugs thudded into the side
of the car. Morgan thrust the door back, grabbed hold,
and vaulted inside. He felt the hot kiss of a bullet
against his neck as he rolled away from the opening.
He wasn't sure the lead had even touched him, but it
had been mighty close.

Surging to his feet, Morgan ran over to the stall
where the buckskin tossed his head in eagerness to
get out. The horse had never minded the sound of
shots or the smell of powdersmoke. Sometimes Morgan thought the buckskin thrived on those things.

"You're better off right where you are, big fella,"
Morgan told the horse as he pulled his Winchester
from the sheath which lay next to his saddle. "You
couldn't do any good out there. There are too many
of them."

The car had doors on both sides. The one on the
side of the bluff where the cannon had been set up
was closed. Morgan eased it open a couple of inches.

Not enough for the outlaws to notice, he hoped, but enough to let him take a look at the situation.

From there he could see the cannon and the men around it. They all wore bandannas tied around the lower half of their faces, and their hats were pulled down partially obscuring the upper half. Morgan couldn't recognize any of them and didn't spot anyone wearing the distinctive outfit Colonel Black had sported that day at the Williams ranch. Most of the men wore long dusters, though, that concealed their clothing, so Black could be up there.

If he was, Morgan suspected he would be somewhere near that big gun. Slipping the barrel of the Winchester through the narrow gap, Morgan drew a bead on one of the outlaws standing beside the cannon.

The rifle cracked sharply and kicked against his shoulder when he squeezed the trigger. The man he had targeted jerked back, then stumbled forward and plunged off the edge of the bluff with a scream. While the wounded outlaw was falling, Morgan worked the Winchester's lever and shifted his aim as fast as he could to another member of the gang. He wanted to bring down as many of them as he could before they realized where the deadly fire was coming from.

His second shot drove into the chest of another outlaw near the cannon and knocked that man out of sight. Morgan cranked off two more rounds and hit a third man before the rest of the owlhoot artillery crew sprang into action. Morgan's eyes widened as he saw the cannon's muzzle swing around and point toward the boxcar.

"Son of a—" he muttered before he leaped away

from the door and threw himself into the stall with
the buckskin.

The cannon's boom was like a particularly loud
clap of thunder. The cannonball smashed through the
boxcar door, shattering it into kindling. The ball continued on at a downward angle, hitting the boxcar
floor and blasting a hole in it as well. Luckily, the
devastating shot missed Morgan and the buckskin by
ten or twelve feet, but Morgan still covered his head
with his arms to protect himself from flying debris.
The buckskin whinnied shrilly as a splinter of wood
nicked him.

Morgan knew he couldn't stay there. The outlaws
would continue to use the cannon to blast away at the
boxcar, since they knew the deadliest shot on the
train was in there.

He had no idea how fast a real artillery crew could
reload and fire a cannon like that, but he hoped the
outlaws wouldn't be as efficient. He grabbed a blanket and saddle and threw them on the buckskin, who
was moving around nervously. The horse might be
accustomed to gunplay, but not an artillery barrage.

Morgan was all too aware of the seconds flying
past. He was in a race against time, a race to get out
of the boxcar with the buckskin before another cannonball came crashing through the wall. He drew the
cinches tight, slung the sheaths that held the Winchester and the Sharps onto the saddle, and then
threw open the gate across the stall entrance. He slid
the door on the far side of the car all the way back.
Shots began to fly through the opening. Morgan
ducked into the stall, grabbed the buckskin's reins,
and swung up into the saddle.

His boot heels dug into the horse's flanks as he yelled and sent the buckskin leaping forward. He had to give the buckskin credit for not even hesitating as the open door loomed in front of them. The horse leaped through it, sailing high into the air as bullets shrilled around them.

At that same instant, the cannon thundered again, and the ball crashed into the boxcar behind them, smashing right through the stall. Morgan glanced back and knew that he and the buckskin had avoided death by only shavings of a second.

The horse landed gracefully, running full blast. They were just outside the gap formed by the bluffs. Morgan whirled his mount and sent the buckskin racing alongside the train, close enough to the bluff so that the outlaws on the near side couldn't hit them from that angle, and the railroad cars shielded them from the riflemen on the far side of the gap.

Morgan saw steam puffing from the diamond-shaped stack on the Baldwin locomotive. The engine didn't seem to be damaged, at least not that he could tell. He rode past the cab and reached the front of the locomotive. The cowcatcher was a tangled, twisted mass of metal. Morgan figured that was where the first round from the cannon had struck. But the rest of the engine appeared to be all right, and the tracks themselves looked undamaged. The engineer must have brought the train to a halt because he thought the tracks were torn up in front of it and he feared a derailment.

Morgan thought the train could still move, so he whirled the horse around and raced back to the cab. The engine still had steam up. The engineer just needed to hit the throttle.

"Move the train! Move the train!" he shouted to a man he saw in the cab who was crouched behind the meager protection of the cab's walls.

"The engineer's dead!" the man called back to him.

Morgan grimaced and reach over to grasp an iron grab bar on the wall of the cab. He swung himself from the buckskin's back into the cab, taking the Winchester with him.

"You know how to run this thing?" he asked as he ducked down behind the other wall, next to the bloody body of the engineer, who had been shot through the head.

"Yeah, but those sons o' bitches up on the bluff will pick me off if I try to work the controls!"

"No, they won't, because I'll cover you," Morgan said. "Now grab that throttle!"

The man, who had to be the fireman, hesitated, but the fierce look on Morgan's face convinced him he would be in even more danger if he didn't do what he was told. As Morgan rose up at the side of the cab and started blazing away at the men on the bluff as fast as he could work the Winchester's lever, the trainman lunged to the engine's controls and shoved the throttle forward. With a burst of steam and a screeching of metal on metal as the drivers engaged, the locomotive lurched forward.

Bullets whined and popped and danced around inside the cab. The train began to pick up speed. Morgan saw the barrel of the cannon moving in an attempt to line up a shot at the engine. He sprayed lead around the big gun and forced the men working it to leap for cover. That gave the locomotive and the coal tender time to clear the gap. The nearly sheer walls on both sides of the tracks fell away.

The outlaws continued shooting at the cars that rolled past, but they couldn't stop the train with rifle fire. The fireman looked back and yelled triumphantly, "We're gonna make it!"

Then he grunted in pain as a slug ripped through his body. He slumped against the brake lever, and once again the train began squealing and skidding to a halt. Morgan whirled away from the side of the cab and grabbed the wounded fireman, jerking him away from the brake. He released it and slammed the throttle forward again.

The train hadn't come to a complete stop, making it easier to regain some speed. Chuffing loudly, the engine kept going, climbing a long slope.

Morgan leaned out to look ahead. The tracks ran in a straight line for a mile or more. He risked abandoning the controls to climb onto the pile of coal in the tender. From there he could see the outlaws on the bluffs, as well as their cannon. The cannon's crew had swiveled the weapon even more, and Morgan knew they were lining up a shot. If they could blow a hole in the locomotive's boiler, they could still stop the train.

The cannon boomed before Morgan could do anything about it. Maybe he imagined it, but he thought he could hear the high-pitched whistle of the cannonball as it flew toward the train.

Chapter 18

There was nothing Morgan could do to stop the cannonball. He threw himself backward, onto the floor of the cab, as the shot fell short and hit the tender instead of the locomotive, smashing into the mound of coal and sending pieces flying everywhere. Some of the chunks pelted the cab like black rain.

But the train kept moving. Morgan scrambled to his feet and checked the tracks ahead. No obstructions, no sharp turns that would require the train to slow down. He shoved the throttle forward as far as it would go.

He didn't want to blow the boiler, but right now his main concern was getting the train out of range of that cannon. The big gun could throw a ball more than a mile, but its accuracy diminished with every yard between the train and the cannon. Morgan thought they were already far enough away so that it would be luck more than anything else if the next shot found its target.

He heard the cannon blast and jerked his head around in time to see the puff of smoke from its muzzle. Then with a crash of rending wood, the cannonball slammed into the last car in the train.

The car where he had left Edward and Glory Sheffield.

Morgan's lips pulled back from his teeth in a grimace as he saw pieces of debris fly high in the air from the impact. He heard a groan and looked down to see the fireman struggling to get to his feet again. The man's left arm hung limp and his shoulder was covered with blood, but at least he was conscious again.

Morgan reached down and grasped the man's right arm to haul him upright. "Can you handle the controls?" he demanded.

The wounded fireman was pale and shaken, but he managed to nod. "Yeah, I think so."

"Good. I've got to go back and check on the Sheffields."

A narrow ledge ran along the side of the tender. Morgan made his way down it carefully. When he reached the first passenger car, he climbed to the top, figuring it would be quicker going that way than trying to get through what was bound to be a lot of chaos and confusion from the frightened passengers inside the car.

Aware that he was making himself a target, he ran toward the rear of the train, leaping from car to car. It was dangerous, especially because the high speed was causing the train to sway a little on the tracks, but he wanted to reach the last car as quickly as he could.

Atop the distant bluff, the cannon boomed again, and Morgan gritted his teeth as he paused to see where the ball would land. It plowed up dirt and threw a cloud of dust in the air to the right of the train. The gunners were losing the range. Morgan started moving again. When he reached the caboose, he climbed down using the grab irons on the side of the car.

As his booted feet landed on the platform at the front of the caboose, the door opened and Edward Sheffield rushed out, nearly running into Morgan.

Sheffield grabbed Morgan's arm. "There you are! My God, did you see what happened? They shelled the train with a cannon!"

Morgan didn't like being grabbed, but at the moment, he was more concerned with what might have happened to Glory. A jolt of relief went through him as he saw her come up behind her husband. He didn't particularly like her, but he had liked the idea of her being splattered all over that train car by a cannonball even less.

He pulled his arm loose from Sheffield's grip and said, "I thought the two of you were still in that last car." He gestured through the open door at the destruction. The cannonball had come through the roof of the car, leaving a gaping hole, and slammed into one of the divans, demolishing it. There was a hole in the floor, too, where the cannonball had gone on through. They were lucky it hadn't hit the wheels and derailed the car.

"We had just started forward to look for you," Sheffield said.

"Are you all right?" Glory put in.

Morgan nodded. "Yeah, I'm fine. Scratched up a little from crawling around under the train, that's all."

Glory's eyes widened. "*Under* the train? What if it had started up again?"

"I'd have been out of luck," Morgan said, although

it was possible he could have stayed where he was and let the train pass over him. As soon as it cleared him, though, he would have been an easy target for the outlaw riflemen on the bluffs.

He leaned out a window and saw that the gap was well behind them. The train was out of effective range of the cannon and well out of range of the rifles. By now the outlaws might be mounted up and coming after them on horseback, but Morgan didn't see any dust to indicate that. More than likely, since the ambush had failed, the gang had given up on stopping the train . . . at least for now.

The blue-uniformed conductor crowded onto the platform behind Sheffield and Glory. "Does anybody know what's going on?" he asked with a note of panic in his voice.

"Your engineer's dead," Morgan told him. "The fireman's at the controls. You'd better get somebody up there to shovel some coal for him. He's wounded, so he can't do that job."

The conductor jerked his head in a nod. "I'll get up there myself, right now. We don't want to start losing steam. Those bushwhackers might try to come after us."

"Even though their ambush failed?" Sheffield asked.

"They were bold enough to attack a train with a cannon," Morgan pointed out. "Maybe we'd better not underestimate them."

The conductor hurried off toward the front of the train. Glory said, "I never heard of such a thing. It's like those outlaws are at war with the railroad."

"That's one more reason I'm convinced Gideon Black is behind this," Sheffield snapped. "These attacks are being carried out like military operations, and he's got the knowledge to do so."

Morgan looked behind the train again and spotted the buckskin galloping after it. The horse couldn't keep up, and was falling farther behind as the train continued to climb into the Dragoon Mountains. Morgan grimaced. He didn't want to lose the buckskin. The horse had been a fine saddle mount.

At that moment, the train began to slow, either because the flames in the firebox had died down and it was losing steam, or because a curve was coming up. Either way, Morgan didn't care. He seized the opportunity as the train's speed fell off to a crawl.

"I'll see you in Titusville," he told Sheffield.

"Wait a minute," the tycoon said. "Where are you—Morgan!"

It was too late. Morgan had already clattered down the iron steps attached to the platform on the rear of the caboose and swung off, landing in a run on the ground. His momentum kept him going for several steps before he came to a stop.

Sheffield glared at him as the train continued to pull away. Glory stood beside her husband with a look of concern on her face. Morgan lifted a hand in farewell to both of them. Then he turned and let out a shrill whistle, calling the buckskin to him.

The horse trotted up to him, then stood there trembling a little, worn out from the effort of trying to keep up with the train. Morgan patted the animal on the shoulder and then took hold of the reins. He couldn't ride the buckskin until the horse had had a chance to rest. He slid the Winchester back in its saddle sheath, then started walking along the tracks, leading the buckskin.

Morgan hoped those outlaws weren't pursuing the train. If he had to make a run for it now, he'd be out of luck. The buckskin couldn't gallop another half mile without collapsing.

Luckily, the sky remained clear of dust behind him. Once the train was out of sight, he was alone in the foothills of the Dragoons.

The walk gave him some time to think. Sheffield was right. The outlaws use of the cannon pointed straight to Colonel Gideon Black. Throw in the connection with the raid on the Williams ranch, and that was more than enough proof for Morgan. The ex-colonel was the man he was looking for.

Finding Black might not be that easy. Morgan wasn't convinced that accepting Sheffield's offer would do any good. A posse of hired guns could tramp around those mountains for weeks without finding any sign of the outlaws. It was easier to avoid a large group of men like that than it was to throw one man off the trail.

The problem was, what could one man do against two dozen outlaws who had gotten their hands on a *cannon*, for God's sake?

He wasn't any closer to an answer to that question when he came in sight of Titusville a couple hours later. He had walked for half an hour to let the buckskin rest, then mounted up and ridden at a slow but steady pace for another hour and a half, following the railroad tracks. That brought him to the settlement, which was tucked into a shallow valley that came to a dead end against the slope of a mountain. Part of the way up the face of that mountain, Morgan saw a number of buildings scattered around a large, dark opening in the face of the earth. That would be the Gloriana Mine, he thought, the source—or rather, one of the sources—of Edward Sheffield's wealth and power.

The damaged train sat at the depot. The engine had been uncoupled and pulled into a roundhouse, where it was turned around and then run back out onto a siding. Men were already working on it, trying to repair the damaged cowcatcher.

Morgan reined to a halt beside the locomotive and asked one of the men working on it, "Do you know where I can find Mr. Sheffield?"

"I expect he's down at the mining company office." The man pointed along the street. "That is, if he's not off somewhere chewin' nails. I never seen the boss so mad."

Morgan nodded his thanks. He wasn't surprised to hear that Sheffield was still upset.

He rode along the street until he came to a red brick building with a sign on it proclaiming it to be the headquarters of the Sheffield Mining Corporation. He dismounted and left the buckskin at the hitch rack in front of the building.

When he went inside, he planned to ask one of the workers if Sheffield was there, but he didn't have to. He heard the tycoon's angry voice coming through an open door behind several desks.

"—absolutely nothing!" Sheffield was saying. "Your men were worthless, Bateman, and that means that *you're* worthless to me!"

Morgan headed toward that door. A man who had been sitting at one of the desks got up quickly and moved in front of him. The fellow was tall and slender, in shirtsleeves, vest, and string tie. He said, "Hold on a minute, mister. Can I help you?"

Morgan nodded toward the door and said, "I'm looking for Sheffield."

"I'm afraid *Mr.* Sheffield is busy right now—"

Morgan stepped around the man. "Sorry. I have to see him."

"Wait! You just can't—"

Sheffield appeared in the open door. "Morgan!" he said. "I thought I heard your voice out here. I was beginning to worry that those outlaws had caught up to you." He turned to look over his shoulder. "Step out here, Bateman. I want you to meet the only man who actually accomplished anything when those outlaws attacked the train."

A man in a brown suit followed Sheffield out of the inner office. He wore a flat-crowned brown hat, and long blond hair fell around his shoulders. Dressed like that, with the long hair, the man bore a faint resemblance to the famous Wild Bill Hickok, and Morgan had a hunch the hombre knew that and tried to play it up to his advantage. The man also wore a pair of ivory-handled Colts.

And at the moment, the anger in his eyes made it clear that he would like nothing better than to pull both of those irons and fill Morgan full of lead.

Chapter 19

"I told you, we'll run those bandits to ground, Mr. Sheffield, if you'll let us," the man said. "So far, you've just had us guarding the trains."

Sheffield snorted. "And a fine job your men did of that today."

"It would have been different if I'd been there."

Sheffield looked like he didn't believe that. "This is Kid Morgan," he said. "I've asked him to take over and lead the effort to find Colonel Black and his men."

"Morgan, huh?" The long-haired man gave Morgan a cool, appraising stare and clearly didn't like what he saw. "I reckon I've heard of him." He spoke directly to Morgan. "And I reckon you've probably heard of me. I'm Phil Bateman."

Slowly, Morgan shook his head. "Nope. Can't say as I have."

A flush crept over Bateman's face as his scowl deepened. As he stepped past Sheffield, his hands hovered over the butts of his guns. "Maybe I ought to show you why you should have," he said, his lips curling in a snarl.

Sheffield snapped, "Damn it, Bateman, stop that. I want you and Morgan to work together, not kill each other."

"I never agreed to work for you," Morgan said.

Sheffield frowned at him. "Now, listen, if it's a matter of money—"

"It's not." Morgan had made up his mind. "I just don't want the job."

He didn't bother explaining to Sheffield that his answer didn't mean he wasn't going after Colonel Black. He had his own reasons for trying to put a stop to the renegade colonel's activities. He had a score to settle for the friends he had lost, and he thought his chances of doing that would be better alone—even with the odds he'd be facing—rather than trying to deal with a stiff-necked hard case like Bateman and a bunch of other hired guns.

Sheffield glared at Morgan. He was a man accustomed to getting what he wanted, and he didn't like it when anyone told him no. He began to sputter, "Blast it, Morgan, you saw that those bastards are capable of—"

"That's right," Morgan said, "I did. That's why I don't want any part of going after them."

Bateman gave a contemptuous laugh. "This is the famous gunfighter you were gonna hire, Mr. Sheffield? First of all, he ain't all that famous, and second, he sounds like a damn coward to me!"

Morgan knew good and well that Bateman was trying to prod him into a fight. Sheffield's words had stung his pride, and Bateman intended to heal it by proving that he was faster on the draw than Kid Morgan.

One advantage Morgan had was that he didn't give a damn whether he was faster than Bateman. He felt fairly confident that he was, but he didn't intend to find out. He wasn't going to risk getting killed before he could settle the score with Colonel Black for what had happened at the Williams ranch.

Sheffield glanced back and forth between the two of them. Judging by the look on his face, he was nervous about the possibility of gunplay breaking out—with him maybe caught in the middle.

Then a woman behind Morgan said, "What's going on here?"

Morgan knew the voice belonged to Glory Sheffield. Her husband looked past Morgan at her and said, "Damn it, Gloriana, I told you to stay at the hotel."

"I would have, but you were over here such a long time, dear."

Glory moved around the men so that she could see Morgan and Bateman—and so *they* could see *her.* She sensed the tension in the room, as did the men who'd been working at the desks. They looked almost as nervous as Sheffield. The clerk who had tried to stop Morgan from going into the inner office had backed off and now stood beside his desk, toying with the inkwell as he watched the confrontation between Morgan and Bateman.

Morgan didn't take his attention off Bateman, but from the corner of his eye he saw the way Glory's breasts began to rise and fall faster. A flush crept over her face. He realized that she was excited by the danger that was in the air. A part of her probably wanted Morgan and Bateman to slap leather.

Morgan wasn't going to let that happen. When Bateman demanded belligerently, "Well, Morgan? Did you hear what I said?" He just smiled faintly.

"I heard you. Think whatever you want, Bateman. It doesn't matter to me."

"So you admit that you're a yellow, spineless coward?"

"I admit that I don't care what somebody like you thinks."

The flat, simple words were so scathing in their dismissal that once again Bateman looked like he was about to reach for his guns. If his hands moved a little more, Morgan was ready to draw. Even though his stance appeared casual, every nerve in his body was taut. He planned to kill Bateman just as quickly as he could, in hopes that the gunman wouldn't get off a shot that might hit an innocent bystander, like one of the clerks—or Glory Sheffield.

"Ah, the hell with it," Bateman muttered abruptly. "I'm not gonna waste a bullet on you, Morgan." He moved his hands away from the ivory-handled gun butts and turned to Sheffield. "Give me the word, Mr. Sheffield, and the boys and I will go out and hunt down those outlaws for you."

Sheffield's mouth tightened into a grim line. "All right, Bateman, I don't suppose I have any choice. Find that renegade, Colonel Black."

"And kill him?" Bateman couldn't quite keep the bloodthirsty eagerness out of his voice.

"Whatever it takes to make sure he leaves my trains alone," Sheffield said. He walked over to his wife and took hold of her arm. "We're going back to the hotel."

She pulled loose from his grip, not roughly but firmly. "There's no need to manhandle me, Edward," she said in an icy tone. "I was hoping to look around Titusville. I haven't been here before, you know."

"There's nothing to see. It's just a town."

She smiled. "I noticed a great many saloons and similar establishments."

"None of which are suitable places for you to visit." Sheffield looked at Bateman. "What are you waiting for? There's still time enough for you to go out there where those outlaws ambushed us and try to pick up their trail."

Bateman nodded. "Yes, sir. Hadn't I better leave some men here to ride guard on the train when it goes back to Bisbee?"

Sheffield looked at Morgan. "Are you going back to Bisbee on the train, Morgan? It ought to be repaired and ready to roll again tomorrow."

Morgan shook his head. "No, I think I'll stay up here for a while. I'd sort of like to look around the town, too."

"See?" Glory said with a triumphant smile at her husband. "I'm not the only one." She stepped over to Morgan and slid her arm around his. "Maybe we should explore Titusville together."

Morgan's jaw tightened. He hadn't expected such scandalous behavior from Glory, but maybe he should have known better, considering what he had seen of her actions so far. She clearly liked goading her husband and flirting with other men as much as she could. He thought about disengaging his arm from hers, but that might just make her more determined to get her way.

"Do what you like," Sheffield snapped. "You always do, anyway. And as long as you're with Morgan, at least I'll know that you're safe from the roughnecks around here." He turned back to Bateman. "Yes, leave some men to guard the train tomorrow, since Morgan won't be on it."

"Yes, sir." Bateman didn't like the implication that Morgan alone would do a better job of protecting the train than his men could. He stalked out of the office, but not before glaring one last time at Morgan.

When Bateman was gone, Glory urged Morgan toward the door. "Come with me, Kid," she said. "I want to see this place."

"I still have work to do," Sheffield said. "I'll be here at the office for a while."

"That's fine, dear." The offhanded way Glory spoke made it clear she didn't care where her husband was or how he was spending his time. A little muscle jumped in Sheffield's jaw as he nodded and turned to go back into the inner office.

With arms linked, Morgan and Glory left the building that housed the mining corporation. "What would you like to look at first?" she asked. "A saloon? A brothel?"

"You're trying to shock me," Morgan drawled. "It's not going to work."

"Are you saying that you can't be shocked, Kid?"

"Nope."

"But it would take more than me to do it, is that right?" She gave him a speculative look. "We'll see about that."

Morgan managed not to sigh in exasperation. "Let's walk over to the general store," he suggested. "I need a new hat."

"I'd noticed that yours was gone. What happened to it?"

"I lost it while I was crawling around under the train. I imagine it's blowing around somewhere out there on the edge of the foothills now."

"Well, I'll be glad to help you pick out another one."

He hadn't asked her to help him pick out a new hat, he thought, but he refrained from pointing that out to her.

Morgan spotted a large building across the street with TITUSVILLE MERCANTILE painted on the sign that hung above its doors. He and Glory started toward it. Morgan was aware that a lot of the men on the boardwalks and in the dusty street stared at Glory with undisguised lust. She was probably the most stunning woman who had ever set foot in the settlement. He was sure that she was aware of the attention, too, and was probably enjoying every minute of it.

She could stir up a lot of trouble if she stayed in a rough-and-tumble place for very long, he thought. It would be a good idea if Sheffield got her back to Bisbee on that train tomorrow.

But that was Sheffield's business, not his, Morgan told himself.

They stepped onto the boardwalk and went into the mercantile. Morgan spotted several hats hung on pegs next to a window and went over to examine them. Since Glory still had her arm linked with his, she went with him.

Morgan reached for a broad-brimmed brown

Stetson similar to the one he had lost under the train. Before he could take it off the peg, Glory said, "No, not that one. It doesn't go with that suit at all."

"I'll probably have to get a new suit, too," Morgan pointed out. "The coat got pretty torn up while I was crawling around on that roadbed."

Glory picked up one of the other hats. "This is the one you need. Try it on."

Morgan turned the hat over in his hands. It was black, with a slightly smaller brim, and the band around the crown was studded with silver conchos. Holding it in one hand, he settled it on his head, then looked at Glory and asked, "What do you think?"

"It's perfect," she told him. "Very handsome. You should get it."

"I don't know how much it costs yet."

"Oh, you don't have to worry about that. Edward owns this store. He owns nearly all the businesses in Titusville."

Morgan frowned. "That doesn't mean I don't have to pay for the hat. I turned down that job he offered me, you know."

"Yes, I know, and I'm still not happy about it. I was hoping we could spend a lot more time together."

He might have tried explaining to her that if he had accepted her husband's offer, he would have been out on the trail of Colonel Black's gang, not spending time with her. Before he could get into that, however, a man's voice said in a mocking tone, "Now ain't that purty?"

Morgan bit back a sigh and thought, *Not again.*

He hoped he wasn't about to have to kill somebody.

Chapter 20

Morgan turned slowly. He had recognized the challenge in the man's voice and knew the comment was intended to either goad him into a fight or humiliate him. It hadn't been that long since Phil Bateman had tried the same tactic, and Morgan was getting damned sick and tired of it.

Two men stood there, hard-bitten hombres with stubbled faces and gaunt cheekbones. They wore range clothes and low-slung guns. One was a few inches taller than the other and had rust-colored hair instead of dirty brown. Those were the only significant differences in their appearance.

Morgan pegged them as two of the men Sheffield had hired to protect his trains. The men who would now attempt to hunt down Colonel Black's band of desperados, under Bateman's leadership.

It wasn't very likely they would be successful, Morgan thought. If Black and his men knew the Dragoon Mountains at all, they would be able to give Sheffield's unofficial posse the slip without much trouble.

"I reckon Bateman must've sent you over here to harass me," Morgan said.

"I'm the one talkin' to you, mister, nobody else," the one with rust-colored hair said. An ugly grin stretched across his face. "And I say that's a mighty purty hat. It looks like somethin' an Eastern dude would wear."

Conrad Browning had been one of those Eastern dudes the hard case referred to, but those days were far behind Kid Morgan. He moved to one side to put some distance between him and Glory. He didn't want her getting hurt if any shooting started. Even as he changed position, though, she sidled after him, as if she didn't want him to get too far away from her.

Morgan saw that from the corner of his eye. His jaw tightened. If he had to be blunt about it, he would.

"Mrs. Sheffield, why don't you go on over to the other side of the store?" he said.

Before Glory could say anything or respond to the suggestion, the shorter of the two hard cases snickered. "You sure you want to do that, dude?" he asked. "Maybe the lady should stay where she is to protect you."

The other one said, "Yeah, I hear she's partial to men who ain't her husband."

Morgan heard Glory's sharp intake of breath. She might not make any bones about the sort of woman she was, but she obviously didn't enjoy hearing two men such as these gun-wolves talking about it.

It got worse, though, as the first man said, "You

know what I call a woman like that? A slut, pure and simple."

The second man laughed. "Then why's she hangin' around with some damn Easterner who probably don't even like women? He looks like a sissy to me."

In a low, angry voice, Glory demanded, "Are you going to just stand there and let them say those things about both of us, Mr. Morgan?"

He noticed that she called him Mr. Morgan again, instead of Kid. But he said, "What do you want me to do, shoot them?"

"Yes," Glory said. "I think I'd like that very much."

Well, that put it right out there.

The two men crouched, poising their hands near their guns, and the movement reminded Morgan of coiling snakes. All they needed was the sound of rattles buzzing to warn of imminent danger.

Everybody in the store knew it, too. There were quite a few customers in the place, and most of them scrambled to get somewhere that they wouldn't be in the line of fire.

"How about it, mister? You gonna draw?"

"Hold on a minute," Morgan said. "I want to look at this hat. I think you may be right about it."

That surprised all of them, including Glory. She said, "What are you doing?"

Moving slowly so as not to spook them into drawing, Morgan reached up and took off the hat. He stepped closer to the window, as if trying to get a better look at it in the light.

"What the hell?" one of the gunmen said.

The next second he yelled a curse as the sunlight slanting in through the window struck the silver conchos on the hatband and reflected right into his eyes, momentarily blinding him. He flung up a hand to block the glare and took an instinctive step back.

At the same instant, Morgan flicked his wrist and sent the hat flying into the face of the other man. Reflex made him flinch as it came straight at his eyes. Morgan kicked him in the groin. The agony that exploded between the man's legs made him forget all about trying to get his gun out of its holster. He screeched in pain, clutched at himself as he doubled over, and then collapsed on the store's plank floor.

The man Morgan had blinded with the sun's reflection from the conchos was still weaving around like he hadn't yet regained his sight. He had his gun in his hand, though, so he was plenty dangerous whether he could see anything or not. Morgan lunged at him, grabbed his wrist, and shoved his arm up just as the man pulled the trigger. The gun roared, but the bullet shot harmlessly into the ceiling.

Still holding tightly to the man's wrist with his left hand, Morgan brought his right around in a looping punch that landed cleanly on the hard case's jaw with enough force behind it to jerk the hombre's head to the side. Morgan twisted the man's wrist so hard that bones ground together under the skin. The man grunted in pain as his fingers opened involuntarily, dropping the gun. It thudded to the floor.

Morgan let go of his wrist and brought that hand up in an uppercut that caught the man under the chin. The man's head rocked back. Morgan chopped the side of his hand against the man's exposed throat.

Gagging and choking and pawing at his throat, the man staggered backward. He blundered into a stack of buckets, tripped and fell, and brought the whole stack crashing down on him. As the hard case struggled to get to his feet, Morgan picked up one of the buckets and brought it down hard on his head. The gunman slumped and sprawled, out cold. His companion lay nearby, curled up in a whimpering ball of pain.

The whole thing had taken maybe ten ticks of the banjo clock on the wall of the store, behind the counter.

"My God," Glory said in an awed voice. "How did you do that? *Why* did you do that?"

Morgan shrugged. "Seemed like it would be easier than shooting them, and less dangerous to everybody else in the store, too. Sorry if I disappointed you." He bent and picked up the hat from the floor. "I think I'm starting to like this hat after all."

He put it on again and turned to see Glory glaring at him. She hadn't liked that comment about disappointing her, he thought. But he knew it was true. She had thought she was about to see the blood and death that had been denied to her earlier in her husband's office, and a part of her had been looking forward to it.

Several of the store's customers and one of the clerks came forward tentatively to stare curiously at the men on the floor. The clerk glanced at Morgan and said, "I never saw anybody move so fast, mister. I think you could've beat 'em both to the draw if you'd wanted to."

"Didn't see any point in getting a lot of blood on the floor," Morgan said with a shrug. "You might've wound up with some bullet holes in the walls you'd have to patch, too."

"Or bullet holes in us."

"That was a risk, too," Morgan agreed. "Have you got any law in this town?"

"Phil Bateman's the marshal."

Morgan grunted. Somehow, that didn't surprise him. Edward Sheffield pretty much owned Titusville, so it made sense that the local law would be one of Sheffield's handpicked men. Morgan was a little surprised that the tycoon hadn't offered him the marshal's badge as well, when Sheffield was trying to hire him.

Morgan pointed at the hat on his head. "How much for the hat?"

"There's no charge," Glory said before the clerk could answer. "I told you, Mr. Morgan, my husband owns this store. I'm sure he won't mind if I give you the hat."

"I'd rather pay for it," Morgan drawled coolly. He took a double eagle out of his pocket and flipped it to the clerk, who deftly plucked the spinning gold piece out of the air without thinking. "Will that cover it?"

"Uh, yes, sir, I reckon,"—the clerk glanced nervously at Glory—"if Miz Sheffield says it's all right."

She flipped a hand impatiently. "If Mr. Morgan wants to be ungracious, that's fine with me, I suppose."

"I don't mean any offense," Morgan said. "I just like to pay my own way and not be beholden to anybody."

"Fine," Glory said again.

Heavy footsteps from the doorway made Morgan glance in that direction. Phil Bateman came into the store, his hands near the ivory-handled revolvers and a look of expectation on his face, as if he hoped he'd have to use the guns. He came to a stop when he saw the two men lying on the floor near Morgan and

Glory, one unconscious, the other obviously not in the mood to cause any more trouble.

"Somebody on the street told me there was a fight goin' on in here," Bateman said. "I should've known you were involved in it, Morgan. Trouble just follows you around, don't it?"

"It seems to," Morgan said, his voice as flat and hard as Bateman's. "I think you knew who was involved, all right, since you sent those two over here after me."

Bateman's eyes narrowed. "What the hell are you talkin' about?"

Morgan nodded toward the two men who had picked the fight. "Are you saying that those men aren't part of the crew that Sheffield hired to guard the railroad?"

"I'm sayin' I never saw those two before in my life," Bateman declared. "I've got better things to do than worry about holdin' a grudge against you, Morgan. If I decide to settle things between us, you can damn well be sure that I'll handle it myself, and I'll come at you from the front."

Even though Morgan had been convinced that Bateman was behind the men's attempt to pick a fight with him, Bateman's words had the ring of truth. Bateman was the sort of man who clearly rated his own prowess with a gun quite highly, and maybe his pride would stand in the way of sending anybody else after Morgan. Morgan hadn't considered that angle of it before.

He decided that he believed what Bateman had just told him. He jerked his head in a curt nod and said, "Fine. But that leaves a question unanswered." He gestured toward the two men. "Who are they?"

"A couple of hombres who just naturally didn't like you?" Bateman gave a humorless laugh. "I can sure understand that feeling."

"Maybe so."

Morgan didn't fully believe it, though. His gut told him there was more to it than just a couple of hard cases trying to harass a man they had pegged as an Easterner, a suitable target for that sort of hoorawing. He would have to get to the bottom of it, otherwise he risked having someone send more men after him.

"I understand you're the local marshal, too," Morgan went on. "What are you going to do with those two?"

"We have a little one-cell jail. I'll deputize a couple of miners to drag them over there and throw them in it. They can cool their heels there until I get back. The justice of the peace can hear their case then."

Morgan knew Bateman meant until he got back from trying to track down Colonel Black's gang. That might take a while, he thought. The prisoners could be in for a long stay in jail.

"What if I don't press charges against them?"

Bateman shook his head. "Doesn't matter. They still disturbed the peace. For that matter, so did you. From the looks of it, their peace got disturbed real good."

"I just defended myself and the lady," Morgan snapped.

"Don't worry, I'm not gonna lock you up. But I reckon it'd be a good idea if you didn't linger around town, Morgan. There's nothing here for you."

Actually, Morgan agreed with him, although he wasn't going to admit that to Bateman. He intended to spend the night there in Titusville.

But come morning, he was going to be on the trail of Colonel Gideon Black.

Chapter 21

By nightfall, the whole town was buzzing about the exploits of the Cannon Gang, as the citizens of Titusville had dubbed the outlaws who had attacked the train. Thirsty passengers and members of the train crew had hit the saloons and spread the story, including the way that the stranger called Kid Morgan had almost single-handedly foiled the daring holdup attempt.

After the violent incident in the general store, Glory Sheffield had lost her enthusiasm for looking around the town with Morgan. She had asked him if he would walk her back to the hotel, which he did. She said her good-byes there, none too warmly. Obviously, she had given up on him as a source of diversion. She probably would have switched her attentions to Phil Bateman, Morgan thought, if Bateman and a large group of men hadn't ridden out of Titusville in the early afternoon, heading to the site of the attack on the train in an attempt to pick up the trail of the outlaws.

The Kid spent the afternoon looking over the town. Titusville appeared to be a prosperous settlement, which meant the Gloriana Mine was successful. All of it represented a steady stream of profits flowing into the pockets of Edward Sheffield. It was easy to see why Sheffield would be a tempting target for outlaws.

Was that all there was to it, though? An uneasy feeling stirred inside Morgan. He sensed there was something he didn't know yet about the situation.

He took a room in the hotel and made arrangements at the local livery stable for the buckskin. After eating supper at what the hotel clerk told him was the best restaurant in Titusville, Morgan walked along the street to one of the saloons, a place called the Birdcage. He wasn't sure why the saloon had been dubbed that. He didn't see a bird or a birdcage anywhere in the big, smoky, crowded room.

Nursing a beer at the bar, Morgan listened to the conversations around him. Not surprisingly, most of them were about the attack on the train by the Cannon Gang. He thought he might pick up some information that could prove useful to him in tracking down the outlaws, but that didn't seem to be the case. None of the men in the saloon knew who the bandits were, or if they did, they weren't admitting it.

After a while, Morgan drifted over to a table where a poker game was going on. When a player dropped out and a chair opened up, the dealer gestured toward it, looked at Morgan, and raised an inquisitive eyebrow. Morgan thought *Why not?* and sat down to take a hand.

His mind wasn't really on the game, but he played skillfully enough that he won a few hands, staying about even. After a while, one of the other players, a miner by the looks of him, threw in his cards and said,

"That's enough for me. I'm leavin' while I still got enough money for a drink of whiskey and a woman."

"Come back any time, friend," the dealer said smoothly as the miner scraped his chair back and stood up.

At the end of the hand, which The Kid won with three nines, another man stepped up and rested a hand on the back of the empty chair. "How about if I sit in, gents?" he asked.

"As long as your money's good, you're more than welcome," the dealer said.

The newcomer placed a stack of coins on the table in front of the empty chair. "Good enough for you?"

The dealer smiled. "More than good enough. Have a seat."

The man settled himself in the chair and said, "I hope this is a friendly game."

Something nagged at Morgan's mind. He hadn't really paid any attention to the stranger, but curiosity drew his gaze to the man's face.

It took every bit of iron-nerved self-control in his body not to show the shock he felt as he recognized the newcomer as Colonel Gideon Black.

Morgan had seen the renegade colonel only one time, when he watched Black and his men from inside the Williams ranch house. Black was dressed differently now. Instead of the fringed buckskin shirt and cavalry trousers and hat, he wore a brown tweed suit and a derby. He looked like a businessman rather than a military commander.

But there was no mistaking the lean, almost satanic face with its dark goatee, as well as the dark hair curling out from under the derby. Morgan managed to keep his face expressionless, as if he had never seen the man who had just sat down at the table with him, but it required quite an effort.

And it took a lot of brass on Black's part to waltz right into Titusville after attacking the train that morning. However, it was possible that no one in town would recognize him, especially dressed like he was. He didn't really look like the same man who had been recruiting gunmen in Bisbee for the past couple months.

"My name is Sayers," Black said. "Joshua D. Sayers. Mining equipment is my line."

"Well, poker is mine, Mr. Sayers," the dealer said. "Welcome to the game."

Black smiled blandly. For a moment, The Kid wondered if he had made a mistake. Was the new player really a mining equipment salesman named Sayers? Was it possible that he just bore a strong resemblance to Colonel Gideon Black?

The Kid leaned forward and held out his hand. "Name's Morgan," he said.

Black . . . or Sayers . . . gripped The Kid's hand. "Joshua Sayers, at your service, sir."

The second The Kid heard those drawled words, he knew he wasn't mistaken. The colonel had said the same thing to Sean Williams back at the ranch, only there he had introduced himself as Colonel Gideon Black, not Joshua Sayers. The voice and the phrasing were identical. For some reason, Black was pretending to be someone else.

"I'm glad to meet you, Mr. Morgan," Black went on. "You're the man everyone in town is talking about, aren't you? The man who saved the train single-handedly?"

"The train crew and some of the passengers were putting up a fight, too," Morgan pointed out. "I wouldn't say I did anything single-handedly."

The dealer was tossing cards in front of each of the players with a deft skill born of long practice. "The game is five-card stud, Mr. Sayers," he told Black. "That suit you?"

"It suits me just fine, sir," Black said as he lifted the corner of his hole card to study it. Then he looked at Morgan again and went on, "You killed several of the bandits and stopped the others from holding up the train. People say that you're a hero, Mr. Morgan."

The Kid shrugged. "I can't stop folks from thinking whatever they want to think."

Had Black come into town looking for vengeance on the man who had ruined his plans? Surely he didn't think he could just walk into the saloon, look around, and kill Kid Morgan. The Kid wasn't going to let that happen, for one thing, and for another, even if by some fluke the colonel succeeded, he would never get away with it.

Unless there was some sort of distraction, like an attack on the town . . .

Morgan stiffened in his chair as he thought about the death and destruction the outlaws could wreak on Titusville if they bombarded the settlement with that cannon. Nestled in the mountains as it was, there was plenty of high ground around Titusville where the big gun could be positioned to fire down on to the town.

"Something wrong, Mr. Morgan?" Black murmured. He was an observant son of a bitch, The Kid had to give him that. He had noticed the reaction when the thought of that potential threat had gone through Morgan's mind.

"No, I'm fine," Morgan said. "And since it's up to me to open the betting . . ." He shoved some double eagles from the pile in front of him to the center of the table to join the ante. "A hundred dollars."

Most of the opening bets since The Kid joined the game had been the five or ten dollar variety. Opening for a hundred was enough to make a couple of the players drop out right away. Black just smiled and matched the bet, as did the other two men, and then the dealer saw the hundred and raised it twenty. He smiled at Morgan and said, "Finally, some real action."

Morgan saw the bet and bumped it up twenty more dollars. Black stayed in, as did the other three. Cards were dealt.

Morgan hadn't paid much attention to the cards in his hand. He didn't care about the money. If you added up all the money in the bank accounts he had from one end of the country to the other, he was worth considerably more than he could ever spend in one lifetime, even if all his holdings never earned another penny, which, of course, they would. He just wanted to get under the man's skin, maybe rattle the bandit leader's composure.

So far, though, it didn't seem to be working. Black still wore a placid smile. He saw the bet and raised again, forty dollars this time. There was a lot of money in the center of the table. One of the remaining players dropped out, but the other one and the dealer stubbornly stayed in.

Morgan had two eights showing. A thought occurred to him, and he lifted the corner of his hole card again. It was an ace, all right. His father had told him one time about Wild Bill Hickok. Frank Morgan had been acquainted with the man some called the Prince of Pistoleers, and seeing long-haired Phil Bateman that afternoon had reminded The Kid of Hickok as well. Now the hand The Kid was being dealt was shaping up to possibly be aces and eights, the same hand Wild Bill had been holding in Deadwood's Number 10 Saloon when Jack McCall came in and shot him in the back of the head.

If Morgan was the sort of man who was inclined to be nervous, he might have started wondering about bad omens along about now.

But he had been through enough tragedy in his life that he knew the worst omen of all was being born in the first place.

"Hell with it," he said when the bet came around to him again. He saw it and then shoved out five more double eagles. "A hundred more."

The man to his left didn't even wait for the next card. "Too steep for me," he said with a shake of his head. "I hate to walk away from a pot that size, gents, but I don't have any choice." He shoved his chair back and stood up.

Black stayed in, as did the dealer, and The Kid caught a three to go with his ace and pair of eights. Logically, he knew that it didn't matter whether he won or lost, and he would have said that his competitive instincts didn't care, either.

But he found himself pondering what to do next as if it really mattered. He had enough money left in front of him to see the bet, but that was all. If either Black or the dealer raised, he would have to drop out.

Of course, he could have written a bank draft, if they would agree to accept it, but he didn't want to have to reveal who he really was. He settled for pushing in what was left of his readily available cash and said, "That's it for me, gentlemen."

Black and the dealer both saw the bet as well, without raising it, then the dealer handed out the final cards. Morgan tried to keep his face expressionless, but he felt the corner of his mouth twitch a little as another ace landed faceup in front of him.

That gave him two pair. Aces and eights, just like Wild Bill Hickok. He flipped over his hole card, and the men who had gathered around the table to watch the outcome of this big game muttered amongst themselves.

"That's quite a hand," Black said. "I'm afraid I have it beat, though." He turned over his hole card and revealed a third deuce to go along with the two already showing.

The dealer said, "Good, but not good enough." He'd had a pair of jacks showing, and the third one was lurking facedown. He revealed it with a flourish. A sigh came from the crowd as he leaned forward to rake in the pot.

Black smiled across the table at The Kid. "Well, Mr. Morgan, it appears that we've been beaten fair and square. I'm just about cleaned out, but I still have the price of a couple of drinks, if you'd care to join me."

Did he really want to have a drink with the man he had sworn to kill, The Kid asked himself?

"Why not?" he said.

Chapter 22

They went to the bar, and Colonel Black told the bartender to bring them two whiskeys. He looked over at The Kid. "I hope that's all right with you."

"You're buying," Morgan said. "It's up to you."

"All right, then." When the drinks came, Black lifted his glass and said, "To the hero."

Morgan frowned. "I told you, there's nothing to that."

Black shook his head and said, "That's not the way I hear it. You not only saved that train from being held up today, you also killed several men down in Bisbee in the past couple of days and probably saved Edward Sheffield's wife from being killed by a shotgun blast. You impressed Sheffield enough that he wanted to hire you to hunt down the men who have been stopping his trains and stealing his ore shipments."

The Kid wasn't sure how Black had heard about all of that. The renegade colonel might have some spies working for him in Bisbee and in Titusville. That was the only explanation Morgan could think of.

He didn't bother disputing what Black had just said. Instead, he threw back his drink and then placed the empty glass on the bar. Black did likewise.

"What did you tell Sheffield?" Black pressed him. "You must have agreed to take the job, or else you wouldn't have come up on the train with him and his wife."

"Not necessarily," The Kid said. "Could be I wanted to get the lay of the land before I told him anything."

"If that were the case, then why get mixed up in that fight earlier today?"

"Because I don't like anybody shooting at me, no matter what the situation," The Kid snapped. "Especially with a damned cannon."

Black gave him a level stare for several seconds, then abruptly chuckled. "I can see where that would be a little annoying, all right. Have you made up your mind?"

"What business is it of yours?"

"I'm curious, that's all. A man who can handle a gun like you . . . well, it's interesting to see which side he'll pick in a fight. Especially when he doesn't know the full story."

The Kid returned Black's cool-eyed gaze for a moment, then signaled to the bartender. "Next round's on me," he said.

"Fine." Black nodded toward an empty table in the corner. "Why don't we go over there so we can have a little more peace and quiet while we talk?"

And a little more privacy, The Kid thought. He didn't know what was going on, but Black had certainly piqued his interest, especially with that comment about him not knowing the whole story. Of course, that was probably exactly what Black had intended by it. But Fate had given The Kid the opportunity to learn more about his quarry, and he wasn't going to turn it down.

When the bartender had refilled their glasses, they picked them up and carried them over to the table Black had indicated. They sat down so that neither man had his back to the door, and once again The Kid was reminded of Wild Bill Hickok. He held his glass in his left hand, and his right slipped the Colt from its holster and leveled it at Black under the table.

For all he knew, Black had a gun on him, too, he thought as he noticed the colonel was also using his left hand to hold his drink. Morgan couldn't help but smile.

"Something amusing, Mr. Morgan?"

"I was just wondering how long we're going to keep up this masquerade."

"Masquerade?" Black raised an eyebrow. "Are you trying to tell me that you're *not* the man called Kid Morgan?"

"Not at all. You're the one who's posing as someone you're not . . . Colonel."

Black looked at him for a long moment, then chuckled and took a sip of the whiskey in his glass. "What gave me away? We've never met before, so I know you didn't recognize me."

"Actually, that's not quite true. We haven't met, but I *have* seen you before."

"Oh? Where?" Black sounded genuinely interested.

"That doesn't matter," The Kid said. "What's important is that we each know who the other is, and we might as well stop beating around the bush. If you've come here to kill me, Colonel, you'll find that it's not an easy job."

"Kill you?" Black laughed again. "You've got me all wrong, Morgan. I came into town and looked you up so that I can ask you to join forces with me."

The Kid couldn't have hidden his surprise if he tried. "I was doing my damnedest to kill you earlier today, out there at the edge of the foothills where you stopped the train."

The colonel didn't try to deny the charge, The Kid noted. Black merely made a small gesture with one hand and said, "That was war. Allegiances can change, and a wise commander knows that."

"War?" The Kid repeated.

"That's right. What else would you call battling against an evil aggressor who has vast forces at his command?"

"You're talking about Edward Sheffield."

The faint smile disappeared from Black's face at the mention of Sheffield's name. "The man is a monster," Black stated flatly. "You have no idea how many crimes he's committed to get where he is."

Morgan thought back over everything he had heard about Edward Sheffield and the man's business practices, back in the days when he'd still been Conrad Browning. Sheffield had a reputation as a sharp, canny, even ruthless businessman, but Morgan didn't recall hearing any rumors that he had engaged in anything criminal.

Of course, it was possible that Sheffield was just good at covering up his less savory practices. Some men were like that.

A fervor crept into Black's voice that made him sound almost insane, as he continued, "All I'm trying to do is set things right. It's a matter of justice, Morgan, plain and simple. Justice . . . and retribution!"

Morgan wanted to ask the colonel how slaughtering Sean, Frannie, and Cyrus Williams had furthered the cause of justice. He kept his own anger under control, though. He could gun down Black right then, but that might not put a stop to the rest of the Cannon Gang. Besides, he couldn't prove who Black was or offer any evidence that the renegade colonel was behind the outrages carried out recently, although Black had just all but admitted it. Morgan wasn't afraid of the law, but he didn't see any point in risking a murder charge, either.

Quietly, he said, "Let me get this straight. You want me to join you, even though I killed some of your men and ruined your plans this morning."

"I've heard a great deal about your exploits, and now that I've seen you in action with my own eyes, I know that we were meant to fight together side by side, rather than against each other. Think of what we could do, Morgan!" Black leaned forward, his eyes burning with the intensity of his emotions. "We could conquer the whole territory!"

Yeah, he was definitely loco, The Kid thought. He didn't know yet what had caused the colonel to go mad, but he had no doubt that Black was insane.

Acting a lot more casual than he felt, The Kid leaned back in his chair and took another drink of the whiskey. As he set the glass on the table, he said, "I don't have any interest in conquering the territory, Colonel, or in conquering anything else, for that matter."

"Then why did you come to Bisbee looking for me?"

Yes, Black definitely had spies operating in that part
of Arizona. It fit right in with the way he evidently regarded his vendetta against Edward Sheffield as a military operation.

"I heard that you were looking for men who were
good with a gun," Morgan replied with a shrug. "I
was curious. I thought I'd see what it was about."

"Then Sheffield swooped in and tried to hire you."

"I didn't take the job," The Kid pointed out.

"And yet you came to Titusville on the train with
him . . . and his wife."

Morgan caught just the faintest hesitation on
Black's part before he mentioned Glory Sheffield.
He didn't know what that meant, but maybe . . .
something.

"I told you, I'm curious. I wanted to see this place
for myself and get a good look at Sheffield's mining
operation. Sometimes men who are supposed to be
rich don't have as much money as they make out
they do."

Black nodded. "Sheffield is rich. Have no doubts
about that, Morgan. But it's ill-gotten gains."

"You keep talking about him being crooked. Do
you have any proof of that?"

The colonel made a curt gesture. "Never mind
about that. I know the truth, and you can take my
word for it. Just answer me this . . . do you have any
intention of going to work for Sheffield?"

"None whatsoever," The Kid answered honestly.
"I've never been much of one for taking orders, even
when the pay might be good."

"Then join forces with me."

"I just told you, I don't like taking orders. Besides,

I'm not sure how the rest of your men would feel about me joining up after I gunned down some of their friends this morning."

"They'll feel like I tell them to feel," Black said confidently. "Besides, they're professional fighting men. They know better than to make close friendships. They'll accept you, I can promise you that."

"And just what is it you're planning to do?"

Black smiled and shook his head. "It would be rather foolish of me to explain all my plans to you before I'm sure that we share common goals, now wouldn't it?"

The Kid shrugged. "I suppose so. But if I don't know what you're going to do, how do I know whether I want to be part of it?"

"Do you want to be a rich man?"

"Everybody would like to have plenty of money," The Kid replied, thinking that in reality, he was one of the richest men west of the Mississippi, just like his father. Those riches hadn't spared either of them from suffering tragic losses in their lives.

"Throw in with me, and before we're through you'll be one of the richest, most powerful men in the territory." Black had that insane gleam in his eyes again. "Everything that belongs to Edward Sheffield will be mine. *Everything.*"

That made a dark suspicion stir in The Kid's mind. It was pure speculation, nothing more, but it fit the circumstances as he knew them and would explain some things. The best way to find out if he was right, he realized, would be to play along with the colonel.

"I suppose I could put up with taking orders for a

while, if the payoff is as big as you make it out to be," he said.

"It will be," Black promised.

"Then I'm in. What do you want me to do?"

"Do you have a room at the hotel?"

"Yeah."

"Go back there and get your things. Meet me on the ridge overlooking the town in half an hour." Black's voice sharpened in command. "No more than that, you understand. You have to be prompt if you're going to be in my outfit."

"Sure," The Kid said. "I'll be there."

"See that you are, or the deal is off. And whatever you do, don't tell anyone what you're doing. Once you're at the appointed place at the appointed time, you'll find out what happens next."

"All right," The Kid said. He pushed himself to his feet. "Just one thing, Colonel . . . don't double cross me. I wouldn't like that."

"I assure you, Mr. Morgan, the feeling is mutual. If you try any tricks, you'll regret them."

"So we're sort of taking each other on our words, aren't we?"

Black smiled thinly. "That's all anyone can do in this world, isn't it?"

He had a point there. The Kid nodded and left The Birdcage Saloon. He walked back to the hotel, taking note of the fact that Titusville's main street was still crowded despite the fact that the evening was wearing on. In a boomtown like that, things might not ever quiet down completely.

When The Kid reached the hotel, he walked upstairs to his room. In the second floor corridor, he stopped short in front of his door and looked down at the place where he had shoved a matchstick between the door and the jamb and broken it off. It was an old trick but an effective one if a fellow wanted to know whether or not somebody had been in his room while he was gone.

In this case, the answer was yes, because the broken matchstick wasn't where he had left it. The tiny piece of wood lay on the floor where there was a gap at the edge of the door. It had fallen straight down when someone opened the door.

Morgan glanced up and down the hall. He was alone at the moment, so he slipped his gun from its holster and held it ready beside his hip. He took out his key and slid it into the lock, not trying to be quiet about it. The key rattled as he turned it.

Then he grasped the knob, twisted it, and flung the door open. At the same time he took a quick step back, then threw himself forward in a lunging dive that carried him halfway across the room, moving low and fast. He hit the floor, rolled, and came up on one knee with the Colt in his hand, ready to pull the trigger.

"Oh, my God!" Glory Sheffield said from where she sat on the side of the bed, eyes wide with surprise. "Do you always come into a room that way, Kid?"

Chapter 23

Morgan came to his feet with a lithe motion and glared at the beautiful young redhead sitting on the edge of his bed.

"Breaking into a man's room is a good way of getting yourself killed . . . or worse," he said.

"A fate worse than death?" Glory shook her head. "I don't think so. Not the way I've been throwing myself at you, and yet you continue to steadfastly ignore me."

The Kid holstered his gun. "I imagine most men find you pretty hard to ignore, Mrs. Sheffield."

"That's true. Generally, they're falling all over themselves trying to give me what I want." She stood up and came toward him. She wore a different gown than she had been wearing earlier, having changed for dinner. This outfit was just as stylish and expensive as the other, and it hugged her body equally sensuously. "You truly don't seem to give a damn, Kid. Maybe that's why I find you so intriguing. And I told you to call me Glory. Calling me Mrs. Sheffield reminds me too much of Edward's first wife."

Maybe she needed a reminder that she was currently married to Edward Sheffield, Morgan thought. He said, "Whatever happened to her, anyway?"

Glory made a face. "She died. She was sick for a long time, and she couldn't be much of a wife to him, if you know what I mean. Not that she would have been, even if she hadn't been sick. She was a dried-up little woman. Very cold-blooded."

"Just the opposite of you."

That brought a wicked smile to Glory's face. "No one has ever accused me of being cold, Kid. Hot-blooded, is more like it."

Morgan could believe that. He asked, "How did you wind up married to him?"

She shrugged. "My father is the Assistant Secretary of War. He has a lot of business contacts with Edward. They thought it would be beneficial to everyone if he and I were married."

So his guess had been right, The Kid thought. Glory's marriage to Sheffield had been a business arrangement as much as anything. He wasn't surprised. A little disgusted, maybe, but not surprised. Over in Europe, the kings sold each other their daughters and sisters and cousins. Here in America, the politicians and the business magnates took the place of royalty.

"What are you doing here in my room, Mrs. Sheffield?"

"Glory, damn it."

"The last time I saw you, you were pretty mad

at me," The Kid reminded her. "You'd gone back to calling me Mr. Morgan."

She shrugged. "I'm easily irritated. It's a failing of mine. But I get over it quickly. Let's face it, you're the most interesting man in Titusville, and quite likely the most handsome, too. I'd rather spend the evening with you than with anyone else."

"What about your husband?"

Glory grimaced again. "Edward barely stopped worrying about business long enough to eat supper, and then he went back to the mining company office. If he did manage to quit worrying about that, he'd be too scared of Gideon to think about anything else."

No sooner were the words out of her mouth than she caught her breath sharply and looked like she wished she could draw them back in. The Kid had already noticed the familiarity with which she had referred to Colonel Black, and it fit right in with the vague theory that had started to form in his mind earlier.

"You and Black know each other, don't you?" he demanded, stepping closer to her.

She moved back and shook her head. "I don't know what you're talking about. I know who he is, of course. He's the outlaw who's trying to ruin Edward's business by holding up the trains and stealing those ore shipments."

"No, there's more to it than that," The Kid insisted. "If your father is the Assistant Secretary of War, that means he has a lot of contacts in the army, too. You knew Black before he retired." Something occurred to him. "Or was he kicked out of the army? Cashiered, as the British say."

Glory's composure had been cracking ever since

she'd made that slip. Now it broke all the way, and she said, "My God, why couldn't you just agree to go after him and kill him? That would solve everything!"

"You'd better tell me what this is about."

She shook her head. "I-I can't."

"That's the only way I can help you . . . Glory."

She drew in a deep, ragged breath and then started pacing back and forth across the hotel room as if she couldn't stay still. Her hands knotted together in front of her and then unknotted. Finally, she said, "Yes, I knew Colonel Black . . . Gideon Black. Have you ever seen him?"

The Kid nodded. "I have," he said, without telling her how recently he had seen the colonel, in fact.

"Then you know that he's a handsome devil. Quite a bit older than me, of course, but still . . . very virile."

The Kid would agree about the "devil" part. He didn't know about the other, but Glory obviously did.

"The two of you were romantically involved?"

"We were lovers." She said it bluntly, with no real inflection in her voice. "I thought I might actually marry him someday and be the colonel's lady. Although he would have been a general sooner or later if . . . if everything hadn't gotten ruined."

"What happened?"

"Gideon was involved in some rather shady dealings connected to the quartermaster corps. My father was part of them, too. But he was more prepared for trouble, and when things began to go wrong, he was able to get rid of all the evidence linking him to what had happened. Gideon wasn't that well prepared."

"So he had to take the blame," Morgan guessed.

Glory nodded. "He was court-martialed. He would

have been sent to prison for years, but my father interceded on his behalf, and in the end, Gideon was only dishonorably discharged. Father thought that Gideon would be grateful to him for his help, but he didn't feel that way."

Morgan wasn't surprised. "He hated your father instead and blamed him for everything that happened. Am I right?"

"Of course. I can see now it was inevitable. I think it made Gideon go a little mad."

More than a little, Morgan thought. Colonel Black was consumed by hatred. But most of it seemed to be directed at Edward Sheffield, and Morgan didn't understand that yet.

"What was Sheffield's part in this? Why does Black hate him?"

"Because Edward was involved in the graft and corruption as well. He was a silent partner in the whole thing. And when it all began to fall apart, Gideon got it in his head that Edward was responsible, too. Actually, he blamed Edward even more than he did my father, because he thought Edward arranged things to ruin him so that . . . so that he could . . ."

"Have you," The Kid guessed when Glory seemed unable to go on.

She caught her bottom lip between her teeth and nodded silently.

The Kid thought she was overacting just a little. She probably wasn't as devastated by the things she had revealed as she pretended to be. Even though he hadn't known her for very long, he was convinced that at heart, she was rather cool and calculating, despite that hot blood she claimed to have.

"So you can see why Gideon hates Edward," Glory went on after a moment. "Because of the court-martial, and because he lost me to Edward as well."

"Did Sheffield blackmail your father into going along with the marriage?"

Glory shook her head, and this time her words sounded completely genuine as she said, "He didn't have to do that. I was perfectly willing to marry him. My God, he's worth a fortune, and he's getting richer all the time. That is, he will be if someone can put a stop to what Gideon's trying to do."

"That's why you wanted me to help your husband."

After backing off from him for a while as she talked, Glory now came toward The Kid again, close enough so that she could lay a hand on his arm. Close enough so that he felt the warmth of her breath.

"After seeing what you did today, Kid, I know you could handle the problem. You could find Gideon and—"

"Kill him?" The Kid cut in.

Anger flared in Glory's eyes. "Yes, damn it! He was a criminal when he was in the army, and he's an even worse outlaw now. Don't make it sound like we're asking you to hunt down and murder an innocent man." She laughed harshly. "Gideon Black is far from innocent, I assure you!"

As he recalled what had happened to the Williams family and their vaqueros, Morgan knew that she was right about that. Gideon Black was cunning and daring, but he was also a mad dog who needed to be put down.

Morgan just wished that in doing so, he wouldn't be

doing a favor for such an unsavory trio as Sheffield, Glory, and her father.

"Well?" she said after staring into his eyes for a moment. "Will you do it?"

The Kid said, "I don't guarantee that I'll kill him . . . but I will see to it that he and his gang are stopped. I'll see that he's brought to justice."

Although if there was any justice in the world, he thought, Gideon Black wouldn't be the only one who was punished. Edward Sheffield and Glory's father had been mixed up neck deep in the criminal activities that had gotten Black court-martialed.

But they weren't running around shooting off cannons, so dealing with them wasn't quite so urgent. Once the renegade colonel had been dealt with, then maybe The Kid could pass the word through Claudius Turnbuckle to some high-level contacts of his own. Sooner or later, there might be an investigation into the dealings between Sheffield and the Assistant Secretary of War. That might wind up hurting Glory as well, but The Kid had no doubt that she would land on her feet.

Or on her back, as the case might be.

Those thoughts went through The Kid's head as Glory threw her arms around his neck and hugged him. "Thank you," she said. "Thank you so much."

"That doesn't mean I'm working for your husband, though," he warned. "We just have some common goals, that's all. I'm not interested in taking orders from him. Anything I do, I'll do in my own way."

"That's fine, as long as we don't have the threat of Gideon Black hanging over us anymore." She still had her arms around his neck, and her body was pressed boldly and brazenly against his. The warm mounds of her breasts prodded his chest as she went on, "You're going to be glad that you decided to help us, Kid. I'm going to make it worth your while. You have my word on that."

She lifted her face to his and kissed him.

Her mouth was hot and sweet and demanding, and there had been a time when he would have taken her to bed eagerly and with great pleasure. But that was before he had met, married, and ultimately lost the only woman he would ever love. Before Rebel.

Instinctively, The Kid's arms had gone around Glory's waist. Now he lifted them and took hold of her arms, intending to unwind them from his neck and step back from her.

"You don't have to—" he began.

"I want to," she whispered. "I want to, and Edward doesn't care. Why don't we just—"

The Kid could have made a guess what she was about to suggest, but he never knew for sure.

Because at that moment, he heard a high-pitched whine, and a second later the wall of the hotel room blew in, blasting them both off their feet.

Chapter 24

The impact was so devastating, the crash so deafening, that for a moment The Kid was stunned, unable to move or even think. Then awareness flickered back to life within him, and he realized that he was lying on top of something soft. Whatever it was moaned and stirred underneath him.

He moved a hand to try to push himself up and realized that he had just gripped a woman's firm, full breast. Surprised, he let go, then his brain began to work even more and he figured out that he was lying on top of Glory Sheffield.

He shifted his hand to the floor beside her and levered himself up. From there he was able to stagger to his feet. The air was full of dust, or maybe it was smoke. Whatever it was he was choking on it, and he couldn't see anything.

With his ears still ringing from the blast, he bent over and grasped her shoulders. He shook her and shouted, "Glory! Glory!" The words sounded odd and muffled to him. She didn't respond. He worried that she was dead.

Then, a moment later, he heard a faint groan that he was pretty sure hadn't come from him. He shook her and called her name again, and she said, "Wha-what happened?"

The Kid slipped his hands under her arms and straightened, hauling her upright. She sagged against him, but there was nothing arousing about the contact. She was only semiconscious. In the haze of dust that filled the room, he barely saw her shaking her head, and he wouldn't have been aware of that if her face hadn't been within inches of his own.

The floor suddenly tilted a little under their feet. Glory cried out in fear. The Kid tightened his grip on her. As his brain began to function better, he had a pretty good idea what had just happened. He didn't know what the extent of the damage was, but he knew they needed to get out of there before the floor collapsed.

With one arm around Glory, he used the other hand to feel his way along the wall until he came to the door, which hung askew on its hinges. He shoved it aside and stumbled into the hotel's second floor corridor. People were shouting curses and questions and frightened cries. Half dragging and half carrying Glory, The Kid turned in what he hoped was the direction of the stairs.

"Kid . . . Kid, where are we?" she murmured.

"Still in the hotel," he told her.

"There was some kind of . . . explosion . . ."

"I know." Somewhere outside, a heavy boom sounded. "Your former lover is shelling the town."

Glory gasped. "Gideon!"

"That's right." The Kid now knew why Colonel Black had insisted that he meet him on top of the ridge overlooking the town in half an hour. Black had already had this attack planned, and he wasn't going to call it off on account of Kid Morgan. If The Kid kept the rendezvous, fine; if not, he could take his chances with the citizens of Titusville when the bombardment started.

Was it just happenstance that the first shot had struck the hotel room where The Kid and Glory Sheffield were? He figured that was probably the case. The hotel was one of the most prominent buildings in town, after all, and as such it would be a tempting target. The Kid wasn't sure if that shot had been a direct hit on his room or if it had landed in one of the neighboring rooms. It was close enough to have wrecked his room, that was for sure, and could have easily killed him and Glory.

"Are you all right?" he asked her as they made their way along the hallway. "Can you tell if you're injured?"

"I-I don't think so." His ears had almost stopped ringing, and he could make out her answer fairly well even with all the hubbub around them. "My legs work. I don't think I'm bleeding anywhere. I just sort of hurt all over."

That didn't surprise The Kid. He felt the same way. He was sure they would both be covered with bruises by the next morning. Assuming, of course, that they survived the Cannon Gang's attack on the town.

Through the walls of the hotel, Morgan heard the big gun boom every couple of minutes. The colonel's gunners were working efficiently up on the ridge, and they were really pounding the settlement. Panic and chaos gripped the whole town.

Instinct wouldn't allow him to remain cooped up inside the hotel while an attack was going on. They reached the stairs and started down toward the lobby. Several guests who were choking and coughing followed them.

As they descended The Kid definitely smelled smoke as well as dust. Some of the strikes must have started fires in town. For all he knew, Colonel Black might even have explosive rounds, as well as solid cannonballs. He had no idea how Black had gotten his hands on a cannon in the first place, let alone what sort of ammunition the outlaws had for it.

Just as The Kid and Glory reached the bottom of the stairs, another wrenching crash sounded from upstairs. Either another round had struck the hotel, or the place was just collapsing from the damage that had already been done to it. Whichever, they didn't want to stay in there.

He closed his hand tightly around her arm and called over the madness around them, "Come on!"

They pushed their way through the crowd of terrified people that had gathered in the lobby and finally reached the street. It was full of shouting, frightened people as well. As they stumbled out of the hotel, The Kid saw several buildings on fire down the street, the flames leaping high into the night sky and casting an orange pall over the entire town.

He looked up toward the ridge, thinking that he might spot the outlaws and the cannon, but he couldn't see anything. Even if he had, his Colt wouldn't do him any good at that range. He needed his Winchester, or the Sharps Big Fifty. They were in the livery stable with the buckskin and his saddle.

Come to think of it, maybe it would be a good idea to head for the stable, he realized. He and Glory would be safer outside of Titusville.

"Where are we going?" she asked as he tugged her along the street.

"To get my horse and maybe a mount for you," he replied. "We're going to get out of here."

"Wait! What about Edward?"

The question surprised The Kid. He hadn't figured that she gave a damn one way or the other about her husband, the way she'd been acting ever since he met her. He would have said that the only thing that mattered to her about Edward Sheffield was his money. Maybe he was wrong. Maybe she was at least a little fond of him.

Morgan glanced toward the building that housed the mining company headquarters. One corner of it had crumpled under the impact of a cannonball, but at least it wasn't on fire. If Sheffield was in there, he was probably still alive.

The mining company was in the opposite direction from the stable, though. "We'll get some horses first," The Kid told Glory. "Then we'll come back to see if we can find him."

She tried to pull her arm free. "Let me go!" she demanded. "I can't let anything happen to Edward! I just can't!"

The Kid didn't relax his grip on her arm. "We'll get him if we can," he promised.

She stopped struggling and let him lead her down

the street to the livery stable. The noise of the shelling and the smoke from the fires had spooked the horses, who whinnied shrilly and lunged back and forth in their stalls. Except for The Kid's buckskin, that is. He looked rather wild-eyed but was still under control.

The two hostlers were trying to calm the maddened horses, with no success. They paid no attention to The Kid as he opened the buckskin's stall and went in to throw his saddle on the horse. He had to let go of Glory to do so, but she took a deep breath and told him, "Don't worry, Kid. I won't run off. I know I'll need your help finding Edward."

The Kid nodded as he worked at the cinches. He wasn't sure they would be able to get Sheffield out of town. He'd counted on being able to saddle one of the other horses, but all of them were too crazed. He and Glory could ride double on the buckskin, but even that stalwart animal couldn't carry the two of them and Edward Sheffield.

When he had his mount ready to ride, he swung up into the saddle and extended a hand to Glory. "Come on!" he told her. "You can ride in front of me."

"What about Edward?"

"We'll find another horse for him on the street, once we've located him."

She seemed to accept that answer. She grasped The Kid's wrist as he took hold of hers, and then with a foot in the stirrup, she raised up onto the buckskin's back. Morgan settled her in front of him, slid his left arm around her waist to hold her securely in place, and used his right to handle the reins. He heeled the buckskin into motion and rode out of the stable.

As they emerged on to the street, Morgan heard

the rattle of gunfire. That didn't particularly surprise him. The Cannon Gang had used their big gun to soften up the town, wreaking havoc and terrifying the citizens of Titusville, and intended to raid the settlement and loot it of everything valuable they could get their hands on. Colonel Black knew that Edward Sheffield owned most of the town. Anything they did to Titusville, they were doing to Sheffield, and that fit right in with Black's insane thirst for vengeance on the tycoon.

It couldn't have worked out better for the colonel, because Phil Bateman and most of Sheffield's hired guns were out of town, searching for the outlaws. Black had known that Titusville wouldn't be able to mount much of a defense.

The Kid couldn't fight the gang alone, either. That was why he wanted to get Glory and possibly Sheffield safely out of there. At least he could keep them alive that way.

As they headed for the mining company headquarters, a group of men on horseback burst out of a side street with a swift rataplan of hoofbeats. In the garish light from the burning buildings, The Kid saw the long dusters, the bandannas masking their faces, the pulled-down hats. The Cannon Gang had invaded Titusville, all right, and they had cut him and Glory off from the building where her husband probably was.

The Kid whirled his horse to head back the other way. "Wait!" Glory cried. "We have to find Edward!"

"Black's bunch is between us and him!" The Kid told her.

"Circle around! We have to save him!"

She was exhibiting a whole lot more concern for

Sheffield than The Kid would have been believed possible. He sent the buckskin toward another side street, hoping to avoid the outlaws that way.

It was a futile hope. Before they reached the corner, another group of riders appeared there, firing six-guns at anybody unlucky enough to get in their way. The Kid bit back a curse and hauled on the reins again. They were caught between the two groups of raiders.

Glory realized that, too. "Kid!" she screamed. "What are we going to do?"

Morgan suddenly spotted Colonel Gideon Black. Unlike the rest of his men, the renegade former soldier wasn't trying to disguise himself. He rode at the head of one of the groups in his cavalry trousers, boots, and hat, as well as the buckskin shirt. He had a saber in his hand, of all things, and he raised it above his head, poised to sweep it down and order a charge.

Before Black could do that, The Kid abruptly sent his horse toward the outlaws. "Colonel!" he shouted as he clamped his arm tighter around Glory Sheffield. "Colonel, look what I've got for you!"

Chapter 25

It was a desperate ploy, but the only one The Kid could think of on such short notice and in such perilous circumstances. As he rode toward Colonel Black, the guns in the hands of the other outlaws swung toward him, and he knew that he and Glory were right on the hair-trigger edge of being filled full of lead.

Black made a slashing motion with the saber. "Hold your fire!" he shouted to his men. "Hold your fire!"

The Kid leaned his head close to Glory's and said in her ear, "Fight me! Make it look real. I'll explain later."

She was quick-witted enough to realize that he had some sort of plan. She began struggling frantically against him, screaming, "No! Let me go, damn you! Let me go!"

She was doing a good job of acting, he thought as he jerked his head to the side so that the elbow she tried to ram into his face barely grazed his jaw. Maybe she wasn't acting. Maybe she was so terrified that the meaning of his words hadn't really penetrated her brain. Either way, Black's men didn't riddle them with bullets as they rode up to the colonel, and that was all The Kid cared about.

"Morgan!" Black exclaimed. "When you didn't show up at the appointed time, I thought you had decided to double cross me."

"I got delayed," The Kid said, nodding toward the squirming, cursing bundle of redheaded female in his arms. "When the shooting started, I figured you must be raiding the town, so I grabbed Mrs. Sheffield and came looking for you. She's one of the things you're after, isn't she?"

Black waved his men on, then brought his horse closer to The Kid's and reached out toward Glory, who flinched away from his touch. "My dear," he said. "It's so wonderful to see you again."

"Get away from me, you bastard!" she cried. "Let me go!" She tried again to reach behind her and hit The Kid. "Damn you, Morgan!"

Colonel Black smiled. "Can you hang on to her, Morgan, or do you want me to take her?"

"I've got her," The Kid said. "Don't worry, Colonel, she won't get away."

"Then we're on the same side, you and I?"

The Kid let a savage grin stretch across his face. "I always like to be on the winning side, and from the looks of it, this isn't even a contest."

Here and there along the street, fires continued to rage. The masked outlaws rode back and forth, their guns spitting death at anyone who dared to oppose them. Not many of the townspeople were doing that anymore. From the looks of it, the Cannon Gang had Titusville just about buffaloed.

"It was never a contest," Black said as a triumphant smile of his own appeared on his face. "Edward Sheffield and his minions were doomed from the moment he betrayed me. It was just a matter of time before I took my vengeance on him and reclaimed what's rightfully mine."

The look he gave Glory made it abundantly clear that he considered her part of the spoils of his victory.

"You're mad!" she told him. "You're out of your mind, Gideon!"

"Don't say that, my dear. You'll soon love me again."

"Never!"

Glory had stopped struggling in The Kid's grip, but tears of rage and fear and futility continued to run down her face. The Kid knew that pretending to join Black's forces was the only way to save their lives, although it was likely that Black wouldn't have allowed Glory to be killed. The Kid was still alive to help her and to continue trying to figure out a way to stop the colonel's reign of terror.

"Follow me, Morgan," Black ordered as he turned his horse. "And be careful not to let that little hellcat get away."

"You can count on it, Colonel," The Kid said. "She's not going anywhere except with us."

They rode through the chaos and confusion that choked Titusville's main street, heading north toward the ridge where the cannon was set up and the Dragoon Mountains beyond it. Black led the way, and as he pulled out a little ahead of Morgan and Glory, she leaned back and asked Morgan in a low voice, "What the hell do you think you're doing?"

"Keeping both of us alive," The Kid told her through clenched teeth. "Black approached me earlier tonight and tried to recruit me for his little owlhoot army. I went along with him. I was supposed to meet him up on the ridge before the attack started, but you caused me to miss that appointment."

"I'm sorry," Glory said coldly.

"Don't be. This might work out even better."

"Better! How could it be better?"

"By turning you over to him, I've convinced him more than ever that I'm on his side," The Kid said. "Otherwise, he would have just killed me and taken you with him anyway."

Glory shook her head. "You don't know how insane he is. You can't trust him, Kid, not for a second."

"I don't intend to. And I'll keep you safe as much as I possibly can."

"That fate worse than death business again?" She laughed, but there wasn't a trace of humor in the sound. "Don't worry, Kid, Gideon can't do anything to me that he hasn't already done."

The Kid didn't figure that was any of his business, but he didn't say anything. He looked around him at the death and destruction that had descended on Titusville, and he was reminded once more of the wanton slaughter that had taken place at the Williams ranch. Colonel Black obviously had no regard whatsoever for human life. He snuffed it out casually, without even thinking about it, any time somebody got in his way or did something to offend his warped sense of justice. He was a monster, and sooner or later, The Kid was going to kill him.

But that would have to wait for the right time, and as the horses began to climb the ridge above the burning town, The Kid didn't know when that was going to be.

It couldn't come soon enough to suit him.

Colonel Black obviously knew the trails in the foothills of the Dragoons, because he led them toward the top of the ridge with ease. Glory knew to continue her pose as a terrified prisoner of her vengeful ex-lover. It didn't take much acting on her part, The Kid thought, because in truth, both of them actually were in a great deal of danger. Trying to fool someone as unstable and violent as the former colonel was a risky business.

So far, though, Black seemed well pleased with the evening's work. Titusville was in shambles, and Glory was in his power.

"What are you going to do to Edward?" she called to Black as she and The Kid rode behind him.

Black turned in the saddle to smile back at her. "Don't worry, my dear. I gave strict orders that he wasn't to be killed . . . yet. I want him to suffer first, as I suffered."

"But you didn't suffer," Glory argued. "You didn't even go to prison, like you easily could have if not for my father."

The Kid didn't think it was a particularly good idea to be reminding Black about that, but as usual, Glory had a mind of her own and wasn't hesitant about expressing it.

The colonel reined in and glared at her. "You think I should be grateful for the treachery practiced by your father and that so-called husband of yours?

They cost me my military career. They stole all the respect that anyone ever felt for me."

"You did that yourself when you decided to become part of a crooked deal," Glory shot back at him, ignoring the warning squeeze that The Kid gave her arm.

"I was drawn into it by the scheming of those two!"

"You knew exactly what you were doing," Glory insisted.

The Kid decided this had gone on long enough. He lifted a hand as if he were about to hit her and growled, "Shut up!"

Instantly, Colonel Black whipped out his revolver. "Morgan!" he snapped. "I appreciate your help, but if you strike the lady, I'll kill you."

The Kid lowered his hand. "Take it easy, Colonel," he said. "I won't hurt her. I just want her to stop her yapping."

Maybe Glory would get the message from that, he thought.

"It's not your place to worry about such things," Black said coldly. "I'm in command here, Morgan, and don't forget it."

The Kid nodded. "Sorry, Colonel. It won't happen again."

They rode on, and thankfully, Glory quieted down. A few minutes later, the zigzagging trail they were following came out on top of the ridge. The Kid spotted the cannon perched near the edge. The area around it was lit by a couple of torches stuck in the ground. The bombardment had ended, and the men who had been working as gunners now stood around the cannon.

The Kid got his first close-up look at the big gun.

It was a massive thing, mounted on two wheels with a sort of cart behind it to give it extra support and absorb some of the recoil. A team of four mules stood off to one side, and The Kid knew that when the outlaws were ready to move the cannon, those mules would be hitched to it. Two mules were already hitched to another cart nearby. The Kid figured it was used to carry ammunition, powder, and everything else the gang needed to fire the big gun.

The cannon's barrel was about six feet long and a foot in diameter. The muzzle itself was six inches wide, The Kid estimated. A cannonball that size would pack a hell of a punch behind it. He had seen for himself the extent of the damage a round like that could do. It was a devastating weapon. The Kid wondered if Colonel Black had stolen it from some military armory somewhere.

Black reined in. The Kid did likewise. With a proud smile, Black waved a hand toward the cannon.

"How do you like my little toy, Morgan?" he asked.

"That's a pretty dangerous toy," The Kid replied.

"Indeed it is. Napoleon thought so, too, when he took it to Russia in 1812 and used it and all its brethren to lay siege to Moscow."

The Kid remembered studying about that at the academy and in college. He gave in to curiosity and asked, "How did you get your hands on it, Colonel?"

"The French army abandoned most of their heavy artillery when Napoleon gave up and began retreating that winter. The entire campaign was riddled with terrible strategic mistakes." The colonel had a note of smug superiority in his voice as he explained. "The Russians claimed the cannon, and later, they were brought to Fort Ross, the Russian settlement in what's now California. When the Russians withdrew from Fort Ross, they left behind several of the cannon, and this one"—Black leaned over in his saddle and patted the big gun's barrel affectionately—"this one passed through a number of hands before winding up in mine. A man who plans to fight a war should be well armed, Morgan."

"You really are mad, Gideon," Glory said quietly.

Black didn't lose his temper. He just shook his head and said, "You'll see how wrong you are about me, Gloriana. You'll see that you should have been loyal to me all along. I'll win you over again, just like I'll win this war against that treacherous husband of yours."

"What are you going to do then?" Glory demanded. "Go to Washington and lay siege to the War Department so you can satisfy your grudge against my father? I'd like to see you try that!"

"Perhaps you shall," Black said, still smiling confidently. "Who knows? Perhaps destroying your husband's empire will be just the beginning. Who's to say that I won't wind up running the entire Arizona Territory? And from there—" Black stopped and shook his head. "Ah, well, it's just a dream . . . for now. In the future, who knows? But those who are loyal to me— and you should listen to this, Morgan—those who are loyal to me will reap great rewards, I promise you that."

"Don't worry, Colonel," The Kid said. "I'll back your play, all the way."

"Very good. Hang on to our prisoner. That's your task for now." Black turned to the other outlaws on the bluff. "Prepare the cannon to be moved. We'll be returning to the stronghold as soon as the others finish in town and join us."

The stronghold. That sounded mighty interesting, The Kid thought. He would have to know where it was, if he was to have any hope of breaking the colonel's power and bringing him to justice. And it looked like if he played along and could manage to stay alive for a while, he stood a good chance of finding out.

While the outlaws began hitching the mule team to the cannon under Black's supervision, The Kid sat there on the buckskin with Glory in front of him. He felt a little tremble go through her and put his mouth close to her ear again.

"It'll be all right," he whispered. "We'll just have to bide our time."

"He really is crazy," she murmured.

"Yeah, but he holds all the cards right now."

Below them, Titusville continued to burn.

Chapter 26

Not long after that, the rest of the gang came boiling up the trail, whooping and shooting into the air in sheer exuberance at the success of the raid they had just carried out. Colonel Black rode out to meet them, followed by The Kid and Glory. "Captain Devlin!" Black hailed one of the men.

The man rode over to join them and pulled down the bandanna that covered the lower half of his face, revealing coarse, hard-bitten features. He was no more a captain than a monkey was, The Kid thought, but Black seemed to like to maintain the façade that the bandit crew was a military outfit.

"Report, Captain." Black issued the command in a brisk tone of voice.

"Mission successful, Colonel," Devlin rasped. "We hit the bank, the stores, the saloons, every place there was money. And we've got bags and bags full of loot to show for it."

"What about the mining company?"

"We stayed away from it, like you said for us to.

There were some lights in there, but nobody came out and offered to fight us."

Black snorted contemptuously. "Of course not. Like all thieves, Edward Sheffield is essentially a coward. He prefers to sneak around, stealing and fouling everything like a rat, rather than confront his enemies in the open."

Glory said, "If you hate him so badly, why don't you just go ahead and kill him?"

Black shook his head. "That wouldn't be sufficient punishment for his sins. As I told you, my dear, that husband of yours will have to suffer before I finally put him out of his misery. I wasn't happy when I saw that one of the rounds from the cannon went astray and struck the mining company building. I checked when we rode into town, and it didn't seem to have done much damage. I'm sure Sheffield was fine. Probably cowering under the desk in his office, wetting himself in fear."

Glory snarled at him. "You son of a bitch."

Black leaned over in the saddle and slapped her, his gauntleted hand coming up so fast that Glory had no chance to get out of the way of the blow. Her head rocked to the side under the impact. The Kid felt it through her body, and anger welled up inside him. He wanted to go after Black, but with an effort, he suppressed the urge.

"That sort of language is unacceptable from an officer's lady, Gloriana," Black said sternly. "You'll learn how to behave properly once we're married. I'll see to that."

"You'll see to this, you—"

More obscenities spewed from her mouth. Black

stiffened in the saddle, and taking a chance, The Kid clapped a hand over Glory's mouth, muffling the tide of invective.

"With the colonel's permission, sir," The Kid said.

Black nodded curtly. "Thank you . . . Sergeant Morgan."

So he was a sergeant now, was he? He supposed that was better than being a private, although he suspected that everybody in Gideon Black's outlaw army was at least a sergeant.

Black turned back to the owlhoot called Devlin. "All right, Captain, we'll be returning to the stronghold now. Pass the order to the men."

"Yes, sir," Devlin said. He didn't salute, but he might as well have.

The mule team was hitched up to the cannon, and men on horseback held the reins of the two leaders. Another man perched on the seat of the ammunition cart to handle that team. The rest of the gang formed up into rows and columns, somewhat to The Kid's surprise. From the looks of it, Black had actually succeeded in imposing a little military discipline on his gun-wolves. They probably went along with it only because they expected a big payoff, but it was still something of an accomplishment.

With The Kid and Glory beside him, Black rode to the front of the gang. He lifted his hand above his head and then swept it forward, calling out in a deep, powerful voice, "Column, *ho!*"

Loaded down with the cannon and the loot they had taken from Titusville, the outlaws set off into the night, bound for their hideout.

Or, rather, their stronghold, The Kid reminded himself.

He couldn't wait to see it.

The stronghold lived up to its name. The sun was rising by the time the gang got there. Garish, orange-red light flooded the valley up which the outlaws rode with their cannon and their prisoner. At the far end of the valley rose an almost sheer cliff, topped by a rounded mound of rock that bore an uncanny resemblance to a human skull. A red skull, in that light. At the base of the cliff was an overhang that shielded a large chamber that had been reinforced and walled off with rock and adobe. A thick adobe wall enclosed an area of several acres in front of the cliff. Gates made of heavy timbers stood open, and through the gap between them, The Kid saw a number of log cabins. The logs came from the scrubby pines that dotted the valley floor. Guard towers also made of logs stood at the front corners of the wall.

"A virtually impregnable fortress," Black boasted to The Kid as the large group of riders approached. "The valley leading up to it is almost two miles long, and from the stronghold, we can cover that entire field of fire. Two more of Napoleon's cannon are mounted up there, and with this one in place as well, we can lay down a barrage that ensures no enemy will ever come close to us."

The Kid had never been a military man, but he could see that Black was right. The men in the stronghold would have every advantage against anyone who wanted to roust them out of there.

By now exhaustion had claimed Glory. She had been dozing in The Kid's arms for several miles as they rocked along in the saddle. Weariness gripped The Kid as well, but he fought it off. He couldn't afford to get careless.

Black's voice roused Glory from her sleep. She lifted her head, which had been sagging forward on her shoulders, and looked around with bleary eyes. "Wh-where are we?" she asked.

"Your new home, my dear," Black told her. He swept a hand toward the compound at the base of the bloodred cliff.

Glory stiffened against The Kid. "It looks horrible," she said. "That big rock looks like a skull."

"The Apaches who used to live in this area called it *El Cráneo Rojo* . . . the Red Skull," Black explained, confirming the impression The Kid had of the bizarre-looking rock formation.

"I suppose it's an appropriate home . . . for a butcher like you," Glory said.

Black reined in to look intently at her. "You'll feel differently about me soon," he said.

"Not unless it's to be relieved that you're dead."

The Kid tightened his arm around her. Clearly, Glory had never learned when it was a good idea to keep her mouth shut. She took the hint that time, though, looking away from Black and not saying anything else.

With Black proudly in the lead, they rode on toward the stronghold. As they came closer, The Kid spotted the two cannon the colonel had mentioned, one at each corner next to the guard towers. There had to be a parapet running around the inside of the wall. It must have been a difficult chore hoisting those heavy guns up onto it. He saw men in the towers as well, and the early morning sun glinting off glass hinted that they were scanning the valley with field glasses.

"I'm looking into getting a pair of Gatling guns," Black commented as they approached the gates. "If I'm successful in that effort, we'll have enough firepower here to hold off any attack that could be mounted against us."

The colonel was living in a dream world if he thought he could stand up to the U.S. Army, The Kid mused. The army had even bigger guns and could stand off at a distance and shell the place into dust, along with everybody in it.

That was pretty unlikely to happen, though, as long as the daughter of the Assistant Secretary of War was Black's prisoner.

The men in the guard towers and on the wall raised their hands in greeting as the column of outlaws rode through the open gates. Black turned his head and called, "Captain Devlin!"

Devlin rode forward quickly. "Yes, Colonel?"

"Thank the men for their faithful service and dismiss them, will you?"

"Yes, sir!" Devlin turned his horse and rode back to join the others.

"Sergeant Morgan, if you'll bring the prisoner and come with me," Black went on.

"I'm with you, Colonel," The Kid said.

"Responding 'Yes, sir,' will be sufficient." Black's tone was cool, a lot cooler than the air that had already begun to heat up as the sun rose.

"Yes, sir." The Kid didn't like kowtowing to the renegade colonel, but at the moment, if he wanted to keep Glory alive and reasonably safe, he didn't have much choice but to go along with whatever Black wanted.

The colonel headed for the dwelling that had been built into the base of the cliff. The Kid glanced over his shoulder and saw that the rest of the gang was scattering behind them. Some of the outlaws rode toward a long, low building that was probably a bunkhouse, while the others headed for individual cabins. The Kid saw women emerge from those cabins . . . some white, some Mexican, some Indian. Obviously a number of the owlhoots had brought their women with them when they joined up with Colonel Black. Some of them might even be legally married. It wasn't that uncommon for an outlaw to have a family, according to what Frank Morgan had told The Kid in the past.

The Kid saw smoke rising from the chimney of a blacksmith shop, and another building had the look of a store or trading post about it. Nearby was what appeared to be a garden patch. There was even a corral with several cattle in it, and their heavy udders told him they were milk cows. It was as if Colonel Black had established his own little settlement there, almost self-sufficient and cut off from the outside world. From this refuge, he intended to carry out his vengeance quest against Edward Sheffield and perhaps even extend his campaign to take over more of the territory.

Sure, the colonel was loco, The Kid thought, but the sooner he was stopped, the less damage he could do with his crazy plans. He had already been responsible for a great deal of death and destruction, and he would continue to spill innocent blood until someone killed him or locked him up.

The Kid had a hunch it would have to be the former. A fanatic like Black would never surrender. He would fight to the death.

An ornately carved door, like the front door of a mansion, was set into the wall that closed off the chamber under the cliff. It swung open, and a stocky Mexican emerged. He saluted Black and said in only slightly accented English, "Colonel . . . good to see you again, sir. Was your mission a success?"

"Yes, it was, Sergeant Lopez," Black answered. "Is the room prepared for our guest?"

"Of course, sir, just like you ordered."

"We'll have another officer staying with us. This is Lieutenant Morgan, my new aide-de-camp."

The colonel must be really grateful to him for capturing Glory, The Kid thought. He had already gotten a promotion in the time it took to ride there, as well as a new assignment. That was all right. If it kept him closer to Black, it kept him closer to Glory Sheffield as well.

Black dismounted and motioned for The Kid and Glory to do likewise. He told Lopez to have their horses tended to, then stepped to the door and held out a hand to usher them inside.

"Welcome to your new home, my dear," he said.

Chapter 27

For a second, Morgan thought Glory was going to spit right in Colonel Black's face. But then, with her chin jutting out defiantly, she strode past the colonel into the cliff house. Black glanced at The Kid and added, "Come along, Lieutenant." The Kid fell in behind him as Black followed Glory inside.

It would have been easy at that moment to draw his Colt, put the muzzle against the back of Black's head, and blow the bastard's evil brains out, The Kid thought. But with thirty or forty bloodthirsty gun-wolves right outside, if he did that it would be the same thing as signing his own death warrant. Not only that, but without Black around, those owlhoots wouldn't show any mercy to Glory. She would die, too, but in a lot slower and more degrading fashion.

No, The Kid told himself, the right time still hadn't come.

Thick, woven rugs covered the stone floor of what looked similar to the main room of a ranch house. It had timber and adobe walls and was furnished with heavy, comfortable armchairs and a divan. It even had windows of real glass that looked out over the compound. The stone ceiling and floor were really the only visible signs that they were in what amounted to a cave.

A middle-aged Indian woman in a long skirt and colorful blouse came through a door in the room's rear wall. She left the door open so that The Kid could see through it into what appeared to be a dining room.

"Señora Lopez," Black greeted her, indicating that she was married to the Mexican major domo. "This is the guest I mentioned we'd be having here, Señora Sheffield. Your husband told me that her room is ready?"

"Sí, señor."

"And this is Lieutenant Morgan," Black went on. "Prepare a room for him as well."

The woman nodded.

"Why don't you take Señora Sheffield to her quarters now?" Black suggested.

Glory glanced toward The Kid in alarm, probably at the prospect of the two of them being separated, and he had a bad moment as he thought she was going to give away the game. She realized what she was about to do, and she turned the look into a glare of hatred.

"I'll never forgive you for this, you . . . you bastard," she practically spat at him.

The Kid kept his face cool and expressionless.

The Indian woman moved to usher Glory out of the room. Glory suddenly jerked away from her, as if to rush toward the front door and make a futile break for freedom. A quick step put Black in her path. She stopped short, and her shoulders slumped in a perfect impression of despair. That probably wasn't far from the truth, despite The Kid's earlier whispered assurances that they would get out of this, somehow.

When Glory and Señora Lopez were gone, Black turned to Morgan and said, "Normally I'd say it's much too early in the morning for a drink, Lieutenant, but since we've been riding all night and I suspect we'll soon be going to bed to get some sleep, it's really more like the end of the evening, isn't it?"

The Kid allowed himself a faint smile. "I can't argue with that logic," he said.

Black went over to a sideboard and picked up a crystal decanter that held an amber liquid. "I think brandy would be the perfect thing right now," he said as he poured the liquor into a couple of snifters. He set the decanter down, picked up the snifters, and carried them over to The Kid. "I don't normally drink with junior officers, but since you're my aide-de-camp and we'll be working together closely, I think an exception is called for."

The Kid took the snifter Black handed him. "Last night in the saloon, we drank to your heroic efforts on the train yesterday morning," the colonel went on.

"You did," The Kid pointed out. "I didn't. I never said I was a hero."

"That doesn't matter," Black said. "This morning we're going to drink to the future . . . a future I intend to share with the lady, and with you, Lieutenant."

The Kid shrugged. "Now, that, I can go along with."

He lifted the snifter and took a healthy slug of the brandy, which was smooth and intensely fiery at the same time. As The Kid lowered his glass, he went on,

"Begging your pardon, Colonel, but this strikes me as a little odd."

Black looked amused. "What does, Lieutenant?"

"Well . . . the fact that I'm suddenly a lieutenant and your, what did you call it, aide-de-camp. I'm not a soldier. Never have been. And less than twenty-four hours ago, I was fighting against you and your men."

"And doing quite a fine job of it, too," Black replied with a chuckle. "When I saw the way you leaped your horse out of that boxcar and then got the train out of the trap I'd laid for it, I knew then that you were a man of great daring, and great ability, as well. I even commented to Captain Devlin that if I had an army of men such as you, there would be no limit to what I might achieve. He agreed, by the way."

Of course he did, The Kid thought. Devlin had enough sense not to argue with a crazy man.

"I knew you had come to Bisbee looking for me, so I thought there was a chance I could make you see the light and realize which side is in the right here, if only I had the chance to talk to you. That's why I disguised myself and visited Titusville yesterday evening. I thought it would be worth the risk to make your acquaintance, Lieutenant."

The Kid took another sip of the brandy. "You still haven't explained about that lieutenant business. I thought I was a sergeant last night."

"A battlefield promotion, so to speak. Completely official."

The Kid supposed that was true enough, since the ranks only existed in Black's demented mind anyway.

"As for why I made you my aide-de-camp," the colonel went on, "I pride myself on being a good judge of character, and I believe that you'll make a fine officer, Morgan. Captain Devlin has proven himself to be an able second in command, but I need someone to serve as my personal assistant. Someone to be at my side during the campaign. Having seen what I have of you in action, I'd be honored to go into battle with you, young man."

So Black was a pompous windbag as well as a loco killer, The Kid thought.

"I appreciate that, Colonel," he said. "I'm honored that you feel that way. I'll try to live up to your faith in me."

"You already have. You delivered Mrs. Sheffield to me." A slight frown appeared on Black's forehead. "Just how is it that you were in a position to, shall we say, apprehend her? And how did you know to bring her to me?"

Morgan thought fast. Those were good questions, and he should have expected the colonel to ask them.

"I guess she was in her hotel room when the shelling started," he said. "I wound up out in the hall-way with her and all the other guests who were trying to get out of there before the place came crashing down around them. When I saw her, I remembered that you had mentioned her in the saloon and talked about how you were going to have everything that belonged to Edward Sheffield." He allowed himself a slight smile. "I had a hunch that included Mrs. Sheffield. Was I right, Colonel?"

Stiffly, Black replied, "At one time, the lady and I were engaged to be married. It's an ugly story, Lieutenant, full of greed and treachery, and I'm not sure I want to share all the details with you."

"No need for you to do that, Colonel, I assure you. I'm interested in your goals for the future, not what happened in the past."

Black nodded. "Very well. Go on."

The Kid shrugged. "There's not much left to tell. Once we got outside, I grabbed Mrs. Sheffield and took her to the stable where my horse was. I knew you had to be responsible for what was happening. I mean, who else in this neck of the woods has a cannon?"

That brought another chuckle and a nod from Black.

"I got the lady on my horse and set out to find you. It didn't take long. Actually, of course, you found us, which is what I thought might happen."

"Then luck was with us all around. Since you didn't show up on the ridge as I'd told you, I thought you weren't going to be joining us after all. If you'd been alone when I spotted you later, I might have ordered my men to kill you. Of course, I couldn't put Mrs. Sheffield in danger, so I ordered them to hold their fire."

"Like you said, Colonel . . . luck."

"Why didn't you keep the appointment? You had time to get your horse and gather your gear before the attack began."

"Sheffield cornered me and tried one more time to get me to work for him. I got away from him as fast as I could, but it wasn't fast enough. Or maybe it was just fast enough, because that way I was in the hotel and was able to get hold of Mrs. Sheffield for you."

"Indeed. Well, it's clear from everything that's happened that you were meant to be part of my campaign, Lieutenant. I'm not an overly superstitious man, but I know an omen when I see one."

The Kid nodded. "Yes, sir. I do, too."

Black drained the last of the brandy from his snifter and then turned to set the empty glass back on the sideboard. "It's been a long night. I believe I'm going to turn in. I'm sure Señora Lopez will be back in a few minutes to show you to your quarters. Get some rest, Lieutenant. Later today, we'll meet with Captain Devlin and a few of the other officers and plan the next move in our campaign."

"What's left?" The Kid asked. "You looted Titusville of pretty much everything that's worth anything and burned down half the town. There might be some ore at the mine—"

Black cut him off with a curt gesture. "You forget, Lieutenant, Mrs. Sheffield is our prisoner, and her husband, despite being a despicable man, is smart enough to realize that once he discovers that she's no longer in Titusville. He's going to gather his hired guns and come after her . . . and we're going to be ready for him."

The Kid didn't like the sound of that. He didn't doubt for a second that the colonel was right. Sheffield would send Phil Bateman and the rest of his gunmen to find his wife. Sheffield might even come along himself. And if Colonel Black had his way, they would ride right into an ambush of some sort. Black might be crazy, but he was a shrewd strategist. That ambush could easily turn into a massacre.

Unless The Kid figured out some way to stop it.

Chapter 28

Almost as soon as Black left the room, before The Kid had a chance to look around, Señora Lopez reappeared. "Follow me, señor," she said in her stolid voice. "Your room is ready."

She led him through the dining room, which was furnished with a long, polished hardwood table that wouldn't have been out of place in a fine mansion back east. They went down a short corridor lit by candles in wall sconces to another hallway running perpendicular to the first one. Just how big *was* this hollowed out, house-under-the-rock, anyway, The Kid wondered?

"Is Señora Sheffield's room back here?" he asked, but the Indian woman ignored him as if she didn't understand the question or hadn't even heard it. He didn't try asking her again. He knew she wouldn't answer.

She opened a door into a small, sparsely furnished, windowless room that reminded The Kid of a monk's cell, although he had to admit that the bed looked pretty comfortable. A single candle in a metal holder burned on a small table beside the bed. There was also a rug on the floor.

"Do you need anything, señor?" the woman asked.

A wave of drowsiness hit The Kid as soon as he saw the bed. The long, action-packed hours of the day before, followed by the night spent in the saddle, were all catching up to him. Wearily, he shook his head and said, "No, señora, I'm fine."

She nodded and left the room, closing the door behind her. As soon as she was gone, The Kid took off his hat, coat, and gunbelt and placed them on the room's single cane-bottomed chair, which he moved over within easy reach of the bed. Then he sat down on the edge of the bed to remove his boots. No sooner had they thumped to the floor than he sprawled onto the mattress. It was all he could do to turn and raise up enough to blow out the candle.

When he did, utter darkness filled the room. Under the cliff like that, no light penetrated at all. The Kid wasn't able to see his hand in front of his face.

Not that he was looking. He had already closed his eyes, and sleep claimed him almost before he could draw a breath.

Morgan slept like a rock, and he had no idea how much time had passed when he gradually came to realize that there was light in the room again. He saw it even through his closed eyelids. With an effort, he pried his eyes open, squinting against the glare of a lantern held in Señora Lopez's hand as she stood beside the bed.

"Colonel Black wishes for you to join him in the dining room, señor," she said.

The Kid sat up and groaned as stiff muscles protested. He hadn't had enough rest to make up for the punishment he had put his body through the past few days. He lifted a hand, rubbed his temples for a moment, then scrubbed his palm across his face. He shook his head in an attempt to dislodge some of the cobwebs. Then he looked up at Señora Lopez said, "I'll be there in a moment."

"In the dining room," the Indian woman reminded him. She took a match from a pocket in her long skirt and used it to light the candle on the bedside table. "And *El Coronel* does not like to be kept waiting."

The Kid nodded and muttered, "Fine, fine." He swung his legs off the bed and reached for his boots.

When Señora Lopez was gone, he noticed that someone had brought a basin and a pitcher of water into his room while he slept, and placed them next to the candle. A frown creased his forehead. He didn't like the idea that he had slept so deeply people could waltz in and out of the room without him even knowing about it. The light from the señora's lantern had woken him that time. Why hadn't it the time before?

He put on his boots, then stood up and poured some water into the basin. Cupping his hands in it, he splashed the water on his face and rubbed it in vigorously. That refreshed him a little. A folded cloth lay on the table with the basin. He picked it up and dried his face.

The faint whisper of a footstep behind him made him whirl around. His hand dipped to the coiled gunbelt on the chair and snatched the Colt from its holster.

Crouching slightly, The Kid faced the doorway with the leveled gun in his hand.

His finger froze on the trigger. A woman stood just inside the door of the room, but it wasn't Señora Lopez. This one was considerably younger, no more than twenty. The faint coppery tone of her skin, the high cheekbones, and the raven-black hair that swept down over her shoulders like dark wings testified that she had Indian blood, too, but her eyes were a startlingly pale blue.

"Oh," she said. "I am sorry, señor. I did not mean to startle you."

The Kid straightened and lowered his gun. "You did more than startle me, señorita. You almost got your head blown off."

"You almost . . . shot me?"

"That's right," The Kid said impatiently. "Don't you see this gun?"

Then he caught his breath as he realized that, no, she didn't see it. Those striking blue eyes hadn't moved or reacted to anything since she came into the room. They just peered straight ahead tranquilly, sightlessly. She had *heard* him spin around and draw his gun.

"You're blind," he said.

"Sí, señor." She smiled. "My name is Elena. I brought you water. Do you require anything else?"

She was used to getting around in pitch blackness. That was how she had been able to come into his room with the pitcher, basin, and cloth without waking him, he realized. She hadn't needed any light.

He recalled that she had asked him a question. He said, "No, gracias, señorita, I'm fine."

She nodded. She was very beautiful, The Kid thought, with striking features and a slender but well-curved body. The short-sleeved white blouse she wore was scooped low enough at the neck to reveal the upper swells of her breasts.

Without saying anything else, she left the room. As The Kid holstered his gun and then buckled on the gunbelt, he thought about her gliding soundlessly around the outlaw stronghold, moving through the darkness like some sort of phantom. The thought was enough to make a little shiver go up his spine.

The Kid put on his hat—the black one with silver conchos on the band that Glory Sheffield had picked out for him in Titusville—and shrugged into his coat. Even though it got as hot as hell's hinges in that part of Arizona, there in those chambers under tons of rock, the air was comfortably cool.

As he emerged from his room, The Kid wondered where Glory was being held. Several doors opened off the corridor into what he assumed were other bedrooms. Since there was no one in the hallway at the moment, he moved along it as quietly as he could, pausing in front of each door and leaning close to see if he could hear anything from the other side. He watched closely as he did so, not wanting the ghostly Elena to slip up on him again.

He didn't hear anyone moving around in the other rooms, and Colonel Black was waiting for him, so he turned and went to the corridor that led back to the dining room.

Black, Devlin, and a couple other members of the gang were seated at the table when The Kid came in.

Black frowned at him and said, "Lieutenant Morgan, you're late."

"My apologies, sir," The Kid said formally. He didn't try to make any excuses, sensing that Black wasn't the sort who would be interested in them.

"Don't let it happen again," the colonel snapped.

"Of course not, sir."

Black waved him into one of the empty chairs. "At ease, Lieutenant. Join us. Señora Lopez has prepared a meal for us. We'll eat, then discuss our plans."

The Kid realized that he was ravenously hungry. He couldn't remember the last time he had eaten anything. As he sat down, he said, "Thank you, sir."

Señora Lopez came through a side door that probably led to the kitchen, followed by Elena. Both women carried platters of food: tortillas, mounds of scrambled eggs, a mixture of strips of beef and peppers and onions. The men helped themselves as soon as the platters were on the table, heaping eggs, beef, peppers, and onions onto the tortillas. The food smelled good, and the even more tantalizing aroma of coffee brewing came from the kitchen. Señora Lopez and Elena left and came back with the coffee pot and cups. The señora poured.

The Kid dug in and indulged his hearty appetite. The food was good, and the coffee with which he washed it down was even better. The food and drink began to make him feel human again, restoring some of the strength that the past few days had drained.

The other two outlaws were Boyd Cranston and Micah Terhune, according to the introductions Colonel Black made. Both men were captains, like

Devlin. Black told them, "Lieutenant Morgan is going to serve as my aide-de-camp, gentlemen."

Terhune's eyes narrowed with suspicion as he looked across the table at The Kid. "You're the fella who was on the train, aren't you? The one who was hell on wheels in that fight?"

The Kid shrugged. "No offense, Captain, but when people shoot at me, I tend to shoot back."

"That's a good answer, Micah," Cranston said with a laugh. "I wouldn't want a man in our outfit who wasn't ready for a fight."

"Yeah, I guess," Terhune said, but he didn't sound wholly convinced.

Devlin said, "The colonel says Morgan's working with us now, and what the colonel says, goes."

Terhune nodded. "Sure. I never figured otherwise."

Devlin turned to Black and asked, "What's our next objective, Colonel?"

Black sipped his coffee and looked smug. "We get to sit back and wait for the enemy to come to us for a change, gentlemen," he said. "Sheffield will want revenge for what we've done, and we have something else he wants, too."

Cranston grinned. He was a tall, handsome man with a shock of blond hair. "You're talking about the lady."

Black saluted Cranston with his coffee cup. "That's exactly right, Captain. By now he's realized that Mrs. Sheffield is no longer in Titusville, and his first thought will be that we took her with us. He may even be able to locate witnesses who saw us riding out of town with her on Lieutenant Morgan's horse.

I imagine at this moment, he's frantically putting together a rescue party."

"How's he gonna know where to look for her?" Terhune asked.

"I'm coming to that, Captain." Black looked up at the majordomo, Lopez, who had entered the dining room and stood unobtrusively to one side with his hands clasped behind his back. The colonel nodded to Lopez, who turned and left the room.

Lopez came back a moment later with a man accompanying him. The newcomer was tall and skinny, with thinning hair and a prominent Adam's apple. He wore a brown tweed suit, and he looked familiar to The Kid. It took a minute for him to recognize the man as the clerk in the mining company headquarters who had tried to stop him from entering Sheffield's private office.

The man had a brown felt hat in his hands, and although he was clutching the hat nervously, he didn't really act like a prisoner, The Kid thought. That impression was confirmed when Black said, "Welcome, Mr. Dunbar. Would you like some coffee?"

Dunbar shook his head and said quickly, "No, I'm, ah, fine, Colonel, just fine. I'd like to be done with this meeting so that I can get back to Titusville."

"What there is left of it, huh?" Black asked with a slight smile.

"The mining company offices are largely intact, and the mine itself is still in operation. There's plenty of work to do."

"The Gloriana Mine . . . isn't that what Sheffield calls it now?"

Dunbar nodded. "Yes, sir. He changed the name last year when he married the, ah, current Mrs. Sheffield."

"Of course." Black waved at one of the vacant chairs. "Sit down, Mr. Dunbar."

The clerk looked like he didn't particularly want to, but he didn't argue. He pulled the chair back and sat down, perching on the edge of the seat with his hat on his lap.

The Kid wasn't really surprised to see Dunbar. He had already figured out that Black had spies working for him in both Bisbee and Titusville. Dunbar was obviously one of those spies. He had probably been feeding information to Black about ore shipments, as well as Sheffield's plans to visit the settlement in the Dragoons. Maybe Dunbar hated Edward Sheffield for some reason, or maybe it was just a matter of money. A lot of men would turn traitor if the price was right.

"If you don't mind my asking, why did you summon me here, Colonel?" Dunbar said. "It's a long ride from town. As it is, I won't be able to get back there before dark."

Black got to his feet and began walking around the table. "I sent for you because I need you to deliver a message for me, Mr. Dunbar."

"What sort of message? To who?"

"I think you know who the message is intended for. Your employer, of course. Your *other* employer, I should say. Edward Sheffield."

Dunbar swallowed hard and nodded. He looked over his shoulder at Black, who had walked behind his chair. "All right," he said. "What is it you want me to tell him?"

"Actually, you won't be *telling* him anything. You're going to take a letter and a map to him."

"I suppose I can do that."

"I'm absolutely certain that you can, Mr. Dunbar," Black said.

With that, he pulled his saber from its scabbard with a smooth motion, grasped the weapon with both hands, and brought the razor-sharp blade around in a hard swing that buried it deep in the side of Dunbar's neck.

Chapter 29

Blood spurted across the table and the remains of the meal as Dunbar screamed and lurched violently forward in his chair. Micah Terhune yelled, "Damn!" as he, Devlin, and Cranston sprang out of their chairs.

The Kid didn't move, his iron will holding him still. It was already too late for him to do anything for Dunbar.

Colonel Black jerked the saber free. Dunbar thrashed around in his chair, pawing at the hideous wound in his neck as blood continued to gush from it. Black set himself and swung the saber again. This time the keen edge of the blade caught Dunbar on the back of the neck and sank deep, grating against bone as the impact of the blow knocked Dunbar forward onto the table.

Black pulled the saber loose and raised it over his head still holding it with both hands. Dunbar's frantic struggles were getting more feeble as his panic-stricken heart pumped more and more blood out of his body through the gashes in his neck.

"Hold still now," Colonel Black said mildly, as if he were admonishing a child.

With a grunt of effort, he brought the saber down in a sweeping blow. The Kid heard the grotesque rasping sound as the blade sheared through Dunbar's spine. Black chopped with the saber twice more, cutting through muscle and skin, and finally Dunbar's head rolled free of his body, which flopped backward into the chair and sat there, arms dangling at its sides, as more blood bubbled slowly from the severed neck.

"Son of a *bitch,*" Terhune whispered into the silence that followed.

Blood had splattered all over the table in front of Dunbar's corpse, as well as the chair where his body sat and the floor around it. If the men across the table from him hadn't jumped back, it would have covered them, too. As it was, this fancy dining room had taken on the look and smell of a charnel house.

Black turned and held his crimson-smeared saber out to Lopez, who stepped forward and took it calmly. "Clean that," Black said.

"Sí, Colonel."

"You have the papers I gave you earlier?"

"Of course." Lopez produced them and handed them to Black.

That would be the letter and the map the colonel had mentioned a few minutes earlier, before the slaughter began, The Kid thought. Black rolled them up and inserted them into a small metal tube he took from his pocket. He screwed the cap onto the tube, then stepped over to the table and reached out to take hold of Dunbar's severed head. He turned it so that he could shove the metal tube into Dunbar's mouth, hammering it home with his fist. The Kid heard teeth shattering, but Dunbar was way past feeling it.

"There," Black said with satisfaction in his voice. "It's much more efficient this way, I think. Lopez will place the head in a small crate, and you'll deliver it to Titusville, Captain Devlin."

"Me?" The word was a startled yelp as it came from Devlin's mouth.

Black's face suddenly hardened. "Are you questioning my orders, Captain?"

At that moment, Devlin, along with everybody else in the room, was probably thinking the same thing The Kid was: how much like Satan himself Colonel Gideon Black had looked as he stood there chopping Dunbar's head off with a saber. With the blood flying and the insane gleam in his eyes, all Black had needed to complete the image were the flames of Hell leaping up around him and giggling, inhuman imps capering at his feet.

"No, sir," Devlin said. "I'm not questioning your orders at all. I'll sure take that box to Titusville for you. You want me to give it to Edward Sheffield?"

"No, you don't have to put it in Sheffield's hands yourself. You've been a fine second in command, Captain. I don't want to risk losing you. Just take the crate into town, find someone who looks dependable, and pay them to deliver it to the mining company office. I'm sure that's where Sheffield will be, if he's not out searching futilely for our trail, which he'll never find without our assistance."

"Which . . . we're going to give him?" Devlin sounded like he didn't fully understand.

"Of course. We want Sheffield to come here. That's why I'm sending him a map."

Cranston said, "But if he knows where we are, won't he just go to the law, or even the army, and get them to help him?"

Black shook his head. "No, because my letter will make it clear to him that he will be under observation, and that if he involves any outsiders, he'll never see his wife alive again." The colonel smiled. "Once he sees that his faithful clerk, Dunbar, was actually working for me, he won't know who to trust. He'll see enemies everywhere, and that's exactly how I want him to feel. I want him to know that his wife is in the hands of a madman, and that the only possible way to save her is to do everything that I tell him, exactly as I tell him. He's under *my* command now."

The Kid felt a chill go through him as he listened to Black. He realized suddenly that the appalling display of violence he had just witnessed wasn't completely the act of a lunatic. Beheading Dunbar had been a calculated act on Black's part, intended to make Sheffield think that he was crazy.

Of course, a man really would have to be loco to come up with something like that. Whether Black believed it was a pose or not, his insanity was the real thing.

The Kid thought he could risk a question. "What is it you're demanding of Sheffield, Colonel?"

Black turned toward him. "That he bring me all the gold and silver ore currently on hand at the mine and at his offices. Also that he sign over to me all of his mining, rail, and other financial interests. When he delivers the ore and those documents to me, I'll turn Gloriana over to him."

"Do you really think he'll give up his entire fortune to save his wife?"

Black slashed a hand through the air. "Of course not. But he'll pretend to go along with me, thinking that he can double cross me the same way he did before. He'll bring the papers with him. He may even give them to me. But then he'll try to kill me . . . and I'll kill him instead. Then Gloriana will be mine, along with everything else he owns, just as I predicted."

"That won't stand up in court."

"I believe it will, because there won't be any witnesses to claim that the transfers of ownership were coerced. Sheffield will be dead, and so will any of those hired guns he brings with him."

"What about people back in Titusville? Everybody in town will hear about that severed head with the note in its mouth. That note will be evidence, and so will the head itself."

"I appreciate you playing devil's advocate, as it were, Lieutenant," Black said, "but I assure you, it's not necessary. I've considered every aspect of this strategy, and I'm confident of its success."

The Kid realized then that he was looking at this all wrong. He was considering Black's plan from the standpoint of logic and reason . . . and those things no longer had any place in the colonel's brain. Black believed it would work because he *wanted* it to work. That was all he needed.

The Kid glanced at the other men in the room. Devlin, Cranston, and Terhune had to have figured out for themselves by now that their leader was out of his mind. Why the hell were they going along with Black's crazy scheme?

The answer burst on The Kid's brain. The other members of the gang didn't *care* if Black's quest for vengeance on Edward Sheffield worked or not. They didn't give a damn about Sheffield or Glory. They had stolen several ore shipments from the train, and they had looted an entire town. They already had a fortune salted away somewhere in this stronghold. The only reason they were still playing along was because they wanted the rest of the ore. Once they had it, they would probably double cross and abandon the colonel.

The Kid couldn't bring himself to feel too bad about that. Whatever happened to Black, it wouldn't be as bad as what he should have coming to him.

But The Kid still had Glory's safety to think about, as well as his own. He had no doubt that Sheffield would show up with a small army of hired guns led by Phil Bateman. Colonel Black was planning an ambush, but even so, there would still be fighting. Glory could get in the way of a stray bullet. There was also the risk that once Black was dead, his so-called "soldiers" would take off for the tall and uncut, taking Glory with them as a hostage. The Kid wanted to prevent that.

The best way for him to accomplish that goal, he realized, was to see to it that he and Glory got out of there before all hell broke loose.

That was going to take some time and planning. It wouldn't be easy, with that heavily guarded wall and gate, plus the whole gang being holed up in the compound. He and Glory couldn't just waltz out, The Kid thought, nor could he shoot their way out against odds like that.

They would need a distraction, or another way to escape.

Luckily, he had some time to work on the problem, because Black turned to Devlin and went on, "It'll take you until sometime tonight to reach Titusville with your . . . delivery . . . Captain. Sheffield won't be able to gather his forces and get back here until late tomorrow afternoon, at the earliest. That will give the men time to rest before the next engagement. Set up a guard schedule that takes that into account."

Devlin nodded. "Yes, sir."

"While you're gone, Captain Terhune, Captain Cranston, Lieutenant Morgan, and I will work out the details of the reception we'll give Sheffield and his men when they get here."

That was good news, The Kid thought. If he knew the details of Black's plan, it would be easier to circumvent it.

"On your way now, Captain," Black continued. He sighed. "I wish I could be there to see Sheffield's face when he opens the package I'm sending him. I'm sure it will be a most pleasing reaction." He looked around the others. "For now, you're all dismissed."

Cranston and Terhune started toward the door. The Kid followed them, but he paused when Black added, "Oh, Lieutenant?"

The Kid looked back over his shoulder. "Sir?"

"I suspect you'd like to take a look around the compound. Don't be gone long, though. We'll have work to do this afternoon."

"Yes, sir, Colonel," The Kid said.

He left the house-under-the-cliff with Cranston and Terhune, but once they were outside in the compound, the two outlaws suddenly stopped and turned to face him. They didn't look too friendly. The Kid glanced around. Some of the other members of the gang were converging on them, and he wondered if this had been planned or if the other men sensed that something was about to happen and were simply curious.

"Something wrong?" The Kid asked coolly.

"Yeah," Terhune replied in a harsh voice. "You're what's wrong, Morgan. You come outta nowhere, you kill some of our partners, and now the boss makes you his aide, for God's sake! It ain't right!"

Cranston added, "You have to admit it's a mite unusual, Morgan."

The Kid shrugged. "I figure the colonel knows what he's doing. Anyway, he's in charge, isn't he? Like Devlin said, if Colonel Black wants us to work together, we need to work together."

"Oh, we'll do what the colonel says, I reckon," Terhune said, "but that doesn't mean we can't find out a little more about you."

"What do you want to know?"

"Just what sort of hombre you are. We know everybody else in the bunch is plenty tough."

"I don't need to remind you of what happened when you attacked the train," The Kid pointed out.

Cranston shook his head. "That could have been luck. We have to be sure of you, Morgan."

"How do you intend to go about that?"

Terhune grinned. "Like this," he said.

He lowered his head and tackled The Kid, ramming into him so hard that Morgan was driven off his feet and came crashing down on his back.

Chapter 30

The attack took Morgan by surprise, and the weight of the beefy Terhune landing on top of him drove all the air out of his lungs. His head bounced hard off the ground and made stars spiral around in front of his eyes. For a couple of seconds, all he could do was lie there, stunned and gasping for breath.

Then he felt Terhune move and realized that the man was about to lift a knee into his groin. His instincts took over as his hips writhed off the ground and twisted to the side. Terhune's knee jabbed into his thigh. That was painful enough, but a hell of a lot better than the alternative.

Self-preservation made The Kid lash out with his left fist. It glanced off Terhune's head just above the right ear. Terhune reached for The Kid's throat and closed his fingers around it, clamping down hard and cutting off what little air Morgan had managed to suck back into his body.

Knowing that he would pass out if Terhune choked him for more than a few seconds, The Kid continued trying to hammer blows to the outlaw's head. Terhune hunched his shoulders, drawing his head down so that The Kid's fists just skidded off his skull and didn't do any damage.

Desperation made The Kid cup his hands and slap them hard against Terhune's ears. He had learned that move back in college, and Terhune howled in pain and loosened his grip enough for The Kid to get his arms between Terhune's arms and tear the outlaw's fingers away from his neck.

The Kid hauled in a breath, then locked both hands behind Terhune's neck and jerked the man's head down. At the same time, he raised his head off the ground, tucking in his chin so that the top of his skull smashed into the middle of Terhune's face. Terhune cried out again as blood spurted hotly from his pulped nose. The Kid shoved him hard to the left and rolled to the right, putting some distance between the two of them.

Still gasping and wheezing, The Kid pushed himself onto his hands and knees and came unsteadily to his feet. He was just in time to see Cranston lunging at him, swinging a mallet-like fist. The Kid tried to get out of the way but was too late. Cranston's punch caught him in the jaw and sent him staggering back.

Knowing that if he went down again, he might never get up, The Kid fought to keep his balance. Cranston rushed him, a confident grin on his handsome face as he threw another looping punch. The Kid ducked under it, stepped in closer, and hooked a right into Cranston's belly. The outlaw's breath huffed out of his mouth. The Kid hit him with a hard left to the heart. Cranston's face turned gray.

Conrad Browning had been on the boxing team in college, so he knew quite a bit about the art and science of pugilism. But Frank Morgan had taught him how to fight for his life, and those were the lessons that stood The Kid in such good stead. He hooked a foot behind one of Cranston's calves and jerked hard, sweeping the outlaw's feet out from under him. Cranston went down, landing hard on his back. When he tried to get up, The Kid hit him again, and that time, Cranston stayed on the ground.

He heard a rush of footsteps behind him and whirled to see Terhune charging him. The lower half of the man's face was covered with blood from his broken nose. The Kid darted out of the way, grabbed Terhune's shirt as he went by, and used the outlaw's own momentum against him as he heaved hard on Terhune's shirt. With a startled yell, Terhune lost control of himself and plunged forward, tripping and plowing up dirt with his face as he hit the ground. The Kid closed in, ready to kick Terhune in the head if necessary to keep the man down, but when Terhune tried to get up, he groaned and collapsed, then didn't move again. He was out cold.

Chest heaving and pulse pounding in his head, The Kid stood there and looked around at the other men, wondering if any of them were going to attack him next.

Instead, he heard the sound of two hands clapping lazily behind him. He turned and saw Colonel Black coming toward him, a smile on his face.

"Excellent, Lieutenant," Black said. "One of the best fights I've seen in a long time. And quite impressive. You had a certain amount of luck on your side, I'd say, but no one defeats men as capable as Captains Terhune and Cranston solely by way of luck. You handled yourself very well."

"You . . . you set this up," The Kid managed to get out.

"I wanted to be sure that I had chosen correctly when I picked you to be my aide, yes," Black agreed. "And the captains were more than happy to help me. They wanted to take your measure, Lieutenant. I daresay every man here felt the same way."

The Kid glanced around, saw some of the other outlaws nodding.

"And what's the decision?" he snapped.

"You're good enough to be one of us," Black said. "I didn't really doubt it, but it's nice to have my judgment confirmed."

"Fine." The Kid looked around, spotted his hat lying on the ground where it had fallen off when Terhune tackled him. He picked it up, slapped it against his leg to get some of the dust off, and put it on. He ached all over from the pounding he had taken, but he wasn't going to let Black or any of the other outlaws see that.

"Why don't you come back inside?" Black suggested. "The dining room has been cleaned and returned to normal. It looks like you have some cuts and scrapes that ought to be taken care of."

The Kid started to shrug and insist that he was fine, but then he realized that there was no point in such false bravado. "All right," he said.

Black led him back into the house and turned him over to Señora Lopez, instructing her to tend to The Kid's injuries. She nodded stolidly and sat him down at the now empty dining room table. She went to the kitchen and Black left through the front of the house, which meant that The Kid was alone in there for the moment.

He didn't know how long Señora Lopez was going to be gone, but he thought he ought to take advantage of the opportunity to have a look around. He stood up and moved along the wall, running his hand over the adobe. Something about it struck him as wrong.

A soft footstep just outside the room made him move back quickly to the chair where he had been sitting. Instead of Señora Lopez, Elena came into the room carrying a tray with a basin of water and a cloth on it.

"Señor Morgan?" she said.

"Right here."

She smiled and started toward him. "I thought I heard you sit down." She came to a stop in front of him and set the tray on the table just as easily as she would have if she could see. "Señora Lopez said you were injured."

"Just some bruises and scrapes," The Kid said. "It's nothing to worry about."

"I will clean them." She reached out and unerringly touched his face. "Let me feel you."

Her fingers were cool and smooth and soft, and as they moved over his face, The Kid felt some of the tension draining from him. Even when she touched the sore spots, the hurt was a good one.

Elena kept one hand on his face and used the other to get the cloth wet. She wiped it gently over his skin, which soothed him even more.

"You are a good man, Señor Morgan," she

whispered. "I can tell it from your face. What are you doing here with these monsters?"

The Kid was surprised that she would say such a thing. She didn't know him. For all she knew, he would tell Colonel Black what she had said, and she might be punished. She couldn't tell what kind of man he was just from touching his face . . . could she?

She leaned closer to him. "Help me," she breathed. "Help me get away from here. Please, Señor Morgan. The men here . . . they are evil."

She wasn't telling him anything he didn't already know. But was she being truthful with him?

Or was this just another test, like the attack on him by Cranston and Terhune? Was Colonel Black using Elena to find out if he could be trusted not to betray the gang?

But as The Kid looked up into Elena's sightless eyes, he knew he didn't have to worry about that. There was nothing on her face except fear, and perhaps a little hope. The Kid had heard it said that the eyes were the windows to the soul, but even though Elena's eyes were blank, he could tell there was no treachery in her soul.

"What do you want me to do?" he asked.

"Take me away from here. I will go with you, do anything you want, if only you will take me away." Her fingers grazed softly over his cheek.

"I don't know how I can do that."

"There is a way," she said.

The Kid felt his pulse quicken. Elena sounded mighty sure about that. The Kid hadn't seen any way out, not without fighting against odds so heavy that they meant certain death.

"What way?" he asked.

"I can trust you?" She caught her breath. "*Aii,* what a foolish question. I know I can trust you. Did I not feel it in your face?"

The Kid didn't know about that. He wanted to re-assure her, so he said quietly, "Yes, Elena, you can trust me. I give you my word I won't betray anything you reveal to me."

"In that case . . ." She set the damp cloth aside and held out her hand. The Kid took it. "I will show you."

He stood up, and she led him over to the wall he had been exploring earlier. His instincts had told him there was something unusual about it. Now he saw what it was as she felt along the wall until she came to one of the support beams. She rested the palm of her hand against it and pushed. The beam, to The Kid's surprise, moved slightly. He heard a faint click.

A section of the wall swung out an inch or so, re-leased by the latch he had heard. Elena slid her fingers into the gap and opened the door even more.

"There are stairs," she said. "They lead to the top of *El Cráneo Rojo.*"

The Kid leaned closer to the opening. The light from the lamps in the dining room penetrated far enough so that he could see a narrow staircase, carved out of the stone of the cliff itself, spiraling up into the darkness. Excitement made his heart slug harder in his chest.

"These stairs go all the way to the top, you say?"

"Sí. Many years ago, before the colonel and his men came, before even the Apaches came to this land, others lived here under the cliff, and they carved these steps so they would have a way to escape from their enemies if they needed to. In the end it did not help. Those old ones are gone now. But the stairs remain."

She was right, The Kid thought. The stairs had an air of antiquity about them, as if they had lurked there unseen behind the wall for centuries. He didn't know anything about those old ones she mentioned, but he felt a surge of gratitude toward them. The hidden stairs were just what he needed.

"Do you know where Señora Sheffield is being held?" he asked.

"Señora Sheffield?"

"The redhaired woman," The Kid said, then realized that description would mean nothing to Elena. "I'm sorry, I didn't think—"

"Do not worry, Señor Morgan. I have never had my sight, so I do not miss it. Are you talking about the colonel's lady?"

"He'd like for her to be," The Kid said, "but she's actually married to someone else."

Elena's lips pursed in disapproval. "I told you the colonel was an evil man. He speaks well, but he does many terrible things."

Remembering what had happened to Dunbar earlier, The Kid knew she sure as hell was right about that.

"I know in which room the woman is being kept," Elena continued. "Why do you need to know?"

"We have to take her with us," The Kid said.

A slight frown creased Elena's otherwise smooth, golden forehead. "Why? Is-is she something special to you, Señor Morgan?"

Was that a hint of jealousy he heard in her voice? The Kid didn't know, but as much as he was depending on Elena's help, he didn't want to risk ruffling her feathers.

"Señora Sheffield is my friend, that's all," he assured her. Even that was stretching the truth a mite—honestly, he didn't like Glory much at all—but he didn't think she deserved whatever Gideon Black had planned for her. He wanted Elena to think that Glory was important enough to him that she would help him get her out of there, too.

"Señora Lopez guards the other señora's room most of the time," Elena said. "You will have to do something with her. Kill her, perhaps."

The Kid grunted in surprise at the casual way Elena made that suggestion.

She heard his reaction, because she added, "Señora Lopez can be very cruel to me at times. She beats me, and—" She broke off with a hiss of breath between her teeth, then said, "The señora comes!"

Chapter 31

The Kid didn't hear anything, but he trusted Elena's hearing, which was keener than his. They both stepped away from the hidden door. Elena pushed it shut. It clicked into place just before Señora Lopez stepped into the dining room.

The older woman spoke sharply in Spanish. The Kid understood enough of it to comprehend that Señora Lopez wanted to know why Elena wasn't tending to his wounds. Elena replied that she had already cleaned them.

"That's right, señora," The Kid said in English. "I'm fine. Elena did a good job of taking care of me."

Señora Lopez sniffed and continued to glare at the young woman. Even though Elena couldn't see that, The Kid had a hunch she sensed it. She had a pretty good feel for most of Señora Lopez's moods and knew when to avoid her if possible.

Señora Lopez snapped at Elena to go to the kitchen. Elena left the dining room, moving with an ease and assurance that made it difficult to remember that she was blind.

The Kid said to the Indian woman, "I'm going to my room to rest some more. Please let me know if Colonel Black requires my presence."

"If the colonel wants you, you will know," she replied. "He will see to that."

The Kid didn't doubt it. He went to his room, lit the candle, and closed the door behind him.

He wished he'd had a chance to talk some more with Elena, so they could work out their plans. He also wished she had told him in which room Glory Sheffield was being held. Until he had that information, The Kid had to rely on Elena. He still didn't think that she had been trying to trick him, but he supposed time would tell about that.

He was tired. He hadn't gotten enough rest before, and the fight with Cranston and Terhune had taken even more out of him. He stretched out on the bed, knowing that he was liable to doze off.

He fell asleep even faster than he expected, almost as soon as his head hit the pillow.

The last thing he thought about was the beautiful face of a blue-eyed blind girl.

The Kid's muscles were stiff when he woke up, but he didn't have any trouble moving around. He put on his hat and gun and went into the dining room.

Glory was sitting at the table.

She leaped to her feet and ran to him as soon as she saw him, practically throwing herself into his arms. "Kid!" she cried. "I didn't know where you were, and that horrible Indian woman won't tell me anything! Are you all right?"

The Kid put his hands on her shoulders and moved her back a little. "I'm fine, Glory," he told her. "How about you?"

She nodded. "I was able to sleep some. I didn't think I could possibly sleep in this awful place, but I did. Have you thought of some way to get us out of here?"

"Keep your voice down," he cautioned her, lowering his own voice to a whisper. "Black's made me his aide. He expects your husband, along with Bateman and the rest of those hired guns, to get here late tomorrow sometime."

"Do we have to stay that long? Can't we try to escape now?"

The Kid cast a glance toward the wall that contained the hidden door. Sure, he could open the door and they could go up those stairs to the top, and if what Elena had told him was true, they would come out on top of the Red Skull and be free.

Yeah, free somewhere in the Dragoons, on foot, with no horses, no supplies, and only a limited amount of ammunition. Plus a whole camp full of enemies who would come looking for them as soon as it was discovered that they were gone. Those weren't the sort of odds that The Kid liked.

They'd be better off biding their time until he could think of a better plan, or at least some sort of plan, period, instead of just rushing up that hidden staircase. Glory might not see it that way, so for now he wasn't going to tell her about the stairs.

"We'll get out, don't worry about that. It might be

better to wait until your husband gets here, though. Black will be more distracted that way."

"Are you sure?" Glory pleaded. "If we stay here, there's no telling what he'll do. I know, I tried to put a brave face on it earlier, but I don't want to have to . . . to have to . . ."

"Maybe it won't come to that," The Kid said.

"If we can get away before Edward gets here," Glory went on, "maybe we can stop him before there's another battle. I can't let anything happen to Edward, Kid. I just *can't!"*

"No offense, but I didn't think you even liked him all that much, what with the way you've been trying to get me into your bed the past few days."

She stared at him, anger smoldering in her eyes. "You don't know anything about it, Kid. One thing doesn't necessarily have anything to do with the other, you know."

He grunted and shook his head. "That's not the way it's been in my experience."

"Anyway, I can't let anything happen to Edward because we haven't been married for eighteen months yet."

The light dawned in The Kid's brain. "You have to be married that long before you get his money if anything happens to him!"

"That's right," Glory replied in a sulky tone. "He said he wasn't going to change his will until he was sure the marriage would last . . . the suspicious bastard!"

The Kid shook his head and laughed. Glory was full of surprises, yet completely predictable.

"So you see, that's why we can't let him be killed,"

she went on. "If you can get me out of this, Kid, and destroy Gideon without Edward coming to any harm, I'll see to it that you're well rewarded. Financially . . . or any other way you'd like."

"You don't give up easy, do you?"

"I *never* give up when there's something I want." Glory's eyes suddenly darted to something behind him. She said, "Kid . . ."

He turned and saw Elena coming into the room. "Señor Morgan?" she asked.

"I'm here, Elena."

"And . . . the Señora Sheffield?"

"Yes, she's here, too."

Elena's voice was cooler than usual as she said, "Señora Lopez told me to find you. She said Colonel Black and his staff will be meeting in here shortly."

"Thank you," The Kid said. "I'll just wait for them, if that's all right."

"I should take Señora Sheffield back to her room. She should not be wandering around. Señora Lopez would not be pleased."

Glory gave a defiant toss of her head that sent her red hair swirling around her face. "I don't give a damn whether that old hag is pleased or not."

"Just go with Elena," The Kid told her. "I'll see you later."

She gave him a look. He saw desperation in her eyes. *Don't forget,* she mouthed.

The two young women left the room, with Elena leading the way even though she was blind. The Kid sat down at the table. He thought about helping himself to a drink. The hour had to be getting late in the day. He decided to wait, figuring that Black would probably order Lopez to pour drinks all around once the meeting got underway. They would probably have dinner, too.

The Kid didn't have to wait long before Black, Cranston, and Terhune came in, accompanied by two more outlaws he hadn't met. Terhune's broken nose was swollen and ugly, but he didn't seem particularly angry at The Kid. He just grunted and said, "Good fight, Morgan. I figured Cranston and me would stomp the hell out of you."

"You were lucky," Cranston said coldly. He seemed to hold more of a grudge than Terhune, although the only visible sign of injury he had was a bruise on his jaw where one of The Kid's punches had landed.

Black shook his head and said, "Luck had nothing to do with it, Captain. I was watching. Lieutenant Morgan acquitted himself quite well."

"Yeah, I guess." Cranston's admission was grudging.

Black waved toward the table. "Sit down, gentlemen. We have work to do. Morgan, this is Lieutenant Harkins and Lieutenant Brill."

The Kid nodded to the other two outlaws. The men took their places around the table. Black stood at the head of the table and addressed them.

"I have lookouts stationed between here and Titusville to keep watch for the approach of Edward Sheffield and his men. They'll send signals so that we'll have plenty of warning before the enemy arrives, probably late in the day tomorrow. We'll position marksmen around the gap at the entrance to the valley so that once Sheffield and his men are in our sights, they won't be able to retreat. I intend to allow

Sheffield to approach the stronghold, but once my business with him is concluded, we shall open fire with cannon and rifles on his men and wipe them out. If any of them attempt to flee, the sharpshooters at the gap will cut them down. I want a clean sweep, gentlemen. No mercy. No quarter. Sheffield and all his men will die." The colonel looked around the table. "Any questions?"

No one spoke. Colonel Black might be loco, The Kid thought, but unfortunately, the plan he had come up with to wipe out Sheffield and his hired gunfighters was a good one. It sounded like it would work.

"Very well, then," Black said. "I want suggestions as to how we can best deploy our forces. I want our ten best rifle shots to close off the gap."

For the next few minutes, Black and the other outlaws hashed out the details of who would be posted where and what the signals would be to start the attack. As the colonel's aide, The Kid would be at Black's side, of course.

At one point, Black glanced at The Kid and frowned. "You should be getting all this down," he said.

"Sorry, Colonel," The Kid said. "I didn't realize I was supposed to take notes."

"As my aide, what did you think your job was?"

The Kid refrained from pointing out that he had never been in the army, let alone served as the aide to a colonel. Instead he said, "When the meeting is over, I'll get paper and a pen from Lopez and write up a report while my memory is still fresh."

Black nodded curtly. "That will be sufficient, but in the future, please be better prepared."

"Yes, sir."

A few minutes later, Black told Lopez to bring in a bottle of wine and also to have dinner served. The Kid had smelled some delicious aromas drifting out from the kitchen, and they reminded him that he still hadn't caught up on his eating.

With the details of the plan worked out, Black picked up the wine glass Lopez had filled for him. The other men picked up their glasses as well.

"If fortune smiles on us, by this time tomorrow evening Edward Sheffield will be dead and all of us will be even wealthier than we are now. I won't forget the services that all of you have rendered in our cause." Black raised his glass. "To good fortune, gentlemen . . . and to the death of our enemies!"

Chapter 32

The Kid didn't see Glory again that evening. He hoped that Black would leave her alone, and an off-hand remark the colonel made gave reason to think that might be possible. While ranting about Edward Sheffield and the way the tycoon had double crossed him, Black said, "Once Sheffield is dead, then Gloriana can truly be mine again!"

It would be just like Black's warped sense of honor to believe that he couldn't molest Glory while she was still married to Sheffield. Once she was a widow, though, it would be a different story.

Either way, there was nothing The Kid could do about it. He remained in the dining room with Black and the other outlaws until the hour was quite late.

Once he had been dismissed and returned to his room, he blew out the candle and waited in the darkness for an hour, until he thought it might be safe to do some prowling in the halls. He went to the door, listened intently, and didn't hear anyone moving around on the other side of it.

The Kid eased the door open and stepped into the corridor. Only a single candle was still lit, and it illuminated the hallway dimly. He wished he knew which room was Glory's . . . if, indeed, any of them were. It was possible she was being held in some other part of the semi-subterranean fortress.

He catfooted along the corridor, once again listening at doors and hearing nothing. He couldn't call out Glory's name, even softly, for fear that someone else might hear. It wouldn't do to be calling Glory's name through the door of Black's room.

Frustrated, The Kid turned toward the short hallway that led to the dining room. He stole along it through the shadows, and as he reached the opening into the dining room, he stopped short at the sight of a ghostly figure moving around in there. All he could see was a moving patch of white.

The figure turned toward him and came closer, and he saw that it was Elena, wearing a long white gown. She must have sensed that someone was there, because she stopped and whispered, *"Que?"*

"It's me, Elena," The Kid whispered back to her.

"Señor Morgan!" She hurried to him. "Señor Morgan, I was about to come to your room. You must leave this place! I just overheard those men Terhune and Cranston talking to the colonel, outside in the compound. They do not trust you. They are trying to persuade him that you should be made a prisoner and killed tomorrow along with the man Sheffield. I think the colonel is going to agree with them!"

The Kid bit back a curse. It looked like he was going to be rushed into action after all, whether he was prepared or not.

"All right," he said. "You have to tell me where Señora Sheffield is being held. We'll get her and take her with us."

Elena hesitated, then said, "Why? That will just anger Colonel Black even more and make him pursue you and kill you."

"I can't leave her here, Elena."

"I heard you earlier today. I heard the two of you talking. She is more to you than a friend."

The Kid's jaw tightened. Elena was jealous, all right. That was just about the last thing in the world he needed.

"Listen to me," he told her. He reached out and rested his hands on her shoulders for emphasis. "Just because Señora Sheffield would like for there to be more between us doesn't mean that there is, or ever will be. I don't want her like that. I just want her to be safe."

"You give me your word on this, Señor Morgan . . . Kid?"

"Of course."

You should feel real proud of yourself, he thought. Leading on a blind girl so she would help him escape from a band of vicious outlaws. But she wanted to get away from them, too, he reminded himself. More than likely she had suffered at their hands, as well as at the hands of Señora Lopez.

"All right," she whispered. "I will show you."

She took his hand and led him out of the dining room, through the door to the kitchen. Another passage branched off from it, and after a moment they were in almost utter darkness. The Kid could barely make out the lightness of Elena's gown. She moved with easy confidence, completely at home in the darkness.

After a few moments, The Kid saw another patch of light ahead of them. They were reaching a turn in the tunnel. Elena paused and put her mouth close to his ear.

"The colonel's quarters are back here, and so is the room where the señora is being kept. We must be very quiet. The colonel is not here. He is with the men in the compound, but Señora Lopez is here, and she has a gun."

The Kid didn't like the sound of that. A gunshot would bring trouble in a hurry, and plenty of it.

"I will tell her that the colonel is looking for her," Elena went on. "You stay here, and when she comes around the corner you can take hold of her and strangle her. Do not let go until she is dead."

The casual way Elena said that made The Kid's eyebrows rise in surprise. For all her gentleness, she could be ruthless, too. He supposed she'd had to learn to be in order to survive.

"Go ahead," The Kid told her. He had no intention of choking Señora Lopez to death, but Elena didn't have to know that.

He put his back against the stone wall of the passage and waited while Elena's slippered feet whispered around the corner. A moment later, he heard soft voices as she talked with Señora Lopez. The Kid couldn't make out the words, but he thought the Indian woman sounded angry. She was still muttering under her breath as she approached the bend in the tunnel. Her footsteps were much heavier than Elena's. The light grew brighter from the lantern she carried. The Kid held his breath as she came around the corner.

She stepped right past him without seeing him at first. Then she caught sight of him from the corner of her eye, and turned toward him, her mouth opened to yell.

Before she could make a sound, The Kid hit her. It was a short, sharp punch with enough power behind it to stun the woman and make her eyes roll up in their sockets. The Kid grabbed the lantern as it slid out of her hand. Señora Lopez fell to her knees and rolled onto her side.

The Kid placed the lantern on the floor of the tunnel and went to work swiftly. He tore strips of cloth from the woman's long skirt and used them to bind her wrists behind her back. He tied her ankles together as well to keep her from moving around. Then he used another piece of cloth as a gag, working it into her mouth and tying it in place with one of the strips. When he was finished, he lifted her and leaned her against the wall in a sitting position.

Her eyelids flickered open, and she glared at him with murderous intensity as she made muffled sounds through the gag. The Kid was glad he couldn't hear what she was saying to him.

He slipped his Colt from its holster and told Señora Lopez, "Settle down, or I'll tap you with the barrel of this gun and knock you out again."

She continued to glare at him, but at least she stopped making so much racket. He stepped around the corner where he could still keep an eye on her and motioned to Elena before he remembered that that didn't do a bit of good.

"Elena," he called softly. "Elena, get Señora Sheffield, and let's get out of here."

For a moment, the girl didn't move, and The Kid thought she might have changed her mind about taking Glory with them. But then Elena reached out and fumbled for a second with the door latch. Such awkwardness was unusual for her, but she probably hadn't had to unlock the door of a room where a prisoner was being held all that often, if ever.

The latch slid back, and Elena opened the door. "Señora Sheffield," she said. "Come. We must leave this place."

The Kid heard Glory ask from inside the room, "What's going on here?" She sounded suspicious, like she wasn't inclined to trust Elena, and The Kid supposed he couldn't blame her for that. Glory had no way of knowing that Elena was on their side.

He took a step along the hallway, past the corner, and called, "Glory! Come on! It's The Kid!"

Glory appeared in the doorway, wearing a green silk gown that Black must have had on hand for her. She stared at him and said, "Kid!"

Then her eyes widened as she glanced past him, and she added, "Look out!"

The Kid whirled around. Somehow, Señora Lopez had gotten to her feet, and her hands were free. The faint candlelight glinted on the short blade of the knife in her hand. The Kid realized that it must have been hidden in her dress, somewhere she could reach it. He hadn't searched her.

She dropped the knife, reached into a pocket, and pulled out a short-barreled pistol. As she swung the gun up The Kid lunged toward her, closing his left hand around the pistol's cylinder so it wouldn't fire and shoving it to the side while he struck her with the barrel of the Colt in his right hand. The blow drove her against the wall. She slid down it, out cold.

Glory and Elena hurried up behind The Kid. "I told you you should kill her," Elena said.

"I don't kill in cold blood," he snapped, which wasn't exactly true. He had, but only under the most extreme provocation.

He shoved the thought of his wife's death out of his mind. He didn't need any distractions. He took hold of Glory's bare upper arm and went on, "There's a way out of here. Elena will show you. I'll get some supplies together as quickly as I can and follow you. We'll meet on top of the Red Skull."

"The-the what?"

"The big rock on top of the cliff. That's where the stairs come out. Wait for me there . . . but if you hear shooting down here, then the two of you get as far away from here as you can, as fast as you can. If you can figure out what direction Titusville is, head for it. You should run into Sheffield and his men on the way."

"You mean you want us to leave you here, Kid?" Glory shook her head. "I can't do that."

"Nor can I, señor," Elena put in.

"Maybe you won't have to." The Kid smiled. "Maybe we'll be lucky—"

The Kid knew better than to tempt fate by saying something like that. No sooner were the words out of his mouth than a heavy roar sounded somewhere outside, followed by a wave of gunfire.

Chapter 33

Glory threw her arms around The Kid's neck in terror. "Oh, my God! What was that?"

"Sounded like one of those cannon," he replied as he disengaged himself from her frantic grip. "From the sound of the gunshots, I'd say the colonel's found himself with a battle on his hands sooner than he expected."

"But-but how?"

The Kid was convinced that Sheffield, Bateman, and the others had found Colonel Black's stronghold and launched a surprise attack on it in the middle of the night. That was the only explanation that made any sense.

"We'll worry about that later," he told Glory. "For now, I want to get you and Elena to someplace safe. Elena, can you take Señora Sheffield up those stairs?"

Elena looked like she didn't care much for the idea, but she nodded. "Sí, señor. You will come to us?"

"As soon as I can," The Kid promised.

He picked up the lantern and the pistol Señora

Lopez had dropped and hustled the two women along the hallway to the dining room, leaving the Indian woman where she was. When they got there, the sound of shots from outside was even louder. The Kid went to the section of wall where the door was hidden and pressed on the beam as he had seen Elena do earlier. The latch clicked, and the door popped open. He swung it back the rest of the way and handed the lantern to Glory, along with the little pistol.

"I'll be along as soon as I can," he told them. "Good luck."

Glory looked like she wanted to fling her arms around his neck again, but her hands were full. She settled for saying, "Good luck to you, Kid."

Elena hugged The Kid instead. "*Vaya con Dios,* Señor Morgan," she said.

Glory frowned at the embrace, then followed Elena up the stairs. The Kid watched until they had made the first turn around the spiral and gone out of sight before he hurried toward the front of the stronghold.

He had heard only the one round from the cannon and was surprised that the other big guns hadn't been brought into action. Maybe the attackers had picked off the gunners and their steady fire was keeping any of the other outlaws from reaching the cannon. He was headed for the door leading into the compound when it burst open and the two owlhoot lieutenants named Harkins and Brill burst in, each with a gun in his hand.

"Morgan!" Brill exclaimed. "You seen that woman you brought in?"

"Mrs. Sheffield?" The Kid said.

Brill jerked his head in a nod. "Yeah. The colonel

ordered me and Harkins to stay with her and watch over her, to make sure that nothin' happens to her."

"What's going on out there?"

Harkins said, "All hell's breakin' loose, that's what's goin' on! Somebody snuck up on us and opened fire. Must be Sheffield and his men, somehow."

"The cannon by the south guard tower got one shot off," Brill put in, "but then the fellas mannin' it went down, and any time somebody else tries to get to it, rifle fire forces 'em back."

"What about the other two cannon?" The Kid asked. "Are they loaded?"

"Yeah, ready to fire. The men in those gun crews are dead, too, though. The sons o' bitches got sharpshooters on top of the Red Skull! They swept the parapets clean. We have a few men left in the guard towers, but everybody else has had to hole up in the cabins."

Harkins said, "What about the woman, damn it? Tell us where she is, Morgan."

"Gone," The Kid said. By now Glory and Elena were probably halfway up the stairs. They would have a surprise waiting for them when they got to the top. Edward Sheffield himself might be up there, although The Kid sort of doubted it. He figured the tycoon would hang back, out of the line of fire. Bateman might well be on top of the Red Skull, though, directing the attack on the outlaw stronghold.

Harkins and Brill stared at The Kid. "What do you mean, gone?" Brill demanded.

"Escaped."

"The hell you say!" Brill's face suddenly twisted with anger. "You let her go! I never did trust you, you son of a bitch! Cranston and Terhune were tryin' to get the colonel to kill you, and I reckon he should have!"

"We'll take care of that right now!" Harkins yelled. Their guns jerked up.

But in the second it took for them to lift their weapons, The Kid's Colt spewed flaming death, roaring and bucking twice in his hand. The bullets smashed into the outlaws and drove them backward with looks of shock and pain on their faces. They collapsed, their blood welling out onto the woven rug. The Kid stepped forward and kicked their guns out of reach before they could try again to shoot him.

Swiftly, with practiced ease, he thumbed three cartridges from the loops on his gunbelt and replaced the two rounds he had just fired, plus slipping a bullet into the chamber he normally kept empty for the hammer to rest on. In the midst of this hornets' nest of enemies, he wanted a full deck from which to deal.

Snapping the cylinder closed, he stepped past the two dead owlhoots and hurried to the door. He looked out, saw lanterns burning in the guard towers and casting their light across the compound. Muzzle flashes lit up the darkness like crimson flowers blooming in the shadows. Some of the men in the towers fired out into the valley where a frontal attack was going on, while others directed their fire toward the riflemen on top of the cliff. Other shots came from the cabins. The air was full of whining, buzzing lead.

The Kid's gaze was drawn back to the cannon mounted in the center of the parapet, with bodies sprawled around it. Brill had said that the big gun by the south tower had been fired, which meant that the other two were still loaded, charged, and ready to wreak havoc.

"Fall back! Fall back!"

The shouted command came from Colonel Black, who led a retreat from the cabins. The outlaws charged out, firing as they ran toward the sanctuary under the cliff. Some of them fell, but most of them made it.

"Colonel!" The Kid called as the men rushed into the stronghold.

"Lieutenant Morgan!" Gideon Black had a bloody gash on his cheek where a bullet had grazed him, but other than that he seemed unharmed. "What happened to Harkins and Brill?"

"A couple of stray bullets got them, right after they ran in here looking for Mrs. Sheffield."

Cranston came up behind the colonel. "He's lying! I'll bet he shot them!"

"He's a damn traitor!" Terhune added.

For a second, The Kid thought Black believed them. Quickly, he said, "If I was a traitor, Colonel, I wouldn't volunteer to go out there and touch off those cannon, now would I?"

Black frowned. "It's sure death to try for those cannon, Lieutenant."

"I can do it," The Kid declared. "Just give me a chance."

Black hesitated, then made up his mind and nodded abruptly. "If you move fast enough, you might be able to reach the parapet. Take a torch with you, so you can fire the cannon as soon as you get there. But Lieutenant . . . I don't think you'll survive this gallant effort."

"Let me worry about that, Colonel."

All The Kid really intended to do was get the hell out of there and reach Sheffield's forces. Then Bateman and the rest of the hired guns could finish off Black and his men. The Kid had hoped to pull the trigger on the renegade colonel himself, so that he could see Black die for what he had done to the Williams family, but as long as Black was blown straight to hell, that was all that really mattered.

"The cannon are lined up on the enemy forces," Black said. "If you could manage to fire them both, that would blow holes in their line and we could launch a counterattack. You'd give us a chance, at least, Lieutenant."

The Kid nodded, eager to be gone from that den of snakes. He hoped that Glory and Elena had reached the top of the stairs and would tell whoever was up there that he was on their side. Maybe they would hold their fire when they saw it was him making a break for it.

"Godspeed, Lieutenant," Black said.

"I still don't trust him," Cranston murmured.

The Kid went to the door. Someone thrust a blazing torch in his hand. He waited for a slight lull in the firing, then burst out into the compound, running for the wall as fast as he could. He planned to go up to the parapet and over the wall, figuring that would be faster and easier than opening the gates.

Even over the crackle of rifle fire, he heard Glory cry, "Don't shoot! It's The Kid!"

Bless her heart, he thought as the shots suddenly died away. She had seen him from up there and recognized him.

In the sudden eerie silence he reached the base of the

stairs that led up to the parapet. Inside the stronghold, Colonel Black figured out what the cease-fire meant. As The Kid started up the stairs, he heard Black shout, "Kill him! Kill Morgan!"

Shots roared out again, but now they were coming from the house-under-the-cliff. Bullets whipped past The Kid, so close he felt their hot breath. He reached the top of the stairs and lunged toward the wall, but shards of adobe flew into the air as a hail of slugs chewed up the top of it. If he tried to climb over, it would be sure death. Instead, The Kid flung himself down into the closest cover—the narrow space between the cannon and the wall.

He was pinned down, but at least the cannon and the carriage on which it rested provided some decent cover. Bullets ricocheted off the cannon's barrel and thudded into the carriage.

The Kid's eyes widened as the parapet suddenly shifted underneath him. He heard a loud crack. The supports underneath it had been hit by a lot of the bullets flying around, and the cannon was really heavy. Another beam cracked. The damage was causing the parapet to give way under the tremendous weight of the big gun.

"Son of a—" The Kid began, but that was all he got out before the parapet fell out from under him and the cannon with a splintering crash. The cannon leaned backward and toppled over, so that the barrel pointed straight up into the air for a second before it crashed on its side, pointing toward the cliff at a slight angle, the broken carriage and parapet wreckage underneath it. The Kid landed on top of it in a shower of debris. The fall wasn't that far, but it was enough to stun him for a second even though he managed to hold on to the still-burning torch.

As his senses came back to him, he saw Colonel Black step out of the stronghold, saber in hand. He twisted his neck to look up at the top of the cliff and screamed, "Gloriana! I did it all for you, Gloriana!" Then as the rest of the gang began to boil out behind him, Black swept the saber toward The Kid and cried, "Kill Morgan!"

"Not before I kill you first, you son of a bitch," The Kid said as he jammed the torch against the touch-hole of the cannon and threw himself desperately away from the big gun.

Chapter 34

In the split-second before he touched off the cannon, he had seen that the barrel was lined up with the front of the stronghold where Colonel Black stood. As he hit the ground, the roar of the shot slammed into his ears and the massive weapon's recoil made it lurch backward in the debris. Lying on his stomach, The Kid watched as the heavy lead ball flew toward the stronghold, rising slightly as it traveled.

It rose just enough to catch Colonel Gideon Black in the belly. The Kid had killed quite a few men in a number of ways, but he had never blown a hole in anybody quite like the hole that cannonball blew through Black. For a second, The Kid would have sworn he could look right through it and see the men standing behind the colonel.

Then the ball tore through them, too, and crashed into the stronghold with a tremendous impact that sent a cloud of dust and chunks of adobe and wood flying into the air. The Kid couldn't even see the cliff anymore.

But he could hear Phil Bateman shouting from the top of it. "The gates, Morgan!" the gunman yelled. "Open the gates!"

The Kid scrambled to his feet and ran to the gates. The bar that held them closed was too heavy for one man to lift out of its brackets, but he was able to shove it enough so that it fell free at one end. The gates swung open then, and some of Sheffield's men rushed through, firing toward the stronghold as they charged.

Exhausted, The Kid reeled over to the wall and collapsed onto the ground. He leaned against the adobe and watched as Bateman's men mopped up the last of the outlaws. The shooting didn't last long, only another minute or so. Then silence descended on the place once more.

The Kid stayed where he was until a buggy rolled through the now wide open gates of the compound and came to a stop not far away. Elena climbed down from the vehicle awkwardly. Someone had draped a jacket around her, over the nightgown she wore. She held out a hand and called, "Señor Morgan! Señor Morgan!"

The Kid put a hand against the wall to steady himself and pushed to his feet. "Here, Elena," he called.

She ran toward the sound of his voice, the long white gown flowing around her legs as she hurried. She came into his outstretched arms and buried her face against his chest.

"Señor Morgan . . . Kid," she said. "You are all right?"

"Just a little tired," he told her.

He looked toward the buggy and saw Glory sitting there next to Sheffield. Someone had given her a coat, too, to cover up the skimpy gown she wore. She gave him a long, intense look, and he sensed that she was saying good-bye to him. She was reunited with her husband . . . and after a few months, she would be assured of someday being rich.

The Kid could have told her that having all the money in the world wasn't what it was made out to be. It couldn't bring back everything that was lost.

"Kid, you saved us," Elena whispered. "You destroyed that monster, Colonel Black, and his men."

"I had a lot of help, and a lot of luck, too," The Kid said. "But we're alive, and that's what matters."

Sheffield said something to Glory, then climbed down from the buggy and walked toward The Kid and Elena. "Mr. Morgan," he said. "It seems I owe you a great deal. Mrs. Sheffield told me how you saved her life more than once."

The Kid left an arm around Elena's shoulders as he turned to face the tycoon. "No offense, Sheffield, but you don't owe me a damn thing. I set out to kill Gideon Black, and I did."

Sheffield frowned. "A personal grudge?"

"You could call it that," The Kid said, thinking of Sean and Frannie Williams and their little boy Cyrus.

"You never said anything—"

"It was my business."

Sheffield shrugged. "Of course. But at the very least, you can accept my thanks. They're heartfelt, I assure you."

"You're welcome," The Kid said with a nod. "Just take care of that wife of yours. And you might tell me how it is that you and Bateman showed up tonight, instead of tomorrow when the colonel was expecting you."

Sheffield smiled thinly. "We were out searching for you and Gloriana, and we were only a few miles from here when we ran into a man heading for Titusville. He had a box with a rather grotesque item in it."

Devlin, The Kid thought. He said, "You figured out that Dunbar was one of Black's spies?"

Sheffield nodded. "That's right. We had to kill the man who was carrying his head. He put up a fight instead of surrendering. Then we found Black's note and the map in the, ah—"

The Kid said, "I know where they were."

"At any rate, once we knew where the hideout was located, Mr. Bateman and I worked out a plan of attack, believing that we could take the outlaws by surprise by striking tonight. Clearly, it was successful."

The Kid looked around at the death and devastation filling the stronghold. "Clearly."

"It would have been much more difficult, without your help, and there's no telling what might have happened to Gloriana in the fighting. As I said, I owe you—but never mind. We've been through that."

"Yeah," The Kid said. "We have."

"I should get back to my wife," Sheffield said. "Thank you again, Mr. Morgan."

The Kid didn't say anything as Sheffield returned to the buggy and climbed up next to Glory. Beside him, Elena tilted her head as if she were actually looking up at him and asked, "Will you take me away from here, Kid?"

"Where would you like to go?"

A shudder ran through her slender body. "Anywhere but here."

The Kid knew the feeling.

No one left until morning, though. By then, the bodies of the dead outlaws had been piled up like cordwood. There were too many of them to haul back to Titusville, and nobody wanted to bury them. Sheffield gave orders for the corpses to be taken into the wrecked stronghold under the cliff. Rocks were piled up in front of the openings, sealing off the place and its grisly contents.

A few members of the gang had survived, along with Lopez and his wife. They would all be taken to Bisbee and turned over to territorial authorities.

The Kid commandeered a horse for Elena and some supplies for them. As they were getting ready to leave that morning, Phil Bateman sauntered over to where The Kid was tightening the cinches on the buckskin's saddle.

"I had a hunch that before this was over, you and I would find out which of us is faster on the draw," the gunman drawled.

The Kid smiled. "It'd be a shame if it had to come to that. This place has seen enough killing."

"Yeah. I was kinda thinking the same thing. But maybe another place, another time—"

"If our trails happen to cross again," The Kid said.

Bateman nodded, touched a finger to the brim of his hat, and turned to walk away.

"That man hates you, Kid," Elena said quietly. "I heard it in his voice. Why?"

"I don't know. Some men just have too much hate in them. It has to come out somewhere." For a while, he had been that way himself, he thought.

Glory had pointedly ignored him since the night before, and that was fine with The Kid. As the group prepared to leave the outlaw stronghold, she sat in her husband's buggy, her face expressionless and her gaze directed straight ahead. But as The Kid and Elena rode past, he saw her eyes flick toward them, just for a second, and he recognized the regret there. She might wind up rich, but she would pay a high price in doing so, and she knew it.

They rode out through the open gates and turned east, while Sheffield, Glory, Bateman, and the others headed south toward Titusville. Their destinations were different. Their trails had parted.

For Kid Morgan, it was a lonely trail and always would be. He glanced over at Elena. She couldn't fill the void in his heart. No one ever would.

But she could travel beside him for a while, until it was time for their trails to part, as well.

They rode toward the rising sun.

Turn the page for an exciting preview of

SLAUGHTER OF EAGLES

by William Johnstone
with J. A. Johnstone

Coming soon, wherever Pinnacle Books are sold!

Chapter 1

From the *MacCallister Eagle:*

Statue of Jamie Ian MacCallister To be Dedicated July Fourth

The noted artist and sculptor Frederic Remington has, for some time now, been busy creating a life-size bronze statue of our founder, the late Colonel James Ian MacCallister. The work was commissioned by the MacCallister City Council and will be paid for by the city of MacCallister and the state of Colorado.

Governor Frederick Pitkin will be present for the dedication, and will be the featured speaker. Colonel MacCallister's children will be guests for the occasion, and will occupy positions of honor on the stage with the governor. It is not mere coincidence that the dedication is to be held on the Fourth of July, for Colonel Jamie Ian MacCallister embodied all that was noble about

> our country and our country's founders. Festivities for the event are now being planned.

Falcon MacCallister read the article as he was waiting for his lunch to be served at City Pig Restaurant. The youngest son of the legendary Jamie Ian MacCallister, Falcon was the biggest of all his siblings. He had his father's size, with wide shoulders, full chest, and powerful arms. And, of all his siblings, he had come the closest to matching his father in reputation.

However, he did have two siblings, the twins Andrew and Rosanna who, in their own field, were just as well-known. Andrew and Rosanna MacCallister were, according to a recent article in the *New York Times*, the "Toast of New York Theater." They had performed for every President from U.S. Grant to Chester Arthur, missing only James Garfield because assassination had limited his term to only seven months. They had also performed for the Queen of England and the King of Sweden.

But they would not be present for the dedication of their father's statue.

That very morning, Falcon had a letter from Andrew and Rosanna, explaining that they would be unable to attend because they would be closing one play on the fourth, and opening a new play one week later. Falcon had visited them in New York a few times, had gotten a glimpse of their world, and though he wished they could be there for the dedication, he could understand why they couldn't. He was going to have to explain that to his other siblings, and he knew they would not be quite as understanding.

"Hello, Falcon, it's good to see you."

Falcon looked up from his paper and saw the Reverend and Mrs. Powell. He stood.

"Brother Charles, Sister Claudia," Falcon said, greeting his old friends with a smile. "How good to see you."

"Please, please, keep your seat," Reverend Powell said. "It's a wonderful thing, isn't it? I mean our town getting a statue of your father."

"Yes," Falcon said. "When I learned what the city council had in mind, I have to admit, I was very pleased."

"I have been asked to give the invocation," Reverend Powell said. He chuckled. "I told them I'm retired now. They would be better off asking young Reverend Pyron."

"I asked that you give the convocation," Falcon said.

Reverend Powell smiled. "I thought, perhaps, that you did. Though I'm sure there are others who are imminently more qualified."

"Nonsense," Falcon said. "Who better than you? You and my father were very close friends, and, like my father, you were one of the founders of the valley."

"I confess, Falcon, that I am both honored and pleased to have been asked to do the invocation. I am very much looking forward to it."

"Won't you join me for lunch?" Falcon invited.

"Claudia?" The reverend deferred to his wife.

"We would be pleased to join you," she said.

Falcon called the waiter over so he could take their order.

"Delay my order until theirs is ready," he said.

"Yes, sir, Mr. MacCallister."

"Now," Falcon said as the waiter left. "Tell me what is going on in your life."

"We are about to be great grandparents," Claudia said. "Any day now."

"Think of it, Falcon. That makes four generations of Powells. What have we loosed on this unsuspecting world?" the Reverend teased.

The Dumey Ranch, Jackson County, Missouri

As Falcon and the Reverend and Mrs. Powell enjoyed their lunch, 750 miles east, at a small ranch in Jackson County, Missouri, young Christine Dumey had come out to the barn to summon her brother, Donnie to lunch.

"Hey, Christine, look at me!" young Donnie shouted at his sister. "I'm going to swing from this loft over to the other one."

"Donnie, don't you do that! You'll fall!" Christine warned, but, laughing at his older sister's concern, Donnie grabbed hold of a hanging rope, then took several running steps before leaping off into space. The rope carried him across and he landed on a pile of loose hay.

"Ha!" Donnie said as he got up and brushed away several bits of straw. "You thought I couldn't do it."

"You are lucky you didn't break your neck," Christine scolded.

"Ah, you are always such a 'fraidey cat," Donnie said.

"Mama said we need to wash up for dinner," Christine called up to him. Donnie was eleven, towheaded and freckle-faced. At thirteen, Christine was beginning to look more like a young woman, than a little girl.

"I'll be right down," Donnie said. He walked over to the edge of the loft and looked out through the big window, toward the main house. He saw three horses tied up at the hitching post. "Hey, Christine, who's here?" he asked. He grabbed on to another rope, then slid, easily, down to the ground.

"What do you mean, who is here?"

"There are three strange horses tied up at the hitching rail."

"I don't know. There was nobody here when I came out to get you. Maybe it's somebody wantin' to buy some livestock."

Donnie shook his head. "We ain't got nothin' to sell right now," he said. "Papa just sold off all the pigs. Got good money for 'em too."

"You look a mess. Come over to the pump. I'll pump water while you wash your face and hands. I wouldn't be surprised if you don't have pig doo on you, somewhere."

"It's on my hands," Donnie said, then, laughing, he ran his hands through Christine's hair. "And now it's in your hair."

"Donnie, stop it!" Christine shouted in alarm.

"Oh, don't get so excited. I didn't really put pig shit in your hair," Donnie said.

"Don't be using words like that."

"Words like what?"

"You know."

"How am I going to know, unless you tell me?" Donnie teased.

"You know exactly what I'm talking about. Hold your hands under the pump."

Donnie stuck his hands under the mouth of the pump and Christine worked the handle until a solid stream of water poured out. Then, wringing his hands to get rid of the water, Donnie and Christine walked into the house. As soon as they got inside they sensed that something was wrong. Three men were standing in the kitchen, while Donnie's mother and father were sitting in chairs over against the wall. Donnie's mother had cooked pork chops for dinner and one of the men was holding a pork chop in his hand. He had just taken a bite and a bit of it was hanging from his moustache. He was, by far, the biggest of the three. The other two men were not much taller than Donnie.

"Mama, Papa, what's going on?" Christine asked, the tone of her voice reflecting her concern.

"Children, these gentlemen are Egan Drumm, and Clete and Luke Mueller," Chris Dumey said.

"The Mueller brothers!" Donnie said.

One of the two small men smiled at Donnie, though the smile did nothing to ease the tension in the room.

"So, you've heard of us, have you?"

"I've heard you rob banks and trains," Donnie said.

"What do you think, Luke? We're famous."

"Shut up, Clete, you damn fool." Luke said.

"Where at's the money?" Eagan Drumm asked. Using his teeth, he tore the last bit of meat from the pork chop bone, then he tossed the bone onto the floor.

"What money?" Chris Dumey asked.

"Tell him what money, Luke," Drumm said.

Luke's pistol was in his holster, but he drew it and fired, in the blink of an eye. The bullet hit Lillian Dumey in her left leg, and blood began to ooze down over her foot. She screamed out in pain, then doubled forward to grab the wound.

"Mama!" Christine shouted, and she ran to her mother.

"You son of a bitch!" Chris Dumey yelled, angrily.

"I know you got a lot of money from selling your hogs yesterday," Drumm said. "So don't be playing dumb with me. I'm going to ask you one more time, where is the money, and if you don't answer, I'll put a bullet in her other leg."

"No, please! All right, all right, I'll tell you! Just don't hurt her anymore! The money is over there, in that vase, under the flowers.

Drumm nodded at Clete Mueller, and he walked over to the vase, picked it up, then threw it on the floor, smashing it. There, in the shards of broken glass, was a packet of bills, tied together with a string into one neat bundle.

"Ha!" Clete said, holding up the money. "Here it is!"

"How much is there?" Drumm asked.

Clete began to count. "Six hunnert dollars," he said after a moment.

Drumm smiled. "That's a pretty good haul," he said. "Two hunnert dollars apiece."

"That's an entire year's work," Dumey protested. "If you take that, how will I feed my family?"

"You won't have to worry about feedin' 'em," Drumm said.

"What do you mean?"

"I mean you'll all be dead." He shot Dumey down, and, laughing, Luke and Clete began shooting as well.

Some time later, Chris Dumey came to. For a moment, he wondered why he was lying on the kitchen floor, then he remembered what happened. Looking around he saw his wife, and both his children, lying lifeless on the floor with him.

There was blood everywhere, and dipping his finger into it, he began to write on the kitchen floor:

WE WAS KILT BY DRUM AND

MUELLER BR . . .

From there the letters trailed off and that was far as he got before he died.

Egan Drumm and the Muellers rode hard away from Dumey ranch, each with two hundred dollars in their pocket. They had ridden for a little better than an hour, when Clete spoke up.

"What do you boys say that the next town we come to we go into town and get us a couple drinks and maybe a woman?"

"A woman, Clete?" Luke replied, laughing. "You want us to all share the same woman?"

"Well, why not? It'll be cheaper if we share one."

"I ain't sharin' a woman with nobody," Luke said. "What about you, Egan?"

"I ain't sharin' 'cause I ain't goin' into town," Drumm replied.

"Why not? We're far enough away, there ain't likely to be nobody aroun' here to know nothin' about what we just done. Fac' is, I doubt there's anyone here 'bout who has ever even heard of the Dumeys."

"That ain't it," Drumm said.

"Then what is?"

"I aim to go out on my own, now."

"Damn, Egan, you don't like us no more?" Clete asked.

"No, it ain't that," Drumm said. "It's just—well, think about it. We just kilt four people back there, and what did we get for it? Two hunnert dollars apiece. Two hunnert dollars, that's all."

"Two hundred dollars ain't nothin' to sneeze at," Luke said. "Hell, if you was ridin' for twenty and found, it'd take you damn near a year to earn that much money."

"I know, I know. That's why I don't ride for twenty and found," Drumm said. "But I think I want to go out on my own, nonetheless. No hard feelin's."

"No hard feelin's," Luke replied.

As Luke and Clete turned their horses in the direction of the small town, Drumm continued to ride on in the same direction they had been going.

"Where do you reckon he's a'goin'?" Clete asked.

"Who knows? He's got a burr in his saddle over somethin'," Luke replied. "Ahh, we don't need him. We'll find someone else to work with the next time we do a job, and when we do, it'll be a lot bigger than this one we just pulled."

"Yeah," Clete said. "We don't need him no more no how."

Brownville, Colorado, one month later

Luke and Clete Mueller were in the Gold Digs Saloon in Brownville, Colorado. Luke was playing cards with three others, while Clete was talking with one of the bar girls. Talking was all he could do because he had already spent nearly all of the money he had gotten from the Dumeys.

The man dealing the cards had only three fingers on his left hand. One of the others had a patch over his right eye, though a few minutes earlier he had removed the patch to scratch his eyebrow, and Luke saw that there was no eye there at all, just a puff of scar tissue. The man with three fingers was Ollie Terrell. Bo Caldwell was the man with only one eye, and the third man was Clarence Poole.

The Muellers had never met Terrell or Caldwell, but they knew Poole because they had served a little time with him in the Missouri State Penitentiary in Jefferson City.

"What the hell you dealin' for, Terrell?" Caldwell asked. "Hell, you can't even hold the cards proper."

"What do you care whether or not I can hold 'em proper? Hell, you got only one eye so you can't see 'em anyway," Terrell replied, and the others laughed.

"I like it when he deals. With no more fingers than he's got on that hand, that means he can't deal off the bottom of the deck," Poole said.

"You can tell he ain't a' doin' that," Caldwell said. "The onliest one of us winnin' is Luke Mueller. If I don't win somethin' soon, I'm goin' to have to get me a job some'eres."

"I've got a job for you," Luke said as he picked up the cards Terrell had just dealt.

"What kind of a job?" Caldwell asked. "'Cause I tell you true, I don't want to be shovelin' no shit out of a stall or nothin' like that."

"Believe me, it is nothin' like that," Luke answered. "It's quick, easy, and there's a lot of money in it."

"Ha!" Terrell said. "Where are you goin' to find somethin' that is quick, easy and has a lot of money? Unless you're plannin' on robbin' a bank."

Luke looked at Terrell, but made no comment.

"What?" Terrell asked. "I'll be damned. That's it, ain't it? You're a' plannin' on robbin' a bank, ain't you?"

"Why don't you just go out in the street and shout it?" Luke asked.

Caldwell looked over at Poole. "You know this fella, Poole. Me'n Terrell don't. Is he serious?"

"You recruitin' people to ride with you?" Poole asked Luke, without responding to Caldwell's question.

"I might be," Luke replied. "That is, if I can find a few good men I can depend on."

A broad smile spread across Poole's face. "You know you can depend on me. I'm in," he said.

"What?" Caldwell asked. "You really are serious, ain't you?"

"Are you in, or out?" Luke asked.

"I'm in. Hell yes," Caldwell replied.

"Me too," Terrell added, excitedly.

"What about Egan Drumm?" Poole asked.

"What about him?" Luke replied.

"Don't he ride with you and Clete? Where's he at?"

"I don't have no idea where he is," Luke said.

"So, what you're a' sayin' is that he ain't a' goin' to be a part of this," Poole said.

"That's what I'm sayin'."

"Good. I never liked that son of a bitch anyway. Don't know why you and Clete ever took to runnin' with him."

"When do we hold up this here bank?" Terrell asked.

Luke fixed a stare at Terrell, then he looked back at Poole. "Does this dumb bastard not know when to keep his mouth shut?"

"Who are you callin' a dumb bastard?" Terrell asked angrily.

"I'm callin' you a dumb bastard," Luke said, coldly.

"Ollie," Caldwell said, reaching over to put his hand on Terrell's shoulder. "Don't get carried away here. You know damn well you don't want to get into a pissin' contest with Luke Mueller."

Suddenly Terrell realized how close he was getting to making a very foolish mistake, and he forced a smile. "Come to think of it," he said. "I guess I can be a dumb bastard from time to time."

Caldwell laughed to ease the tension, then the others laughed as well.

"To answer your question," Luke said. "It'll be tomorrow, over in a place called MacCallister."

MacCallister, Colorado, the next day

The Reverend Charles Powell and his wife, Claudia, were standing just outside the bank when the teller, Clyde Barnes, opened the door to let them in.

"Good morning, Brother Powell, good morning,

Mrs. Powell," the teller greeted. "You're here awfully early today. You must have some business to attend to."

"More pleasure than business," Powell said. "We're going to Denver to see our new great grand-daughter, and I thought we might need a little walking around money."

"Walking around money? You mean you are going to walk to Denver? You aren't taking the train?" Barnes teased.

For a moment Powell didn't get it, then when he did, he laughed out loud.

"No train for us. I figured Claudia and I would just walk along the track 'till we got there," Powell said. "No, sir, who needs an old loud, smelly train?" He laughed again.

"You aren't going to miss the dedication of Colonel MacCallister's statue, are you?" Barnes asked.

"Oh, goodness no, I wouldn't miss that for the world," Reverend Powell said. "But that's some time away, yet. We'll be back in plenty of time for that."

"I didn't think you would want to miss that. I've heard you are giving the invocation."

"I will be giving it, and mighty proud to do so," Reverend Powell said.

"Come on up to the window, Reverend, and I'll give you your money. Have you drawn the draft yet?"

"Yes, I have it right here," Reverend Powell said, pulling the draft from his pocket.

"Well then, we'll have you out of here in no time."

Suddenly the front door burst open and five men came charging into the bank. All five had their guns drawn, and they were so sure of themselves, that none of them were wearing masks. One of them had only one eye, and Mrs. Powell had to turn her head away in revulsion, rather than look directly at him.

"Everybody, get your hands up!" one of the men shouted. He was a small man, but the gun in his hand made him look big enough. "This is a bank robbery. Teller, get behind the cage and give us all the money you got!"

Barnes stepped around behind the counter, opened his drawer, and pulled out a couple hundred dollars. He handed it through the window to the robbers.

"What is this?" the small man asked. "Are you tellin' me this is all the money you've got in this bank?"

"There is more money in the safe, but it's locked and I don't have the combination," Barnes said. "Mr. Dempster only lets me have what he thinks I'll need durin' the day."

The leader of the group, the one who had given the teller his orders, turned his pistol on Claudia Powell and pulled the trigger. The woman let out a cry of pain, then fell.

"Now, you open that safe or someone else dies," the little man with the big gun said.

"What have you done?" Reverend Powell shouted. Even though he was unarmed, he started toward the shooter.

Calmly, and without changing the expression on his face, the little man fired again, and the good reverend went down, collapsing on the floor next to his wife. At that moment a young woman came into the bank, and the little man pointed his pistol toward her.

"No!" Barnes shouted. "Please, don't shoot her! That's my wife! I'll get the money for you!"

The small, evil man smiled. "So, you've suddenly remembered the combination to the safe, have you?"

"Yes, Mr. Mueller. Please, no more shooting."

"Luke, the son of a bitch knows us," one of the other men said. He was only a little taller than Luke.

Luke smiled. "What can I tell you, Clete? When you get as good at something as we are, people learn your name."

"That ain't good, is it?"

"It ain't all bad. If the law in this one horse town knows that it was the Mueller brothers who held up the bank, they'll be too scared to come after us."

Barnes returned from the safe, carrying a sack.

"This is it," he said. "This is all the money the bank has."

"Open the top. Let me look inside," Luke Mueller said.

Barnes opened the top, disclosing several bound packets of twenty dollar bills.

"Now, that's more like it," Mueller said. He smiled, then took the bag. "It's been a real pleasure doing business with you," he said.

Chapter 2

The metal bit jangled against the horse's teeth. The horse's hooves clattered on the hard rock and the leather saddle creaked beneath the weight of its rider.

When Falcon MacCallister rode into town just before noon, he knew that something had happened. It wasn't just some sort of psychic perception, though the clues were so subtle that there are many who would not have picked up on them.

There was no one pitching horseshoes alongside Sikes' Hardware Store.

No one was playing checkers in front of Boots and Saddles.

There were no clusters of women shoppers, standing on the corners, laughing and talking.

In fact there was a pall hanging over the town that was palpable. Wondering what was going on, Falcon stopped in front of the sheriff's office, swung down from his horse, tied it off, and stepped inside. The sheriff and two of his deputies were looking at a map that they had spread out on a table.

"Good morning, Amos," Falcon said, greeting the newly elected sheriff, Amos Cody."

"Ah, Mr. MacCallister, am I glad to see you," the young sheriff said.

"I keep trying to tell you, Amos, call me Falcon."

"Yes, sir, I know you do, but it's just that I grew up hearin' about your pa's exploits, then yours. Well, it just seems hard."

"You are making me feel very old, Amos," Falcon said. He glanced out the window and saw a little cluster of people engaged in an intense conversation. The somber expressions on their faces reinforced his feeling that something bad had happened.

"What's going on, Sheriff?"

"You mean you haven't heard?"

"No, I haven't."

"The bank was robbed this morning," Amos said.

"And the Reverend Powell and his wife was murdered," Deputy Bates added. Bates was a lot older than the young sheriff, and had been a deputy for many years.

"What?" Falcon said in surprise and anger. "Brother Charles and Sister Claudia have been killed?"

"Yes, they were in the bank when it was robbed."

"But I don't understand. Why were they killed?"

Sheriff Cody shook his head. "Who knows?"

"It was Luke and Clete Mueller," Deputy Bates said. "And from all I've heard about them two, they don't really need no reason. Accordin' to Clyde Barnes, the Powells were just standing there in the bank when the robbers came in. Next thing you know, Luke Mueller shot them. Then they got away, clean as a whistle."

"The Mueller brothers, you say?"

"Yes. And three others," Sheriff Cody said.

"Have you ever run across the Mueller brothers?" Bates asked.

"No."

Bates smiled. "I didn't reckon you had. 'Cause if you had, both them bastards would be dead by now."

"Who were the other three?" Falcon asked.

Sheriff Cody shook his head. "We don't know. Barnes recognized the Muellers, but he had never seen any of the other three."

"Are you going after them?"

"By now, they have more than likely left the county," Sheriff Cody said. "That means that even if I found them, I would have to work with the sheriff of that county. But you hold a special deputy's commission from the governor, which gives you authority all over the state, so, I was hoping you might take a personal interest in this. Reverend Powell was a friend of yours, wasn't he?"

"Yes, he was a close friend. He did the funerals for my mother and my father, and he baptized nearly every one of my nieces and nephews. I guess I've known the Reverend and Mrs. Powell for just about all my life. They were among the earliest settlers of the valley, and they were good people."

"He had already retired when I came here," Sheriff Cody said. "But I knew him, of course, and from what I knew of him, he was a good person. And I heard that he could give one stem-winder of a sermon."

"Yes, he could," Falcon said. He remembered, as a young boy, sometimes getting very impatient with the length of the good parson's sermons. Falcon was usually anxious to get to a fishing pond or some such place, and he would squirm until his mother or one of his older sisters would fix him with a steely glare.

"Did anyone see them leave? Do we know which way they were going?" Falcon asked.

"Yes, we had quite a few people who saw them ride out of town. The only thing we know for sure is that they were heading east when they left here. Bates and I went out lookin' for 'em, but didn't see anything.

"I know you probably have other things to do, but I was hopin' you'd take a look around for us, see what you could come up with."

"Sheriff, they killed two people who were as close as family to me. I would go after these men whether you asked me to or not. Yes, I will find them."

It did not escape Sheriff Cody's attention that Falcon said I "will find" them, rather than I "will go after" them.

"Thanks," Sheriff Cody said.

"I told you he would," Bates said with a smile of smug satisfaction on his face.

"Good, good. So, what do we do next? What can I do to help you?"

"The teller was the only witness?" Falcon asked.

"Clyde Barnes was the only witness to the actual hold up, though several saw them riding out of town."

"Let's start with Barnes," Falcon suggested.

For the next half hour, Falcon gathered as much information as he could about the robbers.

"Well, you know what the Muellers look like, don't you?" Barnes said. "I guess just about ever' one knows what they look like. They're little short, dried up, evil looking men. As for the others, one of them has only one eye. That's his left eye. There is nothing but a big old ugly mass of purple flesh where the right eye was. And another one had only three fingers on his left hand. Don't know as I saw anything particular about the third man. I mean, he was pretty ordinary as men go."

"What about their horses?" Falcon asked.

Barnes shook his head. "I didn't see them. I'm sorry."

"That's all right," Falcon said. "You've given me a good description of the men. It will be very helpful."

Falcon was able to get good descriptions on the horses the men were riding from at least half a dozen citizens who had seen them ride out of town at breakneck speed. Two were riding roans, one was riding a black horse, one a white horse, and one was riding a paint.

Falcon examined the ground where the horses had been tied up outside the bank and saw something that made him smile.

One of the horses had a tie bar shoe on his right forefoot.

Riding out to the east end of town, he looked around until he found that same tie bar. He chuckled. They may as well have been leaving a series of arrow shaped signs reading, WE WENT THIS WAY, behind them.

Somewhat farther into the trail, Falcon realized that the Mueller brothers weren't going to make it easy for him. They had been on the run for nearly all their adult life, so they knew how to confuse and disorient anyone who might be tracking them. They took great pains to cover their true trail, while leaving false trails for anyone to follow. To that end the Mueller brothers and those who were with him, rode through streams and over hard rock, trying every trick in the book to throw off anyone who might be following them. But Falcon hung on, doggedly.

The Mueller brothers didn't realize it, but in trying to shake off anyone who might be following them, they were actually helping Falcon. It was always the same five horses who broke the trail, and he had a way of identifying each of them, not just the one with the tie bar shoe. One of the horses had a slight turn-in of its right rear hoof. Two of the horses had noticeable nicks in their shoes, one on the left rear and the other, on both rear shoes. Only one horse had no noticeable features and yet that, in itself, became a way of identifying it. In addition, all the horses had grazed together for the last few days, because their droppings were filled with the same kind of wild, mountain meadow grass.

"Whoever that fella is that's a'doggin' us, is still on our trail," Terrell said.

Luke twisted around in his saddle. "Are you sure?"

"Hell yes, I'm sure. I just got me a glimpse of 'im on the other side of that far ridge."

"That makes him a little more 'n a mile back."

"Ain't they no way we can shake him?" Caldwell asked.

"You got 'ny ideas that we ain't tried?" Luke

replied. "We done ever'thing I can think of, an' it ain't even slowed 'im down none."

"Whoever the hell he is, I swear, he could track a fish through water," Poole said.

"I tell you what we ought to do," Clete said.

"All right, brother, let me hear your idea."

"We ought to just wait behind a couple o' rocks and shoot him, soon as he comes up on us."

"If I thought for certain we would get him, I'd be all for it," Luke said. "But we're not likely to get a clean shot at him out here."

The five men had stopped for a few minutes, not only to discuss the situation of the man on their tail, but also to give their horses a breather. All five were looking back, trying to get a glimpse of the man who was following them. When Luke turned back around, he chuckled.

"I got me an idea," he said.

"What's that?"

Luke pointed to a narrow draw in front of them. "If we can get through that draw, he'll have to follow."

"So?"

"Look at them rocks up on the top there, on the right hand side. Do you see 'em?"

"I see 'em."

"If we push the rocks down, it'll block the draw and he can't get through," Luke said.

"Hell, why don't we just wait until he gets into the draw, then push them rocks down on him?" Clete asked.

"Yeah, all right, we can try it," Luke said. "Come on, let's hurry through the draw."

* * *

Fifteen minutes later, Falcon reached the spot where the five men had halted. He could tell by the tracks that they had stopped there for a few minutes, and he could also tell that they had left that spot at a gallop.

Why?

What would cause them, out there in the middle of nowhere, to suddenly break into a gallop?

Looking ahead, he saw that the trail led to a very narrow draw, so slapping his legs against the side of his horse, he urged the animal on.

"Here he comes," Luke said. "Get ready.

Clete and the others got in position behind the rocks and waited.

"Now!" Luke shouted.

"Now!"

The word rolled down from the top of the rock wall, amplified by the narrow confines of the wall. The word itself got Falcon's attention, and he jerked his horse to a stop. Then, he heard the scrape and clatter of rocks, followed by the thunder of a virtual rockslide. Glancing up, it looked as if the entire wall was collapsing right on him.

"Ha!" Luke shouted. "We got him! There ain't no way he got out of that!"

Clete, Terrell, Caldwell, and Poole stepped up

alongside Luke to look down into the draw. They saw nothing but a large pile of rocks on the floor below.

"Who was it, do you reckon?" Poole asked.

Luke shook his head. "I don't have no idée," he said. "Prob'ly some deputy or somethin'. Whoever it was, it don't make no never mind now, 'cause he's deader than a doornail."

"Ha!" Poole said. "And we've got away clean as a whistle."

"Yeah, what say we divide up our money now, and each one of us go on our different way?" Caldwell said.

"Not yet," Luke replied.

"What do you mean, not yet? Why not?"

"If they was one deputy comin' after us, there's just as likely to be another one. Or maybe two or three more. We'd be better off all stickin' together till we're sure."

From the moment he heard the word "Now," Falcon was on the alert. Jerking his horse around, he was at a full gallop by the time the rocks started falling, and well clear of the draw by the time the rocks started piling up on the floor below. Turning back toward the draw, he watched the dust rise as the rocks closed the passage. He would have to find another way around.

Fortunately he had been there many times before, and he knew another way around, coming out on the other side no more than half an hour later. Once on the other side he picked up their tracks immediately. It was a lot easier following them now than it had been because, thinking they were in the clear, they were no longer making an effort to hide their trail. They were heading in a straight line for the little town of Black Hawk.

The sun went behind the clouds just before noon, and the clouds thickened, and darkened.

"Purty soon it's goin' to commence to rainin' here like pourin' piss out of a boot. And we're goin' to be right in the middle of it," Terrell said.

"What if it does rain? You ain't made of sugar," Clete said. "You ain't goin' to melt."

Poole laughed. "You ain't made of sugar," he repeated. "I like that."

"I ain't goin' to melt, that's true," Terrell said. "But it ain't goin' to be none too comfortable bein' out here in it, neither."

"Let the rain come," Luke said. "The more rain the better."

"What do you mean?"

"Think about it, Terrell. If anybody else is on our trail, why this rain will wash out all the tracks," Luke said.

Terrell was quiet for a moment, then he nodded. "Yeah," he said. He laughed. "Yeah, that's right, ain't it? It would wash out all our tracks. Hell, I say, let the rain come."

"Not yet," Luke said.

"What do you mean, not yet? You just said the rain would wash out all our tracks, didn't you?"

"Yes, I did, and it will. But if it will just hold off for another half hour or so, we'll be to Black Hawk."

"Black Hawk? What's Black Hawk?"

"It's a town me and Clete have already scouted out. No railroad comes to it, there's no telegraph wires, and even if they have heard of us, there ain't likely no one there who has ever seen us. We'll be safe inside, and the rain will wash away the tracks. We can hole up there for a while until they quit lookin' for us."

"And spend some of our money?" Terrell asked, hopefully.

"Yeah," Luke replied with a grin. "We can spend a little of our money there."

"I ain't never been to Black Hawk," Caldwell said. "What's it like?"

"It's got beer, whiskey, food, and women," Poole said. "What else do you need to know about it?"

Terrell chuckled. "Don't need to know nothin' more about it at all, I don't reckon."

It took the better part of a quarter of an hour to reach the town after they first saw it, and they rode in slowly, sizing it up with wary eyes. It was a town with only one street. The unpainted wood of the few ramshackle buildings was turning gray and splitting. There was no railroad, but there was a stagecoach station with a schedule board announcing the arrival and departure of four stage coaches per week. The first few drops of rain started to fall, and the few people that were out on the street ran to get inside before the rain came down in earnest.

"There's where we're headed," Luke said, pointing to a saloon. Painted in red, outlined in gold on the false front of the saloon were the words; LUCKY NUGGET.

The five rode up to the front of the saloon, dismounted, and tied off their horses. Luke reached for the little cloth bag that was tied to his saddle horn.

"You takin' the money in with you?" Terrell asked.

"You don't think I'm goin' to leave it out here, do you?"

"I reckon not. Just think it might be a little strange for you to be carryin' all that money."

"Don't worry about it," Luke said as they stepped onto the porch. Almost as if on cue, the clouds opened up and the rain fell in torrents.

"Ha!" Clete Mueller said, a few minutes later. "I'll just bet you that ole' Egan Drumm is a' wishin' he was with us now. After all the money we just stoled. And here he got to thinkin' he could do better goin' out on his own, so he left. But now here we are. We got us all this money, and he ain't got nothin'."

"We don't know that he ain't got nothin'," Luke said. "We don't know nothin' about him, not even where he is at."

"Yeah, but I'd be willin' to bet he ain't got nothin'," Clete said.

"Speakin' o' goin' out on our own, I think maybe we ought to divide up the money now, and go our own ways," Ollie Terrell said, bringing up the subject again.

"We'll divide the money when I say we divide it," Luke Mueller said. "Anyway, what are you worried about? We got plenty of money to spend now, ain't we? Order whatever you want, we can afford it."

"Yeah," Clete added with a cackle. "We can afford it."

"What about women?" Terrell asked. "What if I'm a' wantin' me a woman?"

"Don't you be worryin' none about gettin' yourself

a woman," Luke said. "They's plenty of women around, and once we start spendin' the money, the women will be comin' out of the woodwork."

Terrell laughed. "Women comin' out of the woodwork. I like that. I ain't never heard nothin' like that before."

"How 'bout we start spendin' some of that money now?" Caldwell asked. "I'm hungry. And I got me a thirst worked up, too."

"Barkeep!" Mueller called. Bring us a couple bottles of whiskey, some glasses, and some food. Lots of food."

"And some women!" Terrell added. "Let's get some women over here."

Three of the bar girls who had been wandering around the saloon, flitting from table to table like bees around flowers, answered the call and within a moment the five bank robbers and three women were having themselves a party.

Though Luke Mueller was the smallest of the men, he turned all his attention to the biggest of the women.

"Ain't that there'n a little big for you, Luke?" Terrell teased, laughing out loud.

As quick as thought, a pistol appeared in Luke's hand, and he pointed it at Terrell, pulling back the hammer.

"You have somethin' to say about what woman I pick?" Luke asked.

The laughter died on Terrell's lips, his pupils dilated with fear, and he held his hand out as if by that action he could ward Luke off. "'Course, you know

I didn't mean nothin' by that, Luke. I was just a' funnin' you is all."

There was a long moment of high tension and absolute silence as everyone watched the tableau. Then, suddenly, a smile spread across Luke's face, and he eased the hammer down and put the pistol back in his holster.

"I didn't mean nothin' neither. I was just funnin' you," he said.

The burst of laughter that followed was precipitated more by the release of tension, than humor.

"What's your name?" Luke asked the big woman.

"Patsy," the woman answered. A moment earlier she had been enjoying her flirtation with the little man, but now he frightened her.

"Tell me, Patsy, what will you charge for me and you to go upstairs?"

"A dollar for one hour," Patsy said. "Three dollars for the rest of the day."

"Here's five dollars. I might want to stay longer than the rest of the day."

Smiling, Patsy took the money and stuck it inside the top of her dress, between her very large breasts. "Oh, honey, we're goin' to have us a real good time," she said. The money had changed her attitude about him.

Luke reached under the table and picked up a cloth bag.

"What's that, darlin', your laundry?" Patsy asked. "Honey, for five dollars I'll give you a very good time, but I ain't a' goin' to be doin' no laundry."

The other soiled doves laughed.

"You can leave your—uh—laundry here, if you want," Clete said.

"That's all right, I'll take care of it," Luke said. "This way, we'll all know where it is, won't we?"

"This way, darlin'," Patsy said, leading Luke away from the table. The others in the saloon watched them go up the stairs.

"Looks like a mouse following an elephant," someone said on the far side of the room. Having seen the lightning draw of the "mouse" though, he made the observation very quietly, and his friend's resultant laughter was just as quiet.

GREAT BOOKS, GREAT SAVINGS!

When You Visit Our Website:
www.kensingtonbooks.com
You Can Save Money Off The Retail Price
Of Any Book You Purchase!

- All Your Favorite Kensington Authors
- New Releases & Timeless Classics
- Overnight Shipping Available
- eBooks Available For Many Titles
- All Major Credit Cards Accepted

Visit Us Today To Start Saving!
www.kensingtonbooks.com

All Orders Are Subject To Availability.
Shipping and Handling Charges Apply.
Offers and Prices Subject To Change Without Notice.